COLTON'S PRIVATE SECURITY

LISA CHILDS

Special thanks and acknowledgment are given to Lisa Childs for her contribution to The Coltons of Dark Canyon miniseries.

Recycling programs for this product may not exist in your area.

ISBN-13: 978-1-335-47191-8

Colton's Private Security

For questions and comments about the quality of this book, please contact us at CustomerService@Harlequin.com.

TM and ® are trademarks of Harlequin Enterprises ULC.

Harlequin Enterprises ULC
22 Adelaide St. West, 41st Floor
Toronto, Ontario M5H 4E3, Canada
www.Harlequin.com

HarperCollins Publishers
Macken House, 39/40 Mayor Street Upper,
Dublin 1, D01 C9W8, Ireland
www.HarperCollins.com

Printed in Lithuania

The minute Cassidy's gaze met his, Mark's breath caught in the back of his throat.

There was such fear in her eyes, but her chin was up, and her hands on Billy Lang's forearm were holding the scissors back as far as she could. She was scared, but she was determined to get away.

And Mark was determined to make sure that she did.

Safely.

But as Lang shoved her forward, she tripped over the prone body of the police officer lying on the floor. And those scissors nipped into her skin, drawing blood and a gasp from her mouth.

Of pain.

That pain struck Mark's heart too. And while he held in his gasp, Lang's head swung toward him.

"Get back!" the man shouted, his dark eyes wild and his face flushed. "Get out of my way or I will kill her."

Dear Reader,

I am so happy to be participating in another Colton continuity, and I am especially excited about The Coltons of Dark Canyon. I visited Utah for the first time last year because one of my daughters moved to Salt Lake City. The area is so beautiful, and I loved that everywhere I turned, I could see mountains in the distance or up close. I enjoy hiking and appreciated that there are so many trails to explore and things to do. I can't wait to return and do more exploring of the trails and all the parks and restaurants, too.

Because I love the area so much, I can't imagine being like the hero in my installment of the series, who couldn't wait to move away from it. But after leaving military service and entering private security, Mark comes home to Dark Canyon and to the chaos and danger his family is currently facing. He knows that they can all pretty much handle themselves, though; it's his former high school sweetheart whom he's worried about protecting. Cassidy Garner can't deny that she might need protection, but the last person she wanted to ever see again is Mark. He's already broken her heart once; she doesn't want to let him close enough to break it again.

I hope you enjoy my contribution to The Coltons of Dark Canyon.

Happy reading!

Lisa Childs

New York Times and *USA TODAY* bestselling, award-winning author **Lisa Childs** has written more than one hundred books. Published in twenty countries, she's also appeared on the *Publishers Weekly*, Barnes & Noble and Nielsen Top 100 bestseller lists. Lisa writes contemporary romance, romantic suspense, and paranormal and women's fiction. She's a wife, mom, bonus mom, avid reader and less avid runner. Readers can reach her through Facebook or her website, lisachilds.com.

Books by Lisa Childs

Harlequin Romantic Suspense

The Coltons of Dark Canyon

Colton's Private Security

Bachelor Bodyguards

Close Quarters with the Bodyguard
Bodyguard Under Siege
Hostage Security
Personal Security
Christmas Security

The Coltons of Owl Creek

Colton's Dangerous Cover

The Coltons of Alaska

The Unknown Colton

Visit the Author Profile page at Harlequin.com for more titles.

With great appreciation to Caroline Timmings; it has been a joy doing these Colton continuities with you.

Prologue

"Cassidy Garner, RN, report to the ER. Cassidy Garner to the ER ASAP."

The message coming over the PA system at Baldwin Memorial Hospital startled Cassidy. She already had her bag over her shoulder and was heading through the plant-filled atrium of the hospital toward the exit. She was supposed to be done for the night.

But she knew she wouldn't have been paged if it wasn't important. Or…

Something that required her security clearance. "Fern!" Fear rushed up, choking her, as she turned around and ran toward the emergency department.

Not Fern. Please don't let it be Fern.

Cassidy's favorite patient had already been through too much after surviving a harrowing abduction by human traffickers who'd kept her in captivity. When firefighter Ryan Colton rescued Fern, she was brought to Baldwin Memorial to recover from a severely broken leg and other injuries she'd suffered during captivity. Cassidy had been her nurse in a private ward until Fern's release.

She'd been doing so well. Cassidy had just gone by Ryan's place not long ago and caught up with her. Fern wasn't just her former patient; she was going to be a lifelong friend.

Tears stung Cassidy's blue eyes, but she furiously blinked them away. A registered nurse for seven years, she was always professional if not exactly detached. She rolled a hairband off her wrist and bound her blond hair up in it as she neared the doors to the ER. Then she drew in a deep breath, bracing herself, before stepping through them. "I'm here!"

"Cassidy!" Dr. Finkbeiner shouted as she entered. "I need your help!"

She sucked in a breath, worried that the attending physician might have had her paged for another reason that had nothing to do with her nursing skills. "I'm not an ER nurse," she reminded him.

"You've done rotations in the ER a lot."

That was how she'd met him when he'd been a resident, but that was at another hospital where she'd done a stint as a traveling nurse. For four years she'd worked as one before coming back to Dark Canyon, Utah, three years ago.

He gestured at a police officer who stood outside one of the ER bays. "And you're the nurse with the security clearance the police require. C'mon, I need help." He jerked aside the heavy vinyl curtain behind the police officer and stepped into the ER bay.

Cassidy followed him. "What do you need?"

"Another set of hands," he said. "Patient has a lot of contusions, cuts and fractures as well as a possible TBI." Traumatic brain injury.

There was blood everywhere.

"What happened?" she asked as she moved to the other side of the gurney from the doctor and studied the long, lanky man lying on it.

"Automobile crash victim," Finkbeiner replied. "Passenger didn't survive."

"And why the police?" Had he been drinking?

"This guy and the one who died are the human traffickers who abducted that woman who escaped some time ago. But it doesn't matter who he is or what he did, we have to help him." Just as he said it, an alarm went off. "Damn, his heart stopped again! Hurry up!"

Cassidy jumped in to help with CPR. She often rotated through different departments in the hospital, so she was able to tune out everything but her training and her instincts. She put aside her fear and revulsion and anger while they worked on the patient. They got him back, his heart rhythm fast but strong. Then they worked on his other injuries. Once the bleeding was stopped, Cassidy had to wheel the patient off for an MRI to check for internal injuries and that possible TBI.

He hadn't regained consciousness since being brought into the ER, so she shouldn't have been afraid of him. But she couldn't forget that this man had hurt Fern, her friend. He'd been apprehended now, though. And the police officer followed close behind her as she wheeled the gurney to the elevator. Even though the patient was unconscious, the officer was intent on making sure that the criminal did not escape. This man would not hurt Fern again.

But still she felt uneasy as she stepped into the elevator with the gurney and with the officer. "I'm Cassidy," she said and waited for the man to introduce himself.

He just nodded.

The officer looked familiar to her, but maybe that was just because he looked so average. Average build, average height. Light brown hair, light brown eyes, but still…

With everything that had been happening in Dark Canyon lately, there had been a lot of police officers in and out of Baldwin Memorial.

"And you are?" she prodded him.

"Officer Olsen."

She nodded. "That's right. I think we've met before."

He shrugged.

"So what happened tonight?" she asked.

He tensed. "I can't tell you."

"I have security clearance," she reminded him. "That was why I was paged for this patient." Because she'd been cleared to treat the other one: Fern, who'd needed protection from the man on the gurney, and whoever he worked for. Who did he work for? Who in Dark Canyon was behind this horrific human trafficking?

He nodded. "This creep and his buddy abducted that woman again and left her for dead in the fire."

She gasped. "Oh, no! Not Fern." She pressed her hand to her madly pounding heart.

"She survived, with the help of the firefighter she's living with," Olsen assured him. "They're on their way to the hospital now for treatment."

"So they're injured too?" she asked with alarm. And she was torn between treating this patient and making sure that her friend was all right.

He shrugged. "Not seriously. I think just smoke inhalation. The firefighter found her pretty quickly. I guess his bodyguard cousin had some tracking device on her or something."

"Bodyguard cousin?" She tensed as her heart began to beat even harder than it had already been. It couldn't be… No, not Mark. Mark wasn't a bodyguard.

"Yeah, he's some former military guy." He shrugged again as if unconcerned.

But Cassidy was very concerned. Former military. So he had to be talking about Mark Colton. She shouldn't have been surprised because she had recently heard that he was back in Dark Canyon. She did not want to see Mark Colton ever again. Fortunately she hadn't run into him whenever she'd visited Fern at his cousin's place. But her heart pounded madly over how close she must have come to seeing him there since he'd helped his cousin protect Fern. Why was he back in Dark Canyon? Just to see his family? Hopefully Mark would leave again soon, like he always had, still the nomad he'd wanted to be. That she'd once wanted to be, but she'd had to come home three years ago. And she couldn't take off again like he did. She had too many responsibilities, too many people she loved who depended on her, while she had learned, from Mark, to never depend on anyone.

"These Coltons..." the officer murmured and shook his head. "Jacob Colton is the reason this guy is here. He and his team caused the crash."

"Jacob stopped a criminal from escaping justice," she said with some measure of censure. That was a good thing. And Mark, with his tracking device, had made sure that Fern was found. The Coltons were heroes. But this officer didn't seem to think so. And Cassidy wasn't sure why.

But then she couldn't think of Mark as a hero either. She could think of him only as the man who'd broken her heart.

Chapter 1

Two weeks later...

Mark Colton carried two cups of coffee through the automatic doors of Baldwin Memorial Hospital. The doors swished shut behind him once he stepped inside the atrium. With its high ceiling, rock formations and abundance of plants, the place was nearly indistinguishable from the world outside. Music played softly as he walked around looking for his cousin Ava.

She waved at him from one of the rock formations that doubled as seating. Her dark auburn hair hung in waves around the shoulders of her navy blue suit. And as he drew closer, her green eyes sparkled with affection and warmth. Ava looked and felt more like his sister than his cousin. His hair was darker than hers and brown, not auburn, but he had the same green eyes.

"You brought me coffee?" she asked hopefully.

He nodded and passed her a cup as he settled onto the rock next to her. "Decaf since it's late." And because his nerves didn't need the caffeine; he was already on edge. He hated the idea of that human trafficker being in the same hospital where his cousin worked.

But Ava wasn't the only person he knew who worked at Baldwin Memorial.

Cassidy Garner.

Mark knew this because another one of his cousins, Ryan, continued to sing the registered nurse's praises over how well she cared for his girlfriend, Fern, when she'd been a patient here. And because she'd been cleared to take care of the victim of human trafficking, Cassidy had also been assigned to care for the human trafficker that Mark's brother Jacob had apprehended a couple of weeks ago.

"As much as I appreciate seeing you, I don't think this is just a random visit," Ava remarked. "So what's up, Mark? You're not leaving again, are you?"

"I've already stayed longer than I intended to," he admitted. His visit home should have been a quick one, just to check on his widowed father and the rest of the family. But there had been more going on in Dark Canyon than he'd realized. And he couldn't walk away if people he cared about could possibly be in danger.

Cassidy Garner's beautiful face popped into his mind. He visualized her as he'd seen her last—eleven years ago, the wind whipping her long blond hair around her face, her blue eyes shining bright either with tears or with temper. They hadn't ended things very amicably when they'd ended their relationship.

Relationship? Had it been that? They'd been so damn young when they'd met in high school that they'd had no idea what a relationship really was. That last summer, after graduation, they'd spent a few weeks traveling together, and they'd learned that they actually wanted different things out of life. He wanted adventure and travel. While she'd claimed that she wanted that, too, she'd also wanted college and an education and a way to give back, or so she'd said.

She could have done that with him, in the military, if she'd really wanted him. But she'd refused to follow him around and had expected him to wait around for her until she was done with college.

And neither had loved the other enough to make a sacrifice or even try to find a compromise. Or maybe they just hadn't wanted each other enough to fight for what they had.

Liar.

Even now Mark tensed with desire just thinking about her. He'd never experienced anything close to the passion he had with her with anyone else. Maybe that was why their arguments had been so heated, though, because of the passion that had always burned so hot between them. Because of how angrily they'd parted ways, he hadn't talked to her since their last fight.

But damn, had he thought of her over the years…

The one who got away. That was what he'd always called her whenever anyone had asked him why he'd never gotten married. Not that he'd ever really intended to get married. He couldn't settle down in one place and didn't want to even try. While other women had claimed, like Cassidy, that they wanted to live that way, eventually they tired of the travel. Or maybe they just got tired of him. After those relationships ended, he rarely thought of them, though, like he thought about her.

"So you are leaving?" Ava asked.

He shook his head. "Not yet. I want to make sure that everyone is safe here in Dark Canyon before I go anywhere." Fortunately, so far, his boss had accommodated his extended leave, but eventually Randy Howard, who was also his former army sergeant, was going to have another assignment for Mark.

Ava groaned and nodded in understanding. "It's been pretty eventful around here the past few months. At least there have been good things happening along with the bad."

"Yes, you have a baby," he said, awed.

She smiled, her green eyes lighting up with love for the child she was in the process of adopting. "Yes, I do." Her smile widened. "And I have Chay."

After all the loss and suffering she'd endured, thanks to a deranged stalker, Ava was finally happy. Mark just wanted to make sure that she was safe. Chayton Bellany, an officer with the Tribal Police, would do his best to protect the woman he obviously loved very much, but Chay couldn't be with her all the time.

He couldn't be with her here.

"Has that trafficker been released from the hospital into police custody yet?" he asked.

"I can't talk to you about a patient," Ava said.

"He's not your patient," Mark said.

She sighed. "No. But he is a patient at this hospital."

"So he's still here?"

Ava sighed again. But she didn't confirm or deny, which was all the confirmation he needed.

"What's taking so long for him to get released into police custody?" he asked, frustration tightening the muscles in his stomach. He wanted that animal behind bars where he couldn't hurt anyone else.

Ava shrugged. "I don't know. I'm a psychologist, not a doctor or a nurse." Her eyes twinkled as she smiled and added, "But there is a certain nurse, one we both know, who might be able to answer your questions."

Mark and Ava were the same age, so she obviously remembered that he and Cassidy had dated in high school. Hell, they'd more than dated; they'd been madly in love. Then, after their summer trip, they'd just ended up mad at each other.

Her last words to Mark were that she never wanted to see or talk to him again. Due to all the close calls he'd had during his years with the army, that wish had nearly been granted. Most of those close calls had been because of the enemy, but one had been because of the incompetence of a certain member of his own squad. He'd survived, but most of his squad hadn't been as lucky as he'd been. The person responsible for all that loss, Rob Coffey, had almost gotten away with what he'd done because his father was a commander and good at cleaning up his son's messes. Anger surged through Mark at the injustice that would have been when so many good people had lost their lives. And for that sniveling coward to not lose anything…

But Coffey hadn't gotten away with it completely. Mark had made sure of that.

"Your face…" Ava murmured. "I would love to know what's going through your mind right now. You look so tense and upset but almost triumphant, too."

He chuckled. "Nice try, cuz, but I'm not going to let you shrink my head."

She reached out and touched the short hair on the top of his head. "Not going to try, though I hope you know if you ever want to talk, I'm here for you."

The seriousness in her tone drew Mark's attention. She was looking at him the same way his dad and brothers had since his return, like she was worried that he might fall apart. Or blow up. Like he was a ticking time bomb of PTSD. He couldn't deny that he had post-traumatic stress disorder. He suspected that anyone would who had seen and done the things he had. But he'd learned to cope with it.

He held up his hands. "I'm fine, Ava. You don't need to worry about me."

"But it's okay for you to worry about me?" she asked.

He nodded. "When there's a dangerous criminal in your vicinity, yeah, it is."

She grimaced.

And a pang of regret struck Mark. "I'm sorry, Ava," he said. "I hate what Daniel Wayne put you through—"

She patted his forearm. "It's over. He'll be in prison for a long time if not the rest of his life. He can't hurt me. And neither will that trafficker, Billy Lang," she said. "There are police officers guarding his room around the clock."

He grimaced now.

"What?"

"From what Ryan and Jacob have learned about Fern's last abduction, it definitely sounds like these traffickers have someone in the police department helping them," he said. And he knew all too well how it felt to not be able to trust a member of his own team.

So, what if one of those officers, instead of guarding Billy Lang, was actually going to help him escape from justice? Or worse yet, hurt more women?

Like Ava…

Or Cassidy…

Cassidy's hand shook as she reached for the package of fresh bandages. With seven years of nursing experience, she wasn't nervous about changing wound dressings. She was nervous about going back into that room with the patient. The human trafficker.

But she grabbed the package from the shelf, drew in a deep breath and turned back toward the door of the small supply closet. As she whirled around, she nearly collided with a body. A squeak of surprise escaped her lips. "What the hell…" she murmured.

Tyler Gibbs, a fellow nurse, held up his hands. "Sorry, Cass, I thought you saw me follow you in here. I didn't mean to scare you."

She shook her head. "You didn't scare me. You surprised me." And she, who had once been so spontaneous when she was younger, didn't care for surprises anymore. At least not since Dark Canyon had gotten so dangerous, especially for single women.

Tyler's thin lips curved into a slight smile, and amusement glinted in his blue eyes. He was blond like she was. Some of the other nurses and the patients compared him to a Ken doll. He was good-looking, and he knew it. But it was the plastic, superficial type of good looks that Cassidy didn't find attractive at all.

And into her mind popped the image of a certain dark-haired, green-eyed man with scruff covering his strong jaw. Cassidy had never outgrown her teenage propensity to fall for tall, dark and handsome.

"Yeah, that's right, nothing scares you, Cass," Tyler said, but there was a mocking tone to his voice. "Except actually going out with me on a date."

She smirked now, like he was, and replied, "I'm not afraid of going out with you, Ty. I just don't want to."

He pressed a hand to his chest, which pressed against the too-small scrubs top that he wore, nearly breaking the seams. "That hurts, Cass. That really hurts."

"Then stop asking me out," she advised him. "And get out of my way so that I can get back to my patient."

"You'd rather work on that scumbag trafficker than hang out in a supply closet with me?"

"Yes," she said. And she wasn't entirely kidding. At least Billy didn't ask her anything since he was still unconscious. However, all the scans indicated that he had no brain trauma, and he was breathing on his own. So was he just pretending to be unconscious?

His neurologist said that although there was no physical reason for him not to have regained consciousness, perhaps there was a psychological one. And the psychiatrist had admitted that could be the case.

But the coma wasn't the only reason he was still in the hospital. He had many wounds from the crash that were still healing. And she had to change his dressings to make sure that the staph infection in one of his wounds wasn't getting worse. The doctor might need to adjust the dosage of his IV antibiotics if there was no improvement.

"So please open the door, Ty," Cassidy said, her voice a bit sharp with the irritation building in her. "I need to get back to my patient."

Tyler sighed. "You're a stubborn woman, Cass."

Instead of being offended, she smiled with pride. "You're not the first person who's told me that." Mark Colton was the first person. But why was she the one who'd needed to put her dreams on hold for him? Why couldn't he have done that for her? Because he hadn't really loved her…

"I'm sure I won't be the last," Tyler said, his voice sharp with irritation now. But finally he turned around and opened the door. He stepped out first.

Then Cassidy followed him out into the hallway,

which was fortunately empty. She did not want any gossip spreading around the hospital about the two of them being alone together in a supply closet. She was not a character on *Grey's Anatomy*. She was a professional.

And maybe it was time she talked to HR about Tyler asking her out so frequently. She hadn't been concerned when he'd asked once, but he hadn't stopped after that rejection. Instead he seemed unable to accept her no as an answer. But, with his good looks, maybe he hadn't been turned down that many times before. And now he saw her as some kind of challenge.

Instead of heading off in the direction of the ward where he was supposed to be working, he walked with her toward the wing of private rooms where she was assigned.

"You don't need to walk with me down here," she said. She knew very well where she was going.

"All kidding aside, Cass, I don't like you having to take care of that creep," he said, and his voice rang now with sincerity. "I worry about you."

And that was why she hadn't reported him to HR. Underneath his Casanova facade, there was a good guy who genuinely seemed to care about others, not just her. He was actually a great nurse, too.

She smiled. "That's sweet but unnecessary. There's a police officer stationed right outside the door. Nothing's going to happen to me."

Tyler shuddered. "Famous last words? You might have just jinxed yourself, Cass."

"I'm not superstitious," she said. But a chill suddenly rushed over her, too.

"And there's your protection," Tyler said as they turned for the hall where Cassidy's patient was.

The officer sat on a chair outside the door, his head

cocked to one side as he dozed. As he nearly toppled off the chair, he jerked awake and gazed around him.

"Now I'm even more worried," Ty said.

"What?" The officer shook his head and blinked. "Ah, Ms. Garner, you're allowed down here. But you can't bring anyone with you."

"I don't want to go in that room," Ty assured the officer. "I was just making sure that Cassidy will be safe here. Need some more coffee, dude?"

A cup sat on the floor next to the officer's chair. "Uh, I'm fine."

The door behind him creaked as it opened, and he whirled around with his hand going for his holster.

"Don't shoot," the doctor said as he raised his hands. "I was just checking on the patient, remember?"

The officer nodded. "Yeah, yeah…"

And Cassidy wasn't convinced he remembered. "Why are you checking on him, Dr. Finkbeiner?" she asked. "He hasn't been your patient since he left the emergency department."

"Dr. Fink was checking on you," Tyler whispered. "No wonder you don't want to go out with me. You're already seeing a doctor."

"I'm not seeing anyone," Cassidy whispered back to the male nurse. But once again that image of Mark Colton popped into her head. She hadn't seen him in person for many years, though, and she hoped it stayed that way. "Not now." But she had once dated Frank Finkbeiner when he'd been a resident. And that mistake had taught her to never date anyone she worked with ever again.

"I wanted to check my sutures," Frank said. "Make sure he was healing. I heard there was some infection."

Cassidy held up the bandages she was carrying. "I was

going to change the dressings now." And she didn't mind the doctor staying with her while she did it.

But the ER physician glanced at his watch. "I'm sorry. I have to get back to the ER now. I just came up here on my break. Guess I wasn't the only one taking a break right now." He pointedly looked from her to Tyler and back.

Tyler grinned. "Lucky for me I caught Cass in the supply closet."

Cassidy turned to glare at him. "That was not lucky for me," she said. "I was just grabbing fresh bandages. Not taking a break. And now if you two will excuse me…" She started toward the door Dr. Finkbeiner had just closed behind himself. But as she drew near to him, she stopped to ask, "How is the patient?"

"Still out," the doctor replied. "Or pretending to be." He must have read the notes, too, that the neurologist had put in the patient's medical records. "I didn't have a chance to check his wounds before I heard talking out in the hall." He gestured at Ty who'd thankfully turned to walk away. "Are you dating him?"

"I'll tell you what I told him, I'm not dating anyone," she said.

"Why not, Cassidy?" he asked a bit smugly, as if he thought he might be the reason. Maybe his ego had convinced him that he'd broken up with her instead of the reality that she'd broken up with him.

"I'm too busy, for one," she said. And not just at the hospital but with helping her widowed sister with her twin boys. "And I have no interest in dating, for another."

"We had fun, those couple of times we went out in Denver," he said.

She'd had more fun with someone else. A *lot* more fun with Mark Colton before they'd blown up their relationship and their plans for a shared future. "I hope that's not why you took the job here."

"You think I followed you here?" he asked, and then grinned. "A little arrogant of you, Cassidy."

Heat rushed to her face with embarrassment that she probably sounded as egotistical as she'd thought he was. "Maybe paranoid," she admitted, and given the things that had been happening lately, she considered paranoia a good thing. "But why did you choose here?"

"You spoke highly of Dark Canyon," he said. "And when I interviewed, I liked what I saw here at the hospital and in the town."

She liked it, too, working at Baldwin Memorial and living close to family again. But there was a part of her that yearned to travel again, to explore new places and meet new people, experience different things from the same old day in and out.

Frank chuckled. "Sometimes I think I like it more than you do."

And maybe he did.

"I better get back to the ER," he said. And like Tyler, he walked away leaving her alone in the hall outside the trafficker's room. The officer was there, but he seemed so sleepy that he was almost unnoticeable.

"Are you all right?" she asked him with concern.

He stretched and yawned and stood up, and as he did, he stumbled a bit.

Was he tired or drunk? Or drugged?

"Should I call someone?" she asked. And she remembered that Jacob Colton had given her his direct cell number. He wanted her to report anything suspicious to him. Was this suspicious, though? It was late. She was tired, too, as her shift was just about over. The officer's shift probably was as well. He'd been working as long as she had. And with as late as it was getting, she really just wanted to change the patient's bandages and get her shift over as soon as possible.

The officer shook his head, and his dark eyes cleared. "No. I'm fine. And I have less than an hour before the officer relieving me gets here."

She nodded. "Okay. Just let me know if you need anything."

"About eight hours of sleep," he said. "But I'll get that when I'm done here."

"Good," she said. She would be lucky to get five, since she'd switched her next shift to the morning so she would be able to pick up the twins from school in the afternoon while her sister Patsy worked late.

"I can go into the room with you," the officer offered. He must have noticed that she was hesitating to open the door.

Billy Lang's lawyer had convinced a judge to rule that his client only had to have the guard posted outside the door and not inside with him. And that he didn't have to be handcuffed to the bed until he regained consciousness.

She wondered how Billy Lang had managed to hire such a high-powered attorney. Lang was definitely working for someone else, someone with much more money and influence than he and his dead partner had wielded. But she'd overheard the police theory was that Lang and his partner must have kidnapped Fern in order to traffic her themselves. She, however, was strong and resilient, and once they'd left her alone, she'd managed to escape.

Cassidy needed to check in on her friend again soon. Make sure that she really had fully recovered from the smoke inhalation she and Ryan had suffered. But right now Cassidy had to treat the man who'd made her friend suffer. She hated this, but she didn't have much choice in the matter unless she wanted to risk her job.

And she needed it and the flexibility her supervisor gave her in order to keep helping her sister with the twins. So she literally sucked it up, drawing a deep, bracing breath before she pushed open the door.

Along with the package of bandages, she'd brought scissors and tape in order to cut off the current bandages and redress the wounds. She also carried a syringe in case she needed to push some pain meds or more antibiotics into the IV. Having the sharp scissors and needle in her pocket made her feel a little better. She could use them as weapons if she needed to. But as she entered, she found Billy Lang as she had every other time she'd come into the room, lying still on the bed.

Was he really unconscious? Or faking his comatose state? Not that he was fully in a coma anymore. Tests had proven that he wasn't deeply unconscious. He had brain activity and was breathing on his own.

He had also reacted to pain stimuli before but hadn't fully regained consciousness, which had made the neurologist question whether the coma was psychosomatic. Maybe it was; maybe he knew that he was going to prison, probably for the rest of his life, if he regained consciousness. No matter how good his lawyer was, he wouldn't be able to escape the justice he had coming to him.

But doling out justice wasn't Cassidy's job. She was only responsible for medical treatment. So she went to work on the bandages on his arm, cutting away the old gauze. The wound beneath was angry and red and oozing with infection.

He was going to need stronger antibiotics.

She would have to call the hospitalist to the room. But before she could reach for the phone, she heard a loud thump outside the door. Had the officer not been able to catch himself this time before falling off the chair?

She started toward the door to check on him, leaving the scissors and the bandages on the tray next to Billy's bed. Realizing her mistake, she whirled around but just like when she and Mark Colton broke up all those years ago, she'd realized her mistake too late. Because Billy Lang was sitting up in his bed with the scissors clenched in his big hand.

Billy had actually regained consciousness a few days ago. Luckily it had been at night with nobody around, so he'd had time to figure out what was going on and where he was before alerting anyone. Then he'd decided it was best if nobody knew he was conscious again, and he had been biding his time since then, waiting until he was healed enough to attempt his escape and for the actual chance to escape. Maybe he wasn't as healed as he should be since his body ached yet from the crash. His wounds itched and throbbed except for the one on his arm that was burning hot. And that heat was beginning to spread over the rest of his skin.

But he couldn't wait any longer. All those damn tests they kept running on him showed that he wasn't really in a coma. Or if he was, it was a trick of his head or something.

It was a trick all right, but he knew exactly what he was doing. Thanks to the painkillers he was on, it hadn't been too hard to keep his heart rate and breathing slow enough to fool everybody that he was still out the past few days. But he doubted he could have lasted much longer keeping his eyes closed every time someone was around. He hadn't fooled everyone, though. Somebody had figured out he was faking, but instead of reporting him, they were helping him escape. And somebody else was going to help him whether or not she wanted to. The nurse turned around and caught him holding the scissors she'd left sitting on the table next to his bed.

She whirled around again and reached for the door. And Billy forced himself to move, jumping over the side railing and rushing to reach her before she could get away. He slammed his free hand against the door, holding it closed while he pressed the sharp nose of those scissor blades against her throat.

"Uh-uh, my sweet little nurse," he said. "You are not getting away from me."

Not like that little bitch Fern had. If only she'd died in that damn fire…

But she was alive and probably chomping at the bit to testify against him. But he wasn't sticking around for his trial. He was getting the hell out of Dark Canyon like he should have when Fern had escaped from the cabin on the reservation.

But he wasn't going alone. He was taking his nurse with him. He was used to her always being around, and because she was always around, he wasn't sure what she'd picked up on, what she suspected. If she knew who was helping him…

And he was already in enough trouble. He couldn't afford to piss off the people he worked for any more than he and Leo already had.

Or he would wind up like Leo: dead.

Chapter 2

Mark had gotten lost for a moment in thoughts of Cassidy and that trip they'd taken the summer after graduating. It had started out so fun and ended so…not fun. For years he'd held on to the anger from their last fight so that he wouldn't have to feel the other things: the loss, the pain, the regret…that they hadn't been able to make it work between them.

"Are you okay, Mark?" Ava asked, and she touched his forearm.

He nodded. "Yeah, yeah…"

"You seemed very far away," she said. "But I guess we should be used to that with you. You are usually very far away from us, and you don't come home very often."

A pang of guilt struck his heart. "I know. I wish I'd been here more for Mom and Dad and…" For everyone else who'd loved his mother, which had been pretty much everyone she'd ever met. She'd been such a beautiful woman inside and out. Even the cancer that had taken her from them hadn't taken away her beauty.

Ava squeezed his forearm. "I miss Aunt Kate, too."

A knot formed in his throat, choking him, and all he could do was nod.

"I don't think you were thinking about your mom,

though, when you grew quiet just now," she said. "You got quiet after I mentioned a certain nurse."

He sighed and admitted, "I haven't talked to Cassidy since that summer after high school."

"After that summer, you left for boot camp and she went to college," Ava said. "Any regrets?"

"About the army?" he asked with a grin. He knew that she was referring to Cassidy. "I got to do what I wanted. Travel the world."

"Did you like what you saw?" Ava asked, and there was that tone to her voice that reminded him that she was a psychologist. But even before she'd become one, she'd been good at getting people to open up to her.

"Not all of it," he admitted. "While I saw some beautiful places, I also saw some very ugly things." Especially on that last thwarted mission where he'd lost so many of his friends.

"Have you talked to anyone about those ugly things?" she asked.

He nodded. "The military has good shrinks, Ava."

"But did you really talk to them?"

"I did what I had to," he said. And he had learned ways to cope, so that he didn't blow up. But he wasn't thinking about those mandatary sessions. He was thinking about getting Rob Coffey dishonorably discharged. That really wasn't punishment enough for what he'd done, because Mark didn't wholly trust Coffey's excuse of simple incompetence. But then after Cassidy, he didn't wholly trust anyone anymore.

"Well, I hope you know that I am always available if you want to talk," she said.

"You are very busy with your career, a baby and a

certain reservation cop," he reminded her, and a pang of envy surprised him.

Not that he wanted a baby or a relationship.

Maybe he just envied that his cousin had so much in her life, and he had…

His career. He really enjoyed working as a bodyguard. The job satisfied his need for adventure and travel. But sometimes he might have liked having someone to share those adventures with. But inevitably that someone would try to change him or make him settle down into a life that he didn't want. No. It was better to be alone and able to do what he wanted than with someone and forced to do what they wanted instead. He'd learned that summer long ago that he just wasn't cut out for relationships. And that was fine.

But what about Cassidy?

Had she found the man who would do what she wanted? And what the hell had she really wanted? Not him. That was the only thing he knew for certain.

Ava smiled. "Yes, I'm a lucky woman," she agreed.

"You deserve every happiness," he told her.

Sadness passed through her eyes for a moment and her shoulders drooped a bit with guilt. "I don't know…"

"Yes, you do," he said. "And nothing that happened was your fault, Ava." Her stalker had ruined her life and taken the life of her fiancé. But somehow Ava had overcome and found happiness again. Mark respected how damn strong she was.

"I'm glad you're home," she said, and she stood up. "And I should be getting home, too. I left my purse in my office. Want to go up with me? My office is on the same floor and not far from the private wing where Cassidy is working."

He stood up, too, and his pulse leaped with the thought of seeing his first love again. Had she changed at all? Or was she still as beautiful as she'd been? As passionate?

"If you want to find out more about Billy Lang..." she trailed off, giving him another excuse to see his ex.

But that was the only reason he would risk seeing Cassidy again. He wanted to make sure that security was really good enough to keep that creep from posing a threat to anyone else. Like his cousin...

Or Cassidy.

"Sure, I'll go up to your office with you," he said. "But don't expect me to lie down on your couch and start spilling my guts."

"Since we're related, you couldn't really be my patient," Ava said. "But you can still talk to me about anything. It would just be a conversation between family, though."

He followed her to the bank of elevators and stepped into one that seemed to be waiting for them with open doors. "I *am* good, Ava," he assured her. "Really." But he couldn't help hearing the hollow tone of his voice that seemed to echo the hollowness he sometimes felt inside himself.

In his heart.

He wanted to blame it on losing his mom or on all the friends he'd lost in failed missions. But that hollowness had been inside him before those losses; it had been inside him since that summer after high school.

After Cassidy.

Ava pressed the button for her floor, and when the elevator lifted, Mark's stomach did as well. He wasn't nervous over the movement; he was nervous over where that movement was carrying him...toward Cassidy. For Ava's sake, he really did want to know when the trafficker was going to be released.

Hell, he wanted to know that for Cassidy's sake, too. No matter how acrimonious their parting had been, he cared about her. He didn't want her to get hurt. Or worse.

He'd already lost too many people he'd cared about, and part of him still cared about her and probably always would. She was his first love.

His only love so far.

Not that he was looking for love. He was looking for answers instead. Who the hell were these traffickers working for? Because someone with more power and influence was definitely calling the shots.

The elevator ground to a stop, but his stomach seemed to keep rising with anticipation that he might be seeing Cassidy soon.

For the first time in eleven years.

The doors swished open, and Ava stepped out first. The elevators opened in the middle of four hallways that each led off in a different direction. She pointed toward one. "My office is down here." Then she turned ninety degrees and pointed down another. "The person you really want to talk to is down that one."

He wasn't sure that he really wanted to talk to Cassidy. Not when he could think of so many other things they'd done better. Like kiss and make love or simply hold each other's hands, their fingers entwined like they were linked for eternity. But eternity hadn't lasted beyond high school except for that summer trip.

Ava glanced at her watch. "Though her shift is probably ending soon." Her lips curved into a slight smile. "You don't have to walk me to my office."

Despite all the dangerous missions he'd been on over

the years, he was reluctant to face Cassidy at least on his own. "You should show me where it is," he said.

She pointed back down the hall to her left. "It's easy enough to find the correct room because there is a police officer sitting outside the door."

"Outside?" Mark questioned. "Why not in the room?"

She shrugged. "I don't know. I've just noticed an officer whenever I pass that hall."

Mark moved to the end of it and peered down the hall himself. The officer she'd indicated was there, but he wasn't sitting. He was lying on the floor next to his chair. Alarm shot through Mark.

"Ava, go to your office," he said. "Lock yourself in and call security to shut down the hospital and to get the police here ASAP."

Ava clutched his arm. "What…what's going on…" She peered down the hall, too, and gasped. "Is he dead?" And she moved forward as if she intended to rush down the hall to check on him.

But Mark caught her arm to hold her back because he could see the door behind that officer's prone body opening. He nudged his cousin in the other direction. Keeping his voice low, he hissed out the words, "Go. Now."

Her green eyes wide with apprehension, she nodded and ran off down the hall she'd indicated first. She had to know what Mark knew—that this trafficker couldn't escape or more women would be in danger.

Mark eased his way down the hall, his back against the wall on the same side as that door. He didn't want the trafficker to see him. He also wanted to check on that fallen officer. And where was Cassidy?

And then there she was, pushed first through that open door. She looked the same as she had all those years ago, same flawless skin, perfect profile and bright blond hair that was escaping from a rubber band on the top of her head.

Her arms were up, tugging on the forearm that was wrapped tightly around her shoulders, as if trying to protect herself from being choked. Or maybe from the sharp point of the little scissors held against her throat, against the artery that would spray her blood all over the crisp white walls and floor if it was severed.

All that would take was a little more pressure, and Cassidy could die.

Cassidy held her breath, scared to breathe, to move, and risk the sharp point of those scissors digging into her skin. The pressure and the sting of those tiny shears against her neck had her heart beating faster with fear.

"Just help me get out of here, and you won't get hurt," Billy Lang had told her moments ago as, behind her back, he'd dressed in clothes his lawyer must have brought him.

She knew the ones he'd worn to the hospital had been cut off him in the ER. The only person, besides medical staff and police officers, who'd been alone with him, as far as Cassidy knew, was his lawyer. She'd thought that was odd since he couldn't confer with an unconscious client, but the lawyer had insisted on checking on Lang. And maybe he'd been there when the patient had regained consciousness. Why hadn't she been? But then she didn't work around the clock. And she'd been so close to being off the clock now.

But Billy was what was too close to her now, his arm wound around her shoulders as he pressed those scissors against her neck. She couldn't move. But she had to in order to get away from him.

And she had to get away from him.

Her sister and her nephews depended on her so much. She had to fight for them. She wasn't sure that her sister could survive another loss. Losing her husband to cancer had nearly destroyed Patsy and the boys.

For them, Cassidy had to escape unscathed from this would-be killer.

For Patsy, Alec and Brian.

She could not let Billy Lang abduct her like he and his partner had abducted Fern and probably other women. At least he was alone now and hopefully weak enough that she would be able to break free once he eased the scissors away from her neck.

"How can I help you?" Cassidy had asked him as she'd stood there while he dressed, knowing that if she'd tried to escape he could have stabbed her with those scissors.

And he'd told her to open the door.

Once she opened it, she expected the officer to jump up from his chair and rescue her. But then she remembered the loud thud she'd heard earlier, and she knew what it had been. The officer lay on the floor in front of the door. He'd been so tired earlier, but falling would have jerked him awake if he'd just been sleeping.

But he obviously wasn't just sleeping.

"What happened to him? Is he all right?" she asked Billy, concern gripping her. She wanted to drop down to check for a pulse, for breath, but Lang was holding her too tightly for her to move.

"No, he's a lousy guard," Billy said with a slight chuckle. "Didn't even notice the sleeping pills slipped into his coffee cup."

Had Billy put them in the cup? Or had someone helped

him? Someone who might still be in the hospital? His lawyer? His boss? Another accomplice?

She glanced around the corridor then and noticed the man pressed against the wall. And her pulse quickened even more. Nearly a dozen years had passed since she had last seen him, but she would recognize Mark Colton anywhere.

His hair was shorter now, the scruff on his jaw thicker than it had ever been, and his body was heavier, more muscular than he'd been as a teenager. But she knew him with her mind and with her body that reacted, too.

With that leaping pulse and a rush of heat.

But maybe that was just the fear that was rushing through her, making her heart pound so fast and hard.

She had to get away from Billy without getting hurt. And she wasn't sure she could do that on her own, let alone if Mark tried to intervene. Instead of saving her, he might get her hurt, too, and it would be a far more serious wound than the one he'd inflicted on her heart all those years ago.

"Ava? Are you all right?"

Ava wasn't surprised that her cousin Jacob answered his cell that way. "You must have found out that I called 911—"

"Lang is trying to escape!" Jacob's breath rattled the cell Ava held in a shaking hand. He must have been moving, hopefully getting into his vehicle and heading this way.

"I…we don't know for sure. We just saw the police officer on the ground and Mark told me to call 911—"

"Mark is there, too?" Jacob asked.

"Yes."

"That's good. He'll keep you safe. You two need to stay locked in your office until you get the all clear."

"I'm locked in my office," Ava assured him. "Mark told me to, but he's not here with me."

Jacob's curse rasped through her phone now. "I don't need to ask you where he is…"

"Cassidy is one of the nurses assigned to Billy Lang's care," Ava said. "And she's on duty tonight."

"Cassidy?"

"Cassidy Garner, Mark's high school sweetheart," Ava said, surprised that Jacob didn't remember his brother's very serious high school relationship. But Jacob was four years older than she and Mark were, so he hadn't gone to high school with them.

"Ah, that's why the nurse looked familiar to me…" Jacob murmured.

"And it's why I knew I wouldn't be able to talk Mark out of trying to help." But she was terrified that he was going to get hurt.

"Maybe it's nothing," Jacob said, as if trying to ease her fear. "Maybe the officer just got sick or something."

But she heard the skepticism and the fear in his voice. "You don't think that any more than Mark did."

"I'm getting there as fast as I can, Ava," he said. "Just stay locked in your office and wait…"

Wait to find out if her cousin and Cassidy were okay.

All the years that Mark had been in the army, Ava had worried about him just as the rest of his family had. They'd never known where he was or what he was doing, just that he was probably in danger.

He had survived all those years in the service, though. And he was home now for however long he managed to stay put. They couldn't lose him now.

Chapter 3

The minute Cassidy's gaze met his, Mark's breath caught in the back of his throat. There was such fear in her eyes, but her chin was up, and her hands on Billy Lang's forearm held the scissors back as far as she could. She was scared, but she was determined to get away.

And Mark was determined to make sure that she did.

Safely.

But as Lang shoved her forward, she tripped over the prone body of the police officer lying on the floor. And those scissors nipped into her skin, drawing blood and a gasp from her mouth.

Of pain.

That pain struck Mark's heart. And while he held in his gasp, Lang's head swung toward him.

"Get back!" the man shouted, his dark eyes wild and his face flushed. "Get out of my way or I will kill her."

Mark eased away from the wall but held up his hands. "I'm not in your way, buddy. Just let her go, and you can get out of here. I'm not going to stop you."

Cassidy gasped again. While she wanted to get away from the man, she obviously didn't want him to escape either. Neither did Mark. But he wanted to make sure

Cassidy didn't get hurt even more than the wound that oozed blood.

Lang snorted. "Yeah, right. I know you're not going to let me go."

Mark kept his hands in the air. "I'm not a cop," he said, speaking calmly and slowly as he eased a little closer to them. "I'm just a civilian bystander here, bud."

"Then get out of my way!" Lang shouted. Then he looked beyond Mark. "All of you! Get out of here!"

Ava must have called for help as he'd directed her, but Mark didn't turn his head to see who had arrived. He stayed focused on Lang and on the woman he held so tightly. Blood trailed down her neck from that wound. But it wasn't gushing. Lang hadn't hit an artery. Yet.

But being as nervous and twitchy as the man seemed, there was a very real possibility he was going to. Maybe accidentally, maybe purposely.

Mark waved a hand behind him, trying to get whoever Lang kept glancing at to back off. "Take me instead of her," he offered. "I'll help you get out of here."

"How?" Lang asked as if he was considering it. "You said you're not a cop. If you're really just a civilian, how the hell are you going to help me? And why would you? What's this nurse to you?"

His first love. The one who got away from him, and he wanted to make sure that she got away from this guy, too.

"The police are on their way," said a voice from somewhere behind Mark. So this man wasn't the police, just someone trying to help. And hopefully he was alone because having too many people around was going to make Lang more desperate to escape.

"You want to get out of here before they arrive," Mark told Lang. "I'll help you get out of here."

"Why? Who the hell are you?" Lang asked.

Mark shrugged. "Just a civilian now. But I was once in the army," he shared.

"I don't need GI Joe to get me out of here," Lang said. "I just need her." And he grabbed the name tag off the pocket of Cassidy's scrubs.

Her security clearance must have been in the bar code on that name tag, and Lang knew it would open the doors he had to open to get out of the building.

Mark stepped back, toward whoever had joined him, hoping to push them out of his and Lang's way. "That's what you really need," he said. "So let's go now. But leave her here."

Lang narrowed his dark eyes and looked at him. "What the hell is your deal? Who are you?"

Mark shrugged again. "Nobody."

"And who is she to you?" Lang asked.

And Mark shrugged again and repeated, "Nobody."

Nobody. The word echoed in Cassidy's head. But she had to push it aside and focus right now. It didn't matter what Mark thought of her, not anymore. It mattered how she was going to get the hell away from Billy Lang.

While she'd allowed her patient to get a hold of the scissors, she still had the syringe in her pocket. All she had to do was move one hand to it, slip off the cap and then…

Where and how could she hit him without those scissors plunging deeper into her neck before she connected?

Figuring that out was what mattered, not what Mark Colton thought of her after all this time. Or even if he'd thought of her at all. She wished she hadn't thought about him. But she couldn't undo the past; all she could worry about right now was the present and getting away from the human trafficker.

Billy Lang had loosened the arm he'd wrapped around her when he'd grabbed her ID badge, but the scissors were pressed so tightly to her throat that it was hard to breathe let alone move.

"Get out of my way!" Lang shouted. "Or I will kill her."

"There's no need for that," Mark said. "We'll get out of here." He turned slightly then, looking over his shoulder at the security guard who'd come up behind him. "Ava Colton, the psychologist on staff here, she's my cousin," he told the guard, his voice deep with an unspoken message.

Back off.

Was that what he was trying to tell the guard?

"She would tell you that we need to de-escalate this situation," he continued. "So you need to step back. And we need to let Mr. Lang get to the elevator."

Cassidy's stomach dropped at the mention of the elevator. The confined space would allow her no room to fight Lang, let alone get away from him. The security guard was no help as he began walking backward, moving away from them. Mark did the same, his gaze back on Lang now. And he beckoned him forward. Mark had been in the military, was a bodyguard now, so she didn't believe that he was really going to help this criminal get away. Lang probably didn't believe him either, which meant that he wasn't going to fall for whatever plan Mark had to stop the escape.

So she was going to have to take care of herself now just as she'd had to after they broke up. She was going to have to do something to make sure she didn't get dragged onto the elevator with Lang. Because she knew better than to trust Mark and trust that whatever his plan was would work. She'd learned long ago to rely only on herself.

"Ah, Mr. Colton," the security guard murmured. "The elevators are locked down. The whole hospital is."

"Unlock it," Mark said. "The smartest and safest course of action for everyone is to let Mr. Lang leave the premises."

Not for her. That wasn't the smartest or safest course of action for Cassidy because it was clear that Lang had no intention of letting her go. And she didn't believe that Mark had any intention of letting Lang go, no matter what he said.

At least he had tried to get Lang to release her and take him instead, not that Lang had any interest in the exchange. Did Mark have no idea that this man was a human trafficker? That he'd kidnapped at least one woman that they knew of and probably many more.

Women like Cassidy, young and single, but unlike those other women, Cassidy had family who would report her missing. Her sister Patsy would be frantic and the boys…

Her heart ached with love for her nephews. She didn't want her family to feel any more loss and pain than they had already suffered. She had to get away from Lang.

With his arm looser around her shoulders as Lang pushed her forward, toward Mark, she let one of her arms slip down so she could slide her hand into the pocket of her scrubs. Her fingers closed around the syringe, and she eased the cap off the needle. The syringe was empty, but the needle was sharp. It wouldn't do much damage, though, unless she could stick it in his eye.

"Get on your phone," Mark told the security guard. "Unlock the elevators and the lobby doors. Now."

The older man was already reaching for his cell phone. Why was he listening to Mark? Just because he was related to Ava? Because he was a Colton?

They were all highly respected in Dark Canyon, especially Mark's dad, Sam, who had been the mayor for many years until his wife was diagnosed with the pancreatic cancer that had eventually killed her. All the Coltons were known for being hardworking, heroic even. And while Mark had been gone a long time, it was well known that he'd been in the army.

Maybe that was why the guard was deferring to him. He spoke into his cell, "Colton said unlock everything. Let him get out. He has a hostage."

"He won't have the hostage," Mark said over his shoulder. "He'll have me. I'm going willingly with him." He turned back to Billy. "So you can let her go."

Billy must have shaken his head because his body moved, and the scissors nipped into her skin again.

Cassidy flinched, and Mark's gaze skimmed over her face and her neck. She was bleeding; she could feel the trickle of it down her skin and could feel the wetness of it where it was soaking into the material of her scrubs top.

"You're hurting her," Mark said, his voice hard like his jaw that he must have clenched. "You need to let her go, Billy. You're not going anywhere if you hurt her."

"I'm not going anywhere if I let her go," Billy said. "You're not fooling me. You're a Colton." He uttered the name like it was a curse or worse. But then it had been a Colton who'd killed his partner and caught him: Jacob. "I know what you're up to…"

Mark lifted his hands. "I'm helping you. I'm getting

them to unlock this place. You can trust me." But as he said that, his gaze slipped from Billy's face to hers, and the look in his green eyes was very intense, very focused, like he used to look at her before he kissed her.

Was he asking Billy to trust him or was he asking her?

She'd made that mistake once, of trusting Mark, and he'd broken her heart. While she was pretty sure that he had some kind of plan to stop Lang from escaping, Cassidy wasn't about to trust him again. Not with her heart or with her life.

Billy knew better than to trust a Colton. They had a way of getting in your way, like that damn firefighter who'd rescued and protected the girl. *Fern*, he thought with a sneer. And that damn special agent with the National Park Service who'd killed Leo and nearly killed Billy, too.

No. There was no way in hell that Billy would ever trust a Colton. But he would use one if he could in order to escape. There was no doubt that the police had been called, and he had to get the hell out of here before they showed up. That was partially because he didn't know which police would respond to this call and which ones he could trust any longer. No. He couldn't trust anyone any more, not just this Colton.

He couldn't trust the cop that was supposed to be helping him, and he couldn't trust the lawyer either. He couldn't trust anyone but himself.

And he knew that he had to get moving. He nudged the girl forward, but he didn't shove her. Colton was right that he couldn't kill her…not until he got the hell out of the hospital anyways.

If he killed her in here, his leverage was gone. He

wouldn't be able to escape. And hell, maybe even after he escaped, he would need her.

His skin was so damn hot everywhere that sweat was trickling down his forehead and down his back. And his legs were shaky, too.

That damn crash.

He was lucky he hadn't wound up like Leo. Dead. But that could still happen if he didn't get away now. And disappear somewhere that nobody would find him.

"Go, Colton," he said. "Get moving, clear my way." Because more people than that security guard had gathered around. Nurses, doctors and patients were peeking out of the doors and around the corner of the hall at them. He would use this Colton to get rid of them all.

And then he would get rid of this Colton.

"Step back, get out of the way," the man said with that kind of authority that some people just assumed, like they were important. Like they'd been born important.

"You can't let him take her," someone remarked, his voice soft as if he didn't want Billy to hear him.

But he did. "She's going to die if anyone tries anything." He focused on Colton then. "Anyone."

The guy nodded as he continued walking backward. "Yeah, we get that, Billy. We hear you. Nobody's going to try to be a hero tonight. We're just going to give you what you want. A way out of here."

Billy snorted at the lies this Colton was spewing. Like one of them wouldn't try to be a hero. Yeah, right.

But the guy was lying to him as much as he was trying to get everyone else to stand down. And Billy needed that. He didn't need some mob trying to take him out. If only he'd dressed faster, he might have already been gone before anyone noticed the stupid cop lying in the hall.

He hadn't planned this as well as he should have. But he hadn't had time, and he hadn't trusted the help he'd been offered either, just like he didn't trust this Colton. But Billy followed him, taking a step forward to each step the guy took backward, like an invisible string was stretched between them, keeping them together.

"We're at the elevators," the guy said like he had eyes in the back of his head or something.

How the hell had he known that?

But there was a sign over their heads, pointing to the elevators, the letters of the word illuminated in red. But when Billy tried to focus on them, they blurred. Everything was getting blurry, and his legs weaker. Instead of just holding the nurse against him, he leaned on her a bit, and when he did, his hand slipped a little with the scissors. Instead of digging them into her flesh, they skimmed down her throat to her collarbone.

The man slapped the down arrow on the wall. "I'm going to go down to the lobby with you, Billy. Make sure that you get out those doors, that nobody tries to stop you."

It wasn't a good idea to let this man into that small space with them. But Billy didn't know what other choice he had. If he didn't, those doors might lock and not open again. But eventually someone would have to let him out. And when they did, they would find a dead nurse.

But still…

If Colton could get him outside…

Billy could get away then. He could disappear.

The doors dinged and opened. And he immediately pressed those scissors against the nurse's throat again. He expected police officers to be standing in the car, but it was empty. But only for a second.

Colton stepped back into it and then gestured for Billy to follow. He pushed the nurse in ahead of him, and then he stepped inside. “Don’t try anything,” Billy warned the other man.

As well as that air of authority, the guy had the muscular build of someone powerful. He’d said he wasn’t a cop but was something ex-military. It might have been better for Billy if he’d been a cop; some of those weren’t bothered about the law. But a military man was used to following orders, or if he’d been higher up, giving orders. No matter what he was saying, he probably already had a plan to stop the escape.

And Billy’s pulse quickened. He’d made another mistake getting into the elevator with him. He was sure of it. But Colton pressed the button with the *L*, and the car descended. The guy didn’t move from where he leaned against the wall.

“This is all going to be fine,” Colton said.

But Billy wasn’t sure if the guy was talking to him, to himself or to the nurse. Despite the close confines of the elevator, his voice started to sound far away to Billy. More sweat trickled down his back and his forehead. Why was it so damn hot?

The elevator seemed to move so slowly, or maybe everything was moving so slowly except Billy’s heart. That was beating fast, like his breathing. Then finally the elevator lurched to a stop, and Billy’s legs nearly gave way. He leaned more heavily on the nurse, and as he did, the scissors slipped down again.

Then she took a step toward the open doors. But he held her back. “You first, Colton,” he told the other man.

If cops were waiting for him out there, he didn’t want to be the first one through the doors. Let them shoot

Colton because he had no doubt that some of them might shoot to kill. To protect their own secrets and the secrets of people far more powerful than either of them.

Colton stepped out and then turned back toward him. "It's clear. Nobody's here yet. But you don't have much time. You have to move."

The doors nearly started to close again, but Colton shot his hand out, holding them open.

"You have to get out of here now," he said.

And Billy lurched forward, shoving the girl ahead of him. She slipped out from beneath his arm, whirled around and swung her hand toward his face. Something sharp pierced the skin below his eye. Pain shot through him, and a howl of fury and agony tore free of his throat. Then he swung his arm with the scissors toward her, intent on taking her down.

On killing the bitch…

Chapter 4

Mark had seen the syringe in Cassidy's pocket, and he'd been worried about just this happening when she tried to use it. About the moment she might try to escape and how Lang would react.

But before the scissors could reach her face, Mark surged forward, throwing his body in front of hers. He moved with such force that she stumbled back and fell to the lobby floor, and he went down with her, covering her body with his. Then he braced himself for the sharp point of the scissors to hit his back.

But Lang just cursed as he moved around them, probably heading toward the exit.

Mark levered himself up to stare down at Cassidy. Her facc was flushed, her blue eyes bright. This was the face that had haunted him for the past eleven years. Maybe her cheekbones were a little sharper, and there was a groove between her blond brows now, too. She used to get a little line there when she was concentrating on something. Or when she was mad.

God, she was beautiful, even more beautiful than when he'd seen her last, in person and in his dreams. His pulse quickened as it always had around her.

But her soft body stiffened beneath his. "Get up," she murmured.

And he snapped out of his momentary trance to remember that she was hurt. He'd seen the blood trickling down her neck. "Are you all right?" he asked with concern.

Her head jerked in a sharp nod. "Yeah, go. Don't let him get away." And she pressed her hands on his shoulders to shove him back.

And he remembered how she'd done that the last time they'd seen each other, when they'd fought, and instead of letting him hug her, she'd pushed him away. She hadn't let him touch her again, not even to hug and kiss her goodbye. She'd been too angry.

And at the time he had been, too. But even when he was mad at her, he'd been inexplicably drawn to her.

"Mark! Go!" she exclaimed.

And he remembered that they weren't teenagers anymore on a carefree summer trip. They were adults with responsibilities. And because of those responsibilities, he couldn't let a criminal get away.

He pushed himself up, but as he did he noticed the blood that had saturated the top of her scrubs and that smeared her skin red on her neck. "You're hurt badly."

She lifted her hand to the wound. "No. It's fine. Go!" Her voice wasn't weak, as if she needed help. She sounded strong and determined to not let that trafficker escape.

Her urgency surged through Mark. He turned and ran toward the lobby doors. But Billy was already there, pushing through them. If only the security guard would have unlocked the elevators but not the front doors…

But Mark was lucky he'd unlocked the elevators. The last thing they'd needed was for Lang to feel trapped and like he had no way out. Then in despair he might have killed Cassidy and then himself.

But she'd gotten away from him.

That was the most important thing.

The second was that Lang didn't escape.

Mark pushed through the doors to follow him out and stopped at the big rock formation in front of the lobby doors. Where was Billy? He couldn't see him now.

But he could hear the sirens and see lights flashing as the police vehicles headed toward the lot. He ran in that direction. Somebody must have brought Lang some clothes or he wouldn't have had anything to wear but the hospital gown after that crash that had killed his partner. So maybe that person had also brought him a vehicle and left it in the parking lot that was out front.

As he rounded the rock formation and headed toward the parking area, Mark caught sight of Billy. He wore dark clothes, but his hair was light enough to make him noticeable. And he was moving slower now. As Mark neared him, he could hear that Lang was breathing hard and fast.

He had not fully recovered yet from the crash. Mark could easily catch him. But just as he increased his speed to close the distance, a police car careened into the lot. The tires screeched as the vehicle braked, and an officer jumped out with gun drawn. Mark kept going, knocking Lang to the ground. The scissors skittered across the asphalt.

But the officer stepped closer and cocked his gun.

"He's unarmed!" Mark shouted. "Don't shoot."

But the gun stayed cocked, the barrel pointed more at Mark now than at Billy whose body was partially under Mark's. "Who the hell are you?" the officer asked.

"Mark Colton," he said, then he explained, "My sister

Ava works in the hospital. And my brother Jacob Colton is the ISB agent who arrested this guy. When I saw him trying to escape, I stopped him. You can put your gun away."

Lang wasn't even fighting to get away from Mark. His body had gone limp; maybe he'd passed out or maybe he was pretending to be back in the coma he'd apparently been faking.

The officer held his weapon up yet, as if he was mentally debating something.

And a chill raced down Mark's back as he remembered Ryan and Jacob telling him that somehow Lang and his partner had gotten a hold of an official badge and impersonated an officer in order to get Fern to leave with them.

"Who are you?" Mark asked.

"Officer Olsen," the man replied.

Mark skimmed his gaze from the officer's face over his uniform. "Wilson PD?" The city was an hour south of Dark Canyon. "What are you doing here?"

"I… I…came here to see if the patient had regained consciousness yet," he said. "I wanted to follow up and see if I could get this guy to talk about the women he abducted from my city."

"Have you talked to my brother Jacob Colton, since he's leading the investigation?" Mark was certainly going to talk to his brother. He pointed at the gun the guy held. "And you can put that away now."

"But the suspect has escaped custody," Olsen said. "He needs to be handcuffed before I put away my weapon."

"I disarmed him," Mark assured the officer. "And I've got him."

The guy must have lost consciousness again, because his body was limp but hot. He was burning up, probably with some kind of infection of his wounds from the crash.

More vehicles rolled into the parking lot, lights flashing, and finally Olsen re-holstered his weapon. If not for the arrival of the other officers, Mark wasn't certain what Olsen might have done. And that made him really uneasy, like it might not have been just Lang who took a bullet from the lawman.

Since one of the new arrivals was his brother Jacob, the special agent with the National Park Service Investigative Services Branch, Mark felt safe enough to jump up. But then he glanced down at Lang lying limp on the asphalt. "He needs medical attention, I think," he told his brother.

"Why? What did you do to him?" Olsen asked the question.

And Jacob looked over at the officer, his blue eyes narrowing with the same suspicion that Mark was feeling. "You're a long way from Wilson again," he remarked.

"Not that far," Olsen said. "And I came here to follow up, to try to get some answers." And he looked at Mark again.

Mark shook his head. "I don't know anything about Lang."

"Not how he got out here in the parking lot?" Olsen asked, and now he looked suspicious, like maybe he thought Mark had helped him. Maybe that was why he'd been so reluctant to re-holster his weapon.

"I'll explain all that but just not right now," Mark said. "I have to check on the nurse Lang was using as a hostage and make sure she's okay."

Blood had been trickling down Cassidy's neck. While she'd insisted the wound wasn't serious, what if it had been? What if she was hurt worse than he'd thought, and he'd just left her lying on the atrium floor?

He would never forgive himself for leaving her. Again.

* * *

The minute Cassidy had sent Mark chasing after Lang she had regretted it. Mark didn't appear to have a weapon on him while Lang had those damn scissors he'd taken away from her. What if he used them on Mark?

She'd pushed herself up from the ground then to go after them. To try to help. She still had the syringe she'd used to stab Lang. Not that it had stopped him much. If not for Mark jumping between them, Lang would have struck her with the scissors. And she might have been hurt worse than the small wounds he'd already inflicted on her neck.

Her fingers were stained with blood from when she'd touched her wound, and blood trickled yet down her neck. She was going to need stitches. But right now she needed to make sure that Mark was all right.

Her legs shook beneath her weight, though, and she moved slowly toward the lobby doors through which both men had disappeared. Then lights flashed outside the glass doors, and sirens wailed, as police vehicles pulled into the parking lot. Her breath shuddered out with relief. Lang wouldn't get away. And hopefully Mark was unharmed.

She wanted to go check but then the elevators behind her dinged as doors opened. And footsteps pounded across the floor as people rushed up to her.

"Cassidy, are you all right?" Dr. Finkbeiner asked the question, his eyes dark with concern. "You're bleeding. We need to get you to the ER now."

"What...what about the officer?" she asked. "Is he all right?" Guilt struck her that she'd just left him upstairs. But Lang hadn't given her a choice. He'd also admitted to drugging the officer with something that had made him sleep. Hopefully that was all he was doing.

"I'm sure someone is treating him," Frank said. "Now let me treat you. You're bleeding. I need to make sure those wounds aren't deep."

"They're not." Or she would be bleeding a hell of a lot worse than she was. And she was more concerned about that officer and Mark than she was herself right now.

The police had arrived. But Mark hadn't come back into the building yet. Had the police arrived in time? Or had Lang hurt him, too?

"Come on, Cassidy," Frank said, urgency in his voice. "We need to get you stitched up. Do you need me to carry you to the ER?"

She snorted. While she was pretty slim, she was five-eight with some muscles from all her years of nursing as much as the yoga and Pilates classes she did with her sister and some friends. She doubted that Frank, who was very slim, too, would be able to lift her, much less carry her anywhere.

But Mark…

He'd been able to lift her all those years ago. And he had even more muscles now, probably from all his years in the military. And wasn't he a bodyguard now?

He'd certainly protected her. She could have been hurt so much worse than she'd been. But what about him?

She peered out the door, but she couldn't see anything other than the flashing lights around that rock formation in front of the lobby.

"Cassidy, do I need to call your sister?" Dr. Finkbeiner asked. "Are you in shock?"

"I'm fine," she said.

"Then let me stitch you up."

"I need to check on that officer…" And Mark.

"I'm sure he's already been brought down to the ER," he said.

Hopefully he had. And if Mark had been hurt, he would be brought there, too. So Cassidy moved away from the lobby doors and back through the atrium toward the rear of the hospital where the emergency department was located.

"I still should call your sister," Dr. Finkbeiner said.

She shook her head. "It's late, and I don't want to worry her." She touched her neck. "Really this is nothing…" But her fingers came away wet from the blood still trickling from the wound.

"It could have been fatal," Frank said. "What the hell was that Colton guy up to? Ordering security to unlock the elevators and the doors?" He shook his head. "That was so damn dangerous. That trafficker could have gotten you out of the hospital."

But he hadn't. And even if she hadn't stabbed Lang with that syringe, she suspected that Mark would have stopped the criminal from taking her anywhere just as he'd stopped Lang from hurting her after she'd stabbed the man with the needle. He had to be hurt, too, so he was bound to wind up in the ER with her and probably back in the hospital as well.

She trembled, and Frank wrapped his arm around her. "You're okay now, Cassidy," he said. "You're safe."

But she didn't feel safe at all. And that had less to do with Lang than with Mark Colton. She pulled away from Frank as they stepped through the doors to the back. Nurses and residents were scrambling around treating the officer who had been brought down to the department. "How is he?" she asked. "Is he breathing?"

Tyler Gibbs glanced up and nodded. "He is. Glad to see you are, too. But you're bleeding, Cass—"

"I've got her," Frank replied, as he slung his arm around her again to guide her into an ER bay. "Lie down and we'll get your wounds cleaned and stitched up."

She shook her head as she settled onto the edge of the gurney. "It's not that bad. Just clean the wound and maybe liquid bandage will seal the cuts."

"I'm the doctor, Cassidy." And Frank, like some other doctors in the hospital, never hesitated to remind the nurses of that when they were doling out orders. "And you're the patient, not the nurse right now."

But she was impatient instead. She wanted to see how the officer was doing and even how Lang was. And Mark…

She just wanted to see Mark again. It had been so long. Despite saying, the last time they'd been together, that she never wanted to see him again, she wanted to see him now. She wanted to make sure that he was okay.

And if he was really as good-looking as she'd imagined he was or if it was just the adrenaline and fear that had her reacting to his presence. To his closeness when he'd lain on top of her.

It had to have been the fear that had had her pulse pounding, her skin tingling. It couldn't have been Mark. Too many years had passed for him to affect her like he once had. They were no longer the hormonal teenagers they used to be. They were adults now.

But then she looked up and found him standing just inside the curtain he must have pulled open again. He was watching Frank treat her wounds, stitching up the bigger of the cuts. He'd already put a butterfly bandage on the smaller one.

Then Mark looked away from Frank, and his gaze slid up her face until his eyes met hers.

And she felt that sharp jolt again. That rush of awareness and attraction. Despite more than a decade passing since that summer, she remembered it so clearly. The sunshine and the heat. The wind blowing through all the open windows of the old van they'd used like a camper. That had been before van life was cool like the influencer flex it was now. But they'd been cool then. Young. Sexy. Passionate.

Maybe too young and too passionate, and the desire they'd felt for each other had been too hot for them to survive. And as her gaze met his, that heat rushed through her again.

But she was older now. Wiser. She wasn't going to let Mark Colton break her heart again.

Officer Olsen's finger twitched like it had on the trigger a short while ago. Lang was a liability that needed to be eliminated. But now he wasn't the only one.

It was bad enough having one Colton breathing down his neck, asking questions like Jacob Colton was asking him now. But now there was another one.

"What are you doing here?" Jacob asked.

"I already told you, I'm just following up on the missing women," Olsen replied.

"At this time of night?"

"I couldn't get here sooner," Olsen replied. But he wished like hell that he had. That he'd gotten to the hospital before Mark Colton had. "What was your brother doing here? He's not in law enforcement, too, is he?"

Jacob shook his head. "No. Ex-military in private security now."

"A mercenary?"

Jacob chuckled. "A bodyguard. Sounds like it was a good thing he was here tonight."

Not for Olsen.

Chapter 5

Mark didn't like the way that dark-haired doctor was touching Cassidy or even the way he was looking at her, like they were more than coworkers. But it was none of his business if they were more. Mark was nothing to her anymore.

But he couldn't say the same about her. She wasn't nothing to him. "Are you all right?" he asked.

"You can't be back here," the doctor said. "You need to leave."

"No, it's fine," Cassidy said.

"Cass, he's a stranger—"

"No, I'm not," Mark said.

"I know you're related to Ava Colton or something," the doctor replied. "But that doesn't give you open access to the whole hospital."

"Cassidy and I go way back," Mark said. Then he turned toward her. "Don't we, Cass?"

A little color chased the paleness from her skin, painting her cheeks bright pink. "Mark and I went to high school together," she told the doctor. "And like I said, it's fine that he's here. But you're done." She spoke for the guy. Maybe she knew that he'd affixed the bandage over her stitches that matched the one near her collarbone. Or maybe she was talking about something else, like whatever might have been between the two of them?

Mark was probably just reading into the situation. But being observant was the reason he was still alive despite all the near misses he'd had in his life, and it was also why he was a damn good bodyguard.

"Lang is being wheeled into the ER right now," Mark said. Jacob had requested medical help in the parking lot before Mark had walked away. "You're probably going to need to treat him."

The doctor clenched his jaw and shook his head. "No. I already saved that animal once, and I regret that now. He could have killed you, Cass."

"I'm fine," she said. "And you can't refuse to treat a patient." She stood up from where she'd been sitting on the edge of the gurney.

And Mark stepped closer as she trembled a bit as if her legs were unsteady. "Careful…"

"I'm fine," she repeated, her voice sharp with impatience. "And I should help."

"Your shift ended ten minutes ago," the doctor said.

"That didn't stop you from paging me the last time this guy was brought into the ER," she said. "You know I am one of the few nurses with the security clearance to treat him."

The doctor sighed but nodded. Then he stepped around Mark, without even sparing him a glance, as he left the area.

When Cassidy moved to follow the doctor, Mark caught her arm. The contact with the bare skin of her forearm sent a jolt through him of awareness, of attraction. She tensed as if she felt it, too.

"You shouldn't be anywhere near that guy," Mark told her. "He could have killed you."

"He didn't," she said. "He was just using me to escape from the hospital."

"I'm not so sure about that," Mark said. "The guy is a human trafficker. You can't be sure what his true motive was for trying to take you with him."

She shuddered. "It doesn't matter what his intention was. You stopped him."

"You stopped him with that needle," Mark said, impressed by how resourceful she was. Then he remembered how the man had lunged at her with the scissors, and he shuddered now. "But you could have gotten hurt worse than he already hurt you."

She shook her head. "I couldn't let him drag me along with him."

"I would have stopped him," he promised, hoping she'd trusted him.

But she just shrugged. "I can take care of myself. And with all the police I saw pulling into the parking lot, I am sure he won't have the chance to get away again."

Mark thought again of Officer Olsen pointing that gun. Had he been aiming at him or at Lang? He wasn't sure which one of them now. Had the officer actually been helping Lang, or had he really just wanted to make sure that he didn't escape?

"You know he's not working alone," Mark said.

"His partner was killed in that crash."

"I'm not talking about his partner," Mark said. "I'm talking about his boss or bosses or coconspirators. It's not safe for you to be around him."

"Cassidy!" that doctor shouted from somewhere close. "I need you over here."

She tugged on her arm, pulling it from his loose grasp. "I have to do my job," she said.

"You're wounded," he said. "And your shift ended. Whoever was supposed to take over for you can step in now."

"They might not be down here," she said. "And I am. And I'm sure there are a bunch of police officers here, too, to make sure that he doesn't get away again. I will be fine, Mark. You have to let me go."

He stepped back, so she could pass him and slip away.

Just like he'd known that summer long ago, he knew now that he couldn't hang on to Cassidy Garner. Once her mind was made up, she didn't change it.

An hour later Cassidy's pride was stung yet over how easily Mark had let her go. And that reminded her of how she'd had to let him go all those years ago. Not that he'd needed her permission or that he'd had any intention of staying. She knew that he'd always intended to leave Dark Canyon; he'd just assumed she would follow him around and wait around for him. But Cassidy had wanted a life of her own.

She had it. All to herself now except for Patsy and Alec and Brian. But they weren't around all the time, so sometimes she was lonely.

But that was her choice. She could have accepted Tyler's invitations to go out. But she didn't want a relationship with anyone she worked with, no matter how casual. She knew that it could get complicated.

And she'd done complicated once with Mark. She didn't want to do that again.

But when she was done helping treat Lang, she found Mark waiting outside the ER bay for her. Or maybe he was just waiting around with his brother Jacob, who stood beside him.

"That's her," Mark said.

Jacob nodded. "I've met Ms. Garner before. She was the nurse for Fern before she was for Lang."

She could have reminded the ISB agent that he had also met her at their house when she'd been hanging out with Mark, studying or watching movies or having dinner with his family. But that had been a long time ago. And she didn't need to think about that time any more than she already did, which was much too often.

"Agent Colton," she greeted him. "Dr. Finkbeiner can let you know the patient's condition." And Frank stepped out of the bay to join her.

"He has an infection in the wound in his arm," the doctor said. "He's going to need IV antibiotics, and we're going to have to watch to make sure it doesn't spread to his blood or his organs."

"It's that serious?" Jacob asked.

Frank nodded. "Unfortunately. I would love to be able to release him to police custody. But that won't be happening."

"You're going to need to increase security," Mark said. "So that he doesn't manage to escape again."

"You were the one encouraging him to walk out the door," the doctor remarked sarcastically. "It's a miracle he didn't escape with Cassidy as his hostage."

"That wouldn't have happened," Mark said. "I had it under control."

Frank snorted. "Cassidy stabbed him with a needle and got away on her own," he said. "I saw the wound on his face."

And Cassidy had explained how Lang got it. But she

wasn't naive enough to think that she would have gotten away from the man. No matter how sick he was, he was stronger than she was. And he was desperate, which made him even more dangerous.

"That was smart thinking," Jacob told her. "I need to take the rest of your report, Ms. Garner. Is there somewhere we can speak privately?" He glanced at the doctor then and even at his brother. Clearly he didn't want either of them to overhear their discussion.

"Cassidy has been through a lot," the doctor answered for her. "I hardly think she's up to an interrogation."

"But she was up to helping you with a patient," Mark shot back at Frank. "And my brother is hardly going to interrogate her."

"I'm fine," she reminded both of the men bickering over her. "And I would prefer to give my report now and get it out of the way." And put all of this, including seeing Mark Colton again, behind her.

Far behind her.

If only she could also put Lang behind her. But he was in no condition to be released to jail. And she was going to have to be his nurse again. The thought had a chill rushing down her spine, and she shivered.

"You're cold," Mark remarked, and he shrugged off the flannel shirt he wore over a T-shirt and handed it to her. "Here, take this."

And she flashed back to all the times he'd given her the shirt right off his back. But then he'd wrapped it around her, wrapping her in his warmth and his scent. She still had one of his old flannel shirts folded up in a dresser drawer. But she wasn't that silly teenage girl anymore. She hadn't been since she'd had to make that tough decision that summer. To follow his dream or to follow her own.

She handed his shirt back to him and insisted, like a broken record, "I'm fine. It's just late, and I need to get going." She glanced around then and indicated an open bay of the ER. "We can talk there," she told Jacob. It wasn't a private room, but the curtains were heavy enough when pulled shut that nobody would be able to hear them unless they were deliberately eavesdropping. And everybody else in the ER was too busy to do that.

Jacob's forehead furrowed a moment, but then he nodded and followed her into the bay. As she pulled the curtain behind them, she noticed that Mark and Frank seemed to have moved a little closer to where they were, as if they'd followed them. Maybe they intended to eavesdrop, or they were just worried about her safety. But unlike Mark, his brother was armed, and she trusted him to protect her.

She trusted Jacob much more than she trusted Mark. Mark had already hurt her once, and if she let him get close to her again, she was certain that he would do it again. Because there was no way he was sticking around Dark Canyon.

And she couldn't leave now even more than she hadn't been able to follow him around eleven years ago. She had people in Dark Canyon who relied on her, people she loved even more than she'd once loved him.

"I'm sorry, Agent—"

"Jacob," he interjected. "Please call me Jacob. Ava reminded me that you used to date Mark back in high school, so we don't need to be so formal with each other."

She forced a smile and nodded.

But then he started firing questions at her, and she realized there was nothing casual about this interview. It did feel more like an interrogation than simply taking her report. "I'm sorry," she said. "I was trying to be careful since we weren't certain if he was really still in the coma, but I wasn't as careful as I should have been. When I heard a strange noise outside the door, I moved toward it and accidentally left the scissors on the tray next to Lang's bed. I'd been changing his bandages…"

"What noise did you hear?" Jacob asked.

"A loud thud. It must have been when the police officer fell off his chair."

"How did the officer look when you passed him to enter the room?"

"Tired," she admitted. "But I thought that was just because it was late and toward the end of his shift. He insisted that he would be fine until the next officer arrived."

"Did you see anyone slip anything into his coffee?"

She shook her head. "No. But Lang admitted that he did."

"How did he do that?"

She shrugged. "I don't know. It must have happened when I was getting the new bandages from the supply closet."

"So you'd stepped away from Lang's room?"

"I'm not in there around the clock," she said. "I just go in to check on him, on his vitals and to change his bandages."

"So you had no indication that Lang was conscious?"

She sighed. "The neurologist knew he wasn't in a physical coma but the word *psychosomatic* was being used."

"Which means?"

"That there could have been a psychological reason that he hadn't regained consciousness yet. Your cousin Ava could explain that to you better than I can," Cassidy said, and she nearly yawned as exhaustion suddenly overwhelmed her. "I can only answer to what I did tonight. I screwed up leaving those scissors there. I hope you believe me that it was an accident." Because she was beginning to worry that the agent thought she'd helped Lang, that she was working with him. "But I understand if, after this, you no longer want me to be the nurse for this patient."

Jacob shook his head. "That's not the case at all, Cassidy. I'm just trying to figure out how this happened so we can make sure that it doesn't happen again."

She doubted that was something he could promise. Lang was desperate to escape, so desperate that he would undoubtedly stage another attempt. That chill rushed over her again at the thought, and she wished she'd accepted Mark's shirt. But having his warmth and his scent wrapped around her would have made it even harder for her to ignore her reaction to him, her attraction to him.

"I will make sure that I am more careful in the future," she said because she was not going to be the reason that her sister or nephews suffered another loss. But she wasn't just going to be more careful around Lang; she was going to be more careful around Mark, too.

"That's a good plan," Jacob said. "We don't know who all is working for this trafficking ring. You shouldn't trust anyone right now."

"I won't," she agreed.

Jacob grinned. "Except me. And you can trust my brother, too. Mark is a bodyguard now. He already told me that he intends to drive you home tonight and check out the security at your place. He will make sure nothing will happen to you."

She shook her head, rejecting the idea of being alone with Mark, of having him in her home. "No. Mark and I aren't..." Lovers, like they'd once been, but she wasn't about to use that word with his brother, so she floundered for the right word. "We're not…we're strangers now. There's no reason for him to act as my bodyguard."

"Like I just said, we don't know who all is working with the traffickers, Cassidy," Jacob said. "We don't know how Billy got the sleeping aid he put in the officer's coffee or how he got the clothes he was wearing."

"His lawyer has visited him," she said, "which I thought was odd with him being in a coma."

"I will be questioning him, too, but I want to talk to everyone in the hospital who's had access to Lang's room, too," Jacob said.

"You think someone working in the hospital helped him?" she asked.

Jacob shrugged. "We don't know anything for certain yet. Ordinarily I would have an officer drive you home tonight, but I think it's a better idea for Mark to drive you and make sure that your place is secure."

Her heart pounded hard and fast again like it had when Lang had grabbed her scissors. And when she'd seen Mark again. "You don't think I can trust one of the officers?"

"It's smart to be careful right now," Jacob said. "You've had a hell of a night. Let Mark drive you home. Maybe I can talk him into handling security here at the hospital, too, while you're working."

Cassidy shook her head again. "No. That's not necessary. I don't need a bodyguard." And if she did, the last man she would want on the job was Mark Colton.

The last man she would want was Mark Colton. Or the last man she *should* want was Mark Colton. But part of her yearned for him to touch her again like he used to, to kiss her again…to make her come apart in his arms like she used to.

* * *

The man waited in the shadows outside Baldwin Memorial Hospital. He'd been waiting for a while and watching. And his patience paid off when two people walked out. A tall man with short dark hair and the woman with bright blond hair. She wore scrubs, stained with blood, and the man wore a flannel shirt and jeans.

He didn't look like what he was: ex-military and a bodyguard. He didn't look like the pain in the ass that he was. Always rushing to the rescue, getting in the way, causing trouble.

Somebody needed to make him pay for his interference. And soon someone would.

Chapter 6

Mark glanced across the console at Cassidy. Even though she hadn't said a word since settling into the passenger's seat, she wasn't quiet because she'd fallen asleep. Despite how late it was and the dark circles beneath her pretty blue eyes, she was wide-awake. Her body was stiff, her fingers digging into the armrest on the door as if she was tempted to push it open and jump out while the SUV was moving.

"You can relax. I'm not taking you hostage like Lang did," he said.

"Feels a little like you have," she said, her voice harsh with resentment. "Your brother didn't give me much choice."

"Because he wants to make sure you're safe," he said. And so did Mark.

"Lang is not getting out of the hospital tonight," she said. "Not with all the police there."

Mark snorted.

"What?" she asked. "Your brother acted like that, too, like he seemed to think I was safer with you driving me home than with another officer."

Mark nodded. "He does think that, and so do I."

"Why?"

"Lang had somehow gotten a hold of an official badge when he abducted Fern."

"You and your brother think there's an officer working with Billy Lang?"

"With the traffickers that Billy and his partner were working for," he clarified.

"Who?"

He shrugged. "Jacob is working on figuring it out. But I think he hopes he's wrong. That it's not an officer." Mark understood that; a betrayal from a person who was supposed to be on your side was hard to understand and made it even harder to trust again.

He wasn't thinking just about Rob Coffey now but about Cassidy, too. How she'd backed out of their plan for the future and out of their relationship. He glanced across the console at her again. "Does this remind you of that summer?" he asked.

She tensed again, her fingers digging even harder into the armrest. "How? What do you mean?"

"Our road trip across the country," he said. "Me driving. You riding shotgun in that old van of yours."

She snorted now. "You did always have to drive."

He caught the resentment in her voice. "I thought that was what you wanted, because you loved staring out the windows and taking pictures. You didn't want to miss anything."

She breathed in deeply. "I didn't then, and I certainly don't miss *anything* from that trip."

He sucked in a breath now at the jab of pain over her making it clear she hadn't missed him. He wished he could say the same, but he had missed her over the years. Too much.

"That was a long time ago," she said. "We were just kids then. Naive and idealistic."

She didn't sound like either now. She sounded as cynical as he sometimes felt.

"You don't miss being naive and idealistic?" he asked.

"No. I like being an adult," she said again with that resentment.

"It was easier being a kid," he said.

"But being naive and idealistic just led to disappointment," she said.

Was that all their breakup had been to her? Just a disappointment? Like what she would feel over not being able to get tickets to a concert or something? Disappointment didn't begin to describe the heartbreak he'd felt.

He had been devastated. Fortunately boot camp had been so hard and left him so tired that he hadn't been able to wallow in his misery. He'd had to push his way through it to the other side. He sighed. "Yeah, you're right."

He forced thoughts of the past from his mind and focused on the drive from the hospital to her home, which was a town house not far from Baldwin Memorial. As he followed the directions she'd given him, he kept an eye on the rearview mirror, checking to see if anyone was following them from the hospital. Headlights were consistently behind them, shining in the back of the SUV. But the road between the hospital and her condo subdivision was a busy one. It might have just been coincidence.

"Do a lot of people who work at the hospital live in this complex?" he asked as he turned into the community of three-story-tall, brick-and-stone townhomes.

"Quite a few," she said. "It's close, making it an easy commute especially in the winter when the roads are snow-covered and slippery."

So some of the lights behind them could have just been another hospital employee heading home after a shift. But still…

The short hairs on the back of his neck bristled as tension wound through him. What if someone had followed them? And why had they?

"This is my condo," Cassidy said, pointing toward the unit on the farthest end of a cul-de-sac street. Tall pines towered next to it, dimming the glow of the streetlamp and the light burning next to the door.

And he was very glad he'd driven her home. "This place isn't very safe," he said.

She made a slight growling sound. "It is a very safe neighborhood."

"Maybe the neighborhood," he acknowledged. "But your unit is on the end next to the woods. Anyone could come out of the woods and try to get into your place."

"How?" she asked.

"You have windows on that side," he said. "Maybe a door to a patio. It gives an intruder easy access points."

She made that growling sound again.

So he knew that he was right, and she couldn't argue with him. Because if she could have, she would have. Despite being more than a decade older, she clearly hadn't changed quite as much as she'd said. While she might not have been naive and idealistic anymore, she was still argumentative. He'd once found that so sexy. Actually, from how fast his heart was beating, he still did.

But he had to focus on keeping her safe, not how damn sexy she was. "Do you have a security system?" he asked.

"No," she said, her jaw taut.

"Then I do need to go inside with you and make sure the place is safe," he said.

"That's not necessary."

"I told Jacob that I would," he said. Not because his brother had asked him to but because Mark had insisted on making sure that her home was secure, that she would be in no more danger than she'd already been tonight.

"I don't care what you promised your brother," she said. "It isn't necessary for you to go inside. It wasn't even necessary for you to drive me home."

She clearly didn't want him in her home. Why? Was there someone inside waiting for her that she didn't want him to meet? A husband? Children?

If she'd been at all friendly with him, he would've asked her questions like two old friends catching up would do. But they weren't two old friends. They were two old lovers.

An image flashed through his mind of making love with her, their naked bodies entwined on the mattress in the back of her old van. Skin sliding over skin, her breasts bumping his chest, her nipples taut, her core slick as he slid inside her. In and out, thrusting as the passion gripped him so tightly he felt like he was going to explode. And then he had.

And she'd joined him, screaming his name.

"Mark!" she yelled his name now with impatience, probably because she'd called for his attention more than once.

He blinked, trying to clear that memory from his mind and the tension from his body. But he could think of only one way he could do that, with her, *in* her.

Cassidy wanted to get rid of Mark. Now. Before she did something stupid, before she let herself remember what it had been like between them all those years ago.

The passion had burned so hot between them. But they'd had even more than passion.

They'd had love, too, or so she'd thought. She'd had so much fun with him. They'd talked endlessly about their dreams, about the bright future they saw together. But they hadn't actually agreed on how to get to that future.

She wanted to go to college and nursing school while he'd joined the army and shipped off all over the world. She could have followed him, but that would have meant putting her dreams on hold. And he could have waited for her but that would have meant putting his dreams on hold. Neither of them had been willing to make the sacrifice for the other.

"Cassidy, just let me look around, make sure that all the doors and windows are locked and that there is no easy way for someone to get inside," he urged her from where he sat yet in the driver's seat.

She should have opened the passenger door and hopped out already. But it did seem so dark outside the SUV, the pine trees blocking out whatever light might have penetrated from the streetlamp and the fixture next to her front door. And she was chilled yet from what had happened tonight, of how close she'd come to getting abducted just like her friend Fern had been. Thankfully Fern hadn't been sexually abused, but physically she'd gone through hell with her broken leg, and her spirit had nearly been broken, too.

But she was doing so much better now. Fern was strong, and she had the love and support of Mark's cousin Ryan. And the protection.

Cassidy lived alone. Usually she was happy that she did. She liked coming home to decompress in silence after a rough shift at the hospital. And tonight had been the roughest. But, except for the light next to the front door, the town house was dark. She shivered at the thought of stepping into the place, of not knowing if she was going to be alone or have to fight someone off like she'd fought Lang off a short while ago.

"Damn you..." she muttered. "I think you're making me paranoid." Which was the least of the things he'd made her actually. He'd also made her cynical and resentful, too.

"It's smart to be cautious, Cassidy," he said.

He was right. But if she was truly going to be cautious, she wouldn't have let him drive her home. But now that he was here...

She sighed. "Fine," she said. "You can check the condo to make sure that it's safe." And that nobody was waiting in the dark for her.

Not that anyone would have a reason to do that. But she was on edge, paranoid, and not just because of Mark. Human traffickers were operating in Dark Canyon and one had nearly abducted her tonight. She would have been naive and idealistic if she wasn't a bit paranoid. And, as she'd told Mark, she wasn't naive and idealistic anymore. Not since that summer. Not since he'd broken her heart.

"You can open that passenger door now," Mark said. "The entire time I was driving here I kept thinking that you were going to open it and jump out while the SUV was moving."

She couldn't fight the smile that curved her lips. "That obvious?"

"Yes." He leaned a bit over the console now, staring intently at her mouth. "Yes..."

And now it wasn't just a smile that she was fighting. It was the urge to lick her lips and then lean over to meet his mouth with hers. To see if his kisses were as incredible as she remembered.

Fear of giving in to temptation, of getting hurt again jolted her. She fumbled with the handle and pushed open the door, desperate for some space between them. When she hopped out onto the drive, her knees nearly folded beneath her weight, her legs shaking.

He had been the only one able to do that to her, to make her tremble with desire. She'd thought it was just because she'd been a teenager when she'd fallen for him. She'd thought it was something she'd just outgrown and that was why no other man had affected her like that.

But it was him.

"Damn him..."

"Damning me again?" he asked, his voice a deep rumble close to her ear.

She jumped, startled that he'd gotten so close to her without her noticing. And that he'd overheard her that time when she hadn't intended him to hear her. Because she didn't want to explain.

"Sorry," he said. "I didn't mean to scare you."

But he did frighten her so very much. It was a different fear than what she'd felt when Lang had threatened her with those scissors. She wasn't afraid for her life now; she was afraid for her heart.

She released a shaky breath. "It's been a hell of a night," she said. "And I'm working the morning shift."

"Then let's get you to bed," he said, his voice even deeper now while his eyes twinkled in the faint light.

She shook her head. "I'll get myself to bed," she said. "You just need to check my doors and windows."

He muttered now, but it sounded as if he said, "That's too bad..."

The last thing she wanted was Mark Colton flirting with her. Because that was how it had started all those years ago when she'd been the new girl in their high school after her parents moved their family to Dark Canyon. Or maybe she'd been the one flirting with him then. He'd been so cute that she hadn't been able to help herself.

And now that teenage boy had grown into an even more attractive man. She forced herself to look away from him as she headed toward her front door.

He stuck close, as if he was trying to use his body as a shield to protect hers. But his closeness unsettled her so much that she couldn't find her keys in her purse. The leather satchel was all she'd grabbed from her locker because he'd been waiting for her. But her keys had to be in the bag.

"You should always have your keys out in your hand when you come up to your door or your vehicle," he said.

"Yes, Dad," she said sarcastically. "Usually I drive straight into my garage and shut down the door before I step out." She pointed toward the garage door that was next to the front door.

"Don't tell me you leave the door between the garage and the house unlocked," he said, groaning.

Heat rushed to her face. "Why…why would that be a problem?"

"Because it's so easy to reprogram garage door openers. It wouldn't be hard for someone to get into your garage and then into your house."

The keys jabbed her fingers, and she pulled them from the bottom of her bag. "Here they are." But what he'd said was making her shake so badly that she probably would not be able to get them into the lock.

He took them from her, his skin brushing over hers,

making her tingle with even more awareness of him, of his closeness, of his hotness.

"You need a security system with a programmable lock for your door," he said as he held the keys in the pool of light from the fixture next to her door. He chose one of the keys, inserted it and turned the knob to pop open the door.

She had keys for other places on that key chain. Patsy's door. Her parents'. A storage unit. "How did you do that?" she asked suspiciously.

He shrugged. "No special powers or parlor trick. Teeth of the key match the teeth of the lock," he said.

As he drew it out, she looked at the key and then the lock. She didn't see much difference between the key and all the other ones on her chain, but she was so tired she could barely see the front door despite its bright red color. She reached to push it open wide enough for her to step inside, but he caught her arm and stopped her from entering.

"Let me go first but stick close to me while I make sure the place is clear."

"I can wait outside," she said. Not that she wanted him inside her home without her.

He shook his head. "Might not be safe out here either."

She shivered. "You *are* making me paranoid."

"Cautious," he said as he stepped into the foyer and flipped on the light. "And trust me, it's better to be cautious than to be dead."

He held up a hand, holding her back, as he checked behind the door and in the closet. Next he opened the unlocked door to the garage, tsked, and shook his head. The garage was only one stall and empty now that her vehicle was still at the hospital. So he could see everything from the door, that he closed again and locked. Then he waved her into her own home.

She hesitated a moment before stepping over the threshold. "Your brother told me not to trust anyone," she said.

He chuckled. "Except for him and for me."

She stepped inside, and he closed the door behind her and locked that one, too. She said, "You were eavesdropping."

He nodded but turned away from her. He checked the small guest bath although there was no way anyone could hide in there. There wasn't even a shower or tub. Then he moved into the kitchen with its bright white cabinets, shiny, stainless steel appliances and crisp white countertops.

"Yes, I eavesdropped," he said. "I wanted to know what happened tonight, how the cop got knocked out and how Lang got your scissors."

"Did you think I helped Lang?" she asked, curious if he could have doubted her.

He snorted. "No. You tried stabbing him in the eye with a needle."

She flinched as she remembered doing that. If she hadn't been desperate to save herself, she wouldn't have ever hurt another person. But knowing how Lang and his partner had hurt Fern had compelled her to do whatever necessary to defend herself. "I missed."

He chuckled again. "Disappointed?"

"No," she said. "I just wanted to get away, not mortally wound him."

"Sometimes you have to mortally wound someone in order to survive," he murmured. He'd moved to her kitchen window, checking the lock, and now to the sliders that opened onto a small patio.

"They're locked," she said even as he tugged on the handles.

"Yeah, but these locks are flimsy. Sliding doors are easy to force open. You need a bar in the track here." He pointed to it. "That way the door can't be forced."

"I don't have a bar."

He moved back to her kitchen, reached over the sink and pulled down the small curtain rod. After taking off the cute teal blue curtain that coordinated with her plates and countertop appliances, he jammed that into the track of the slider. "This'll do for now."

But she had no curtain over her kitchen window.

He walked to the two-story living room, checking the windows there. One was unlocked. He tsked again like he had over the garage door and locked it, too. Then he headed toward the stairs to the second story.

"That's everything on the main level," she said. "Nobody can get upstairs if they can't get in here."

"Unless they're already up there."

She shivered again and followed him. The second story had two bedrooms with en suite bathrooms. She had decorated the one over the garage for her nephews when she'd moved back here three years ago. It had twin beds with bright-patterned bedspreads and matching curtains at the windows and stuffed animals on both beds. The boys claimed now that they were too old for them, but yet every time they stayed over, they cuddled with them at night.

"You have kids?" Mark asked, his voice gruff, his green eyes wide with surprise when he turned back to her.

She could have explained that the bedroom was set up like this for her nephews. But it wasn't any of his business for whom she'd decorated this room. She also liked that he'd realized she could have moved on after their breakup, that she could have gotten married and started a family. Her ego liked him thinking that she'd left their relationship and him in the past even though she actually hadn't.

"Cassidy?" he prodded.

She shook her head. "This isn't a high school reunion where we're catching up on what has happened in each other's lives," she said. And she was happy about that because it wouldn't have taken her long to catch him up on what she'd done. School. Work. Her family. "You're just here to check that my home is safe from human traffickers."

He sighed. "And it's really not, Cassidy. I think I should stay the night."

"You put my curtain rod in the sliders and locked all the windows and doors. I'm safe," she said, and she yawned. "And I'm tired. I need to get to bed."

"Let's check that room next," he said. But he poked his head into the bedroom the boys used before striding into her suite.

He opened the door and turned on the light from the small chandelier over the queen-size bed. With its pale pink walls and bedding, the room was ultrafeminine. And as he moved around the space, he looked even more masculine. For a moment she could imagine him lying in that bed with her. Naked. His hair dark against the pillows and sheets.

Fortunately he went into her bathroom then, checking the shower and the walk-in closet. His gaze moved along the line of her clothes. Was he checking for intruders? Or checking to see if there were any men's clothing hanging among hers?

He had to know that she was single from looking at her stuff. But when he came back into her bedroom, he picked up a picture from the bedside table. It was of her and the boys from a few years ago. Patsy had taken the photo of them, their heads close together as they sat on her couch watching one of their favorite movies.

"Twins," Mark remarked, his eyes narrowed as he studied the picture.

The boys had darker hair than hers, and their eyes were hazel. They looked more like their dad than they did Patsy. Her sister claimed it was comforting, like a piece of her beloved husband lived on in their children. Patsy treasured her memories of Brian senior.

Cassidy, on the other hand, had cursed the memories she had of Mark, of their time together. Of the passion they'd shared, the passion that had eluded her with anyone else. Even now she could envision them rolling around in the back of the van he'd mentioned earlier, their naked bodies entwined. And him filling what had been a hollow ache inside her the past eleven years.

Tears of frustration stung her eyes, and she blinked them away.

"You love them," he murmured, obviously misconstruing the tears.

She cleared her throat. "Again, not your business, Colton," she reminded him. "You've checked my house. It's safe. I'm safe."

She really wasn't safe, not with him and not with the memories chasing through her mind, warming her body, making her skin tingle and her pulse race. She wanted to blame those sensations on a rush of adrenaline over nearly being abducted earlier. But she knew that it was him, just like it had been back in high school. And he made her feel like a teenager again: immature, reckless, impulsive.

She needed him out of her bedroom now. Before she did something stupid, like drag him down onto that bed with her.

Jacob was so damn glad that Mark was home and not just because he'd missed his brother. Mark would make sure that nothing happened to Cassidy Garner. A twinge of guilt struck Jacob over the ordeal she'd just suffered. But she was one of the few nurses with the security clearance necessary to treat Fern. So that had also made her one of the few able to treat Billy Lang.

Jacob stood over the guy's bedside now, staring down at him. Lang had bandages on his arms and IVs pumping antibiotics in him. He also had a small bandage on his cheek from where Cassidy had stabbed him with a needle.

She was tough, so hopefully she would have no trauma over what had happened to her tonight. And she had Mark making sure that she got safely home. Jacob couldn't remember what the story between them was, why they'd broken up. He would ask Mark when he had the chance.

But right now he was focused on his case. And on Billy Lang.

The guy's lids moved, twitching slightly before opening a slit.

Jacob chuckled. "You can give up the act, Lang. Nobody's buying your *coma*."

Lang groaned. "I'm burning up, man."

"You have an infection," Jacob said.

"Yeah, from you trying to kill me like you did Leo," Lang said.

Jacob shrugged. "You and your partner needed to be

stopped before any other women were hurt. But then you tried to hurt your nurse tonight."

"I had to get out of here," Lang said.

"Why?"

Lang snorted. "You know why."

"You might be able to strike a deal," Jacob said, "if you start talking. If you tell us what you know about the human trafficking ring."

Lang snorted again, then coughed. "You just don't get it at all."

"What?"

Lang moved his head back and forth on his pillow, shaking it. "There are certain people who you don't cross. Or get in their way."

"Talk to me and we'll get you witness protection," Jacob offered.

Lang released a ragged sigh of resignation, as if he didn't believe there was any way that Jacob could protect him. How powerful was the person in charge of the human trafficking? "Don't worry about me," Lang said. "Worry about your brother now."

"What?"

"That was your brother tonight, right?" Lang asked. "The one who stopped me?"

Jacob's stomach muscles tightened, but he couldn't deny Mark's relationship to him. "Yeah."

"He's going to regret getting involved in this," Lang said. "He's going to need protection now."

"I'm not worried," Jacob said. Mark was a survivor. And now he was a bodyguard. He protected other people, so of course he would be able to protect himself.

But despite what he'd just said, Jacob found himself

worrying about his brother. Could he have survived all his missions in the army and his assignments as a bodyguard and wind up losing his life at home?

Chapter 7

Bleary-eyed from lack of sleep, Mark stumbled down the back staircase to the kitchen. Sunshine poured in through the many windows, and he squinted against it, trying to adjust his eyes to the brightness. After some blinking, he managed to focus on his dad standing at the granite island in the middle of the kitchen.

Sam chuckled. "Reminds me of old times with you stumbling down the stairs like that in the morning. Rough night?" he asked as he poured a mug of coffee and pushed it across the counter to Mark.

Mark wrapped his hands around the mug and lifted it to his mouth. He gulped down a couple of scalding sips before clearing his throat. "Just a late one," he said.

His dad chuckled again. "That reminds me of old times, too. You staying out too late with Cassidy Garner. I'm surprised her dad didn't threaten you with a shotgun."

"I always got her home on time," Mark insisted. "She had negotiated a later curfew than mine." He grinned and teased, "Her dad was easier-going than the ogre who raised me."

Sam snorted. "Yeah, right. I might have been an ogre if your mother had ever let me enforce any punishment on you boys. She had the softest, biggest heart."

A twinge struck Mark's heart at the thought of his sweet mother. "Yes, she did." Mark glanced around the kitchen then, yearning to see her here where she'd spent so much time. "It feels weird to be here without her."

"Yes, it felt weird to me too for so long," Sam said.

Felt.

Apparently he'd gotten used to it. Or he'd moved on… with a neighbor no less. That was probably why he hadn't sold the house because Susan Baylor lived so close.

Guilt pricked at Mark for thinking that. He should have been happy that his dad was doing better. As devastating as it had been for Mark to lose his mother, it had to have been hardest on Dad. Sam had loved her so much. He and Kate had had the kind of marriage most people wanted, loving and supportive.

Mark and Cassidy had always talked about having more than that kind of relationship, though. They hadn't wanted to settle down in the big family house with the white picket fence where Mark had grown up, where Mark's dad still lived. They'd wanted a life on the road. A life of adventure.

Or so he'd thought until she'd backed out of the plan.

"So where were you last night?" Sam asked. "Out with one of your brothers or cousins?"

Mark sighed and shook his head. "No."

"You don't have to tell me," Sam said. "I know you're not a teenager any—"

"I was with Cassidy," Mark interjected.

And his dad laughed. But when Mark didn't laugh with him, he stopped and stared at him. "You're seeing Cassidy Garner again? Is that why you're sticking around Dark Canyon?"

Mark snorted. "No. And last night was the first time

I've seen Cassidy since I got back." Since that summer they'd broken up actually. She hadn't even attended his mother's funeral like so many of his friends from school had. Someone had said then that her parents had moved away and she hadn't come back after college.

But she was here now.

Why?

"When's the last time you've seen her?" he asked his dad. Maybe his father knew if the boys in the picture on her bedside table were hers and if she was married or divorced. Probably divorced, he would guess, since there had been no evidence of a man's presence in her bedroom. And the boys hadn't been asleep in their beds at her house. So maybe they went back and forth between her home and their dad's.

His father sighed. "I don't know. I guess it would be that summer after you and she graduated high school."

"Yeah, me, too," Mark murmured.

"So did you just run into her somewhere last night?" his dad asked.

Mark nodded. "At the hospital when I was checking in with Ava."

"You were talking to Ava?" his dad asked, his dark brown eyes narrowed as he studied Mark's face.

Mark grinned. "Not like that," he said. "Not in a professional capacity. I was just checking on my cousin to make sure she was safe with that human trafficker in the hospital."

Sam shuddered. "That's a horrible business. Horrible. How was she? Is that trafficker still in the hospital and not in jail yet?"

"He tried to escape last night," Mark admitted. "And he was trying to take Cassidy with him." His stomach pitched at the thought of what might have happened had Mark not been there, had Lang gotten away with Cassidy.

"I take it that *you* made sure that didn't happen," Sam said.

Mark shrugged. "Not sure how much I did," he said. "Cassidy is still a fighter." She'd certainly fought a lot with him while they'd been going out. But their arguments had been passionate and sometimes funny, like fighting over which movie to watch or where to travel or who loved whom more. Not serious arguments until that last one when they'd realized that neither of them loved the other enough to fight for their relationship.

"That's good," Sam said. "I know your brother is working hard on finding out who all is involved in this trafficking ring, but—"

Mark's cell rang and he pulled it out of his pocket to see the screen lit up with his brother's name. He swiped to accept the call. "Speak of the devil," he greeted his brother.

"Lang?" Jacob asked.

"You," Mark said. "But I was filling in Dad on what happened last night, so I guess we were talking about Lang, too." And about Cassidy.

Which Mark had not needed to do since she was all he'd thought about last night. Even when he'd finally fallen asleep, he'd dreamed about her, and in his dreams she hadn't been just in his head. She'd been in his bed, moving over him, around him, raining kisses on him… loving him like she used to. But had she ever really loved him at all?

She must have moved on, gotten married, had kids with someone…

"Mark?" His brother called his name with the same

impatience that Cassidy had last night, so he must have been talking while Mark zoned out thinking about her.

"Your brother looks like he did most Saturday and Sunday mornings when he was in school," Sam chimed in on the conversation.

"You were out late with Cassidy?" Jacob asked.

"Yeah, I checked her place, made sure nobody had gotten inside, and made sure it was locked up tight when I left," Mark said. But he wished he'd stayed and not just to make sure that nobody got inside.

But she hadn't wanted him there.

"She really needs a good security system, though," Mark said. Especially with the hours she must work at the hospital, coming home late, getting up early.

He'd driven her home last night. How was she getting back to the hospital? He should have offered to drive her there this morning.

"I'm calling because I've been informed that you might need some extra security, too," Jacob said.

"What? Why?" their dad asked the question.

Jacob's sigh rattled the phone. "I don't want to worry you, Dad," he said, and there was an edge to his voice. He probably wished that Mark hadn't put him on speaker.

"Too late for that," their dad said. "I worry every day about my boys."

And given their chosen professions, probably with good reason. Jacob worked in law enforcement, Mark had been in the army for years, and Noah, the youngest, worked with search and rescue when he wasn't doing investigative journalism.

"I'm between assignments right now," Mark said. "Why would Dad have to worry about me?"

"Lang said some stuff last night when I was interviewing him—"

"Who he's working for?" their dad interrupted to ask, his dark eyes bright with hope. Clearly he wanted the traffickers caught as much as everyone else did.

Jacob sighed again. "Unfortunately, he did not tell me that. He's too afraid of whoever he's working for to talk about them."

"What did he say?" Mark asked.

"He just made a comment that you were going to regret getting involved in this," Jacob said.

Mark snorted. "The old 'you'll be sorry' line," he said and chuckled. Rob Coffey had told him the same thing, but Mark hadn't been sorry at all. He'd just shrugged off the threat and the accusation that he'd had anything to do with Coffey's incompetence getting exposed. But he had. He'd had everything to do with it.

Sam chuckled, too. "Sounds like the schoolyard bully when someone finally stood up to him."

Their dad, a lawyer and former councilman and mayor, had taken on his share of bullies over the years. Despite how much he'd loved serving Dark Canyon, when their mother got sick with cancer, he didn't run for reelection. He'd said taking care of her, like she'd taken care of all of them for years, was all he'd wanted to do. Mark's heart swelled with pride and love for the man he would always admire most.

"I don't think that Lang is the bully," Jacob said. "He's just a toady, working for someone else. Someone who is the bully."

"Someone who is used to wielding power to get what he wants," Sam murmured.

"What?" Jacob asked. "Dad, do you have some idea who could be behind this?"

"No," Sam said. "Just remembering my days in politics and the reason why some people entered them."

"For the power," Mark said. "Some people in the army were like that, too."

"Is that the reason why you chose not to re-up?" his dad asked.

Mark remembered that last mission, the horror of it, the casualties. The friends he'd lost. He closed his eyes and shook his head. "No, I had other reasons." Then he returned his attention to his cell phone, asking his brother, "Hey, Jacob, did Lang say anything else to you? Something you can use?"

"No," Jacob said. "Like I told you, he's too afraid of whoever he's working for to give them up."

"Maybe *they* were the reason he tried to escape last night more than the thought of going to jail," Mark mused.

"That definitely sounds like the case," Jacob agreed.

"So he's going to try to get out again," Mark warned him. And would he try to use Cassidy to do it?

"I'm putting extra guards on duty at the hospital until he's released to go to jail."

"Can you trust these guards?" Mark asked.

Jacob sighed. "I'll make sure that I can. Right now I have Mae, uh, Dr. Copeland running tests on the officer's coffee cup and the clothes that Lang was wearing. We're trying to figure out who helped him with his escape last night."

"I know you're doing everything you can," Mark assured him.

"Yes," their dad agreed. "I hope you got some rest, too, unlike your brother here who looks exhausted."

"I'll sleep when this case is closed," Jacob said.

"What about eating?" Sam asked. "Susan would love to have you all here for dinner one night."

"Susan?" Jacob asked as if he didn't know that their father was dating their divorced neighbor.

"Yes, Susan," Sam repeated.

"You know, Mrs. Baylor," Mark said.

"They're divorced," Sam reminded them. "Something Susan wishes she'd done long ago. Susan and your mother were friends. Your mother was there for her when Susan lost her son Andrew, because Susan's husband, Kenneth, certainly wasn't there for her."

Mark winced, remembering the loss of their young neighbor. Andrew had only been eight when he died of leukemia. Mark had been about the same age at the time, and the death had hit him hard. He couldn't imagine how hard it must have hit the little boy's mother. "That was really sad," Mark said.

"But Susan is so strong," Sam said. "She misses her son every day but she still manages to go on, to run her catering business, to live her life to the fullest. She got me living again, after your mother died. She's become very important to me."

And his sons were well aware of that and that was the problem. They were not ready yet to see their father with someone besides their mother. But Mom wasn't coming back.

"Dad, I'm really busy right now," Jacob said.

His dad looked at Mark then.

He shrugged. "I don't know when I'm leaving for my next assignment. But before I do, I want to make sure that Cassidy is safe, that these traffickers aren't going to come after her." He would try again to convince her to let him stay with her, but he knew how hard it was to change her mind about anything.

"Make sure they don't come after you," Jacob warned.

"Ditto," Mark shot back at his brother.

"I've gotta go," Jacob said, his voice lilting with excitement. "Mae—Dr. Copeland is calling. She might have something."

Mark suspected that she did have something, something that attracted his older brother. Jacob's voice seemed to change whenever he mentioned her.

Did Mark's voice do the same thing whenever he mentioned Cassidy? Over the years, whenever someone had pried into his personal life, asking him why he never got married, he'd talked about her. He'd used the excuse that if he hadn't been able to make it work with her, he wouldn't have been able to with anyone else either.

But maybe it was her fault that he'd never made it work with anyone else. Maybe he'd idealized the passion between them so much that nothing he'd had with anyone else had ever come close. As she'd said, they had been naive and idealistic then.

After all the places he'd been and things he'd seen, he wasn't wide-eyed and hopeful anymore. So why couldn't he let her go like she'd let him go all those years ago? He had to forget about her, forget about what they'd had. But he couldn't do that until he made sure that she was safe. And he had this uneasy feeling that she wasn't.

Or maybe he was the one who wasn't safe, and not because of Lang's not-so-veiled threat but because of Cassidy.

Cassidy blinked against the blast of cold water from the showerhead. Goose bumps rose on her bare skin, but she didn't turn the heat up. She needed the cold to wake up after a short night, and she needed it to cool off from the hot dreams she'd had when she had finally succumbed to sleep.

Damn him…

She muttered the words to herself, and unlike last night, he wasn't able to overhear her. But part of her wished he had, that he was here with her in the shower, naked skin pressed against naked skin. He could soap her up, shampoo her hair with his big hands, and then lift her against the shower wall and make love to her. Her body throbbed with need.

How long had it been since she'd even had a date let alone more? She couldn't remember when she'd been out last. She had offers. Many offers from Tyler. And when he'd first started working here, Frank Finkbeiner had asked her to go out for drinks. She always refused with the excuse that she didn't want to date a coworker at a job where she intended to stay. It had been different when she'd still been a traveling nurse and had purposely kept her contracts short. If things hadn't worked out, and they never had, she hadn't been around long enough for things to get awkward.

But if she'd really wanted to start dating again, she could have gotten on an app or something to meet someone outside the hospital. She used the excuse that she didn't have the time. Between work and helping Patsy, she was just too busy.

Patsy…

Cassidy had asked her sister to pick her up this morning, after she dropped the boys at school, and drop Cassidy at the hospital on her way to work. So she needed to be ready when she got here. She turned off the water, which was so cold that she should have been shivering.

But thinking about Mark had heated her up. She'd told him last night that she wasn't naive and idealistic anymore, but maybe she had built up what they'd had into something of a fantasy. It wasn't real. That kind of passion, attraction…it couldn't be.

She reached for a towel and wrapped it around herself before stepping out of the shower. As she stepped onto the mat, she heard something. A creak. A light thud.

Someone was moving around downstairs. If Patsy was here already, she hadn't dropped the boys at school yet, so she would have been in too much of a hurry to come inside. She would have waited for her in the driveway. Maybe texted. Maybe even blown the horn.

So that wasn't Patsy in the town house with her.

It was an intruder.

The nurse's house sat at the end of a cul-de-sac with woods on one side of it. He'd already tried the doors and windows. They were locked, but they would be easy enough to force open. The problem might be the wall that she shared with the town house next to her. Would that resident be able to hear through the wall if she screamed?

If she fought…

That was a risk that might be worth taking.

Chapter 8

That sudden urgency to see Cassidy compelled Mark to shower fast, so that he could get over to her town house and check on her. To make sure that she was okay.

That the threat Lang mentioned to his brother didn't also extend to her. She had stabbed the guy with a needle; he might want revenge on her. Or maybe the people he worked for would.

Or maybe, being human traffickers, they might just want her. Cassidy was beautiful. So damn beautiful that Mark had never been able to stop thinking about her.

He was in such a hurry to get out the door that he nearly ignored his cell when it rang again. Probably Jacob calling back to warn him again about Lang's stupid threat of retribution.

For what? For stopping him from escaping? Or stopping him from getting killed?

Because if Mark hadn't been there, he wasn't sure that Officer Olsen wouldn't have fired his weapon. With Lang clutching those stupid scissors, the officer might have even been able to claim self-defense. Or maybe the officer wouldn't have shot anyone; maybe Mark was just too mistrusting of everyone.

As he headed toward the SUV he'd parked in the driveway, he grabbed his cell and glanced at the screen. Then he groaned and swiped accept, "Hey, boss."

"Ah, so you haven't quit, then," Randy Howard said.

"Of course not, Sarge," Mark assured his boss and former drill sergeant. He unlocked the SUV and jumped into the driver's seat.

"Then you're ready to take on a new assignment?" Randy asked. "Because I have a job for you. This one would take you Down Under."

"Australia..." He sighed longingly at the thought of traveling to one of his favorite places. "When is this?"

"You'd need to leave tomorrow—"

Panic jabbed him. "I can't, boss," he said. "Not that soon."

"You've already been off a couple of weeks, Mark," Randy reminded him.

"I know," he said. "And I'm sorry to ask, but I really need to extend my leave right now. I just need a little more time with my family in Dark Canyon."

"Everything all right at home?" Randy asked, his voice deep with concern.

Mark sighed. "A lot has been happening around Dark Canyon," he said. "I think people I care about could be in danger." Cassidy.

"I'm worried that you could be in danger, too," Randy said.

And Mark groaned but he couldn't deny it although the greatest threat posed might be from Cassidy. "My big brother talking to you, too?" he asked.

"Your brother? No, I'm pretty sure he would know where you are," Randy replied.

Mark furrowed his brow. "What do you mean?"

"Somebody's been trying to find you," his boss warned

him. "Not sure if it's friend or foe but since I figure your friends, like your family, would know where you are, I'm leaning toward foe."

Given all the friends he'd lost over the years, he was leaning toward foe, too.

"Or maybe it's someone trying to track you down to steal you away from my agency," Randy continued. "You're not off because you're interviewing for new positions?"

"No, absolutely not," Mark assured him.

"So you are coming back, right?"

"Yeah, sure, once I'm certain everything's okay here," Mark replied. Hopefully Jacob and his mysterious Dr. Copeland would find something to lead them back to whoever was behind the human trafficking. Because right now there was more darkness in the area than just the canyon. "My family's just been through a lot lately, and there's still a threat here, at home," Mark explained. "I have to make sure everyone stays safe."

"That is a bodyguard's number one priority," Randy agreed. "But make sure you stay safe, too. Be careful."

Randy wasn't just a good boss; he was a good friend, too.

"Always am," Mark replied.

"I'm not sure if you've been careful or lucky," Randy said with a chuckle. "I hope it's careful because eventually luck runs out."

"I know." That was why he had to make sure that Cassidy was safe. He couldn't rely on luck to protect her. Or on anyone but himself. After disconnecting the call, he started the ignition and headed toward her place.

That urgency was back, and he pressed harder on the accelerator. He had the uneasy feeling that he might already be too late.

* * *

Cassidy knew she should have called the police, but part of her wondered if it was Mark who'd broken into her house just so that he could prove his point that he should have spent the night. So to prove to him that she could take care of herself, Cassidy pulled on her robe, with the collar pulled tightly around her neck, and slipped quietly down the stairs armed with the can of pepper spray from her purse. It would serve him right if she sprayed him for scaring her like this.

But the person who jumped in front of her as she descended the last step wasn't Mark. She jerked the can down before she accidentally sprayed her sister in the face. "Patsy! What are you doing here?"

Patsy wrinkled her forehead. "What do you mean? You texted me last night asking me to swing by to give you a ride to the hospital today," her sister reminded her.

"Yeah, but you're early," Cassidy said. "Aren't you supposed to be dropping off the boys now?"

Patsy smiled. "Another parent took them this morning. We've been divvying up drop-offs so that neither of us have to do it every day now."

"That's great." Also strange that her sister hadn't mentioned it to her.

"What happened to your car?" Patsy asked. "And why are you armed with pepper spray?"

"My car is fine," Cassidy said. "I just left it at the hospital last night."

"Ah, did you finally go out with that hunky male nurse or the dark-haired doctor?"

Cassidy shook her head. "No. Neither. And that's never going to happen." Seeing Mark again had just reinforced to her that the attraction wasn't there between her and

Tyler or her and Frank. Not like it was between her and Mark, not that she would ever act on that attraction.

"Then who brought you home last night?" her sister persisted. "And you still haven't explained why you're armed with pepper spray."

"Mark Colton brought me home last night," she admitted.

Patsy's eyes, the same blue as Cassidy's, widened with shock. "Mark Colton? Your first and only love?"

Cassidy snorted. "I wouldn't call him that."

"What would you call him?"

"Youthful stupidity," she said.

Patsy laughed. "That youthful stupidity was super hot. Did he get fat and bald?"

"I wish." Then she might have gotten some sleep last night instead of lying awake thinking about him, wanting him.

Patsy laughed again. "So how did Mark Colton wind up bringing you home and is he still here?" She peered around Cassidy, as if trying to see upstairs.

"No," she said. "He wanted to stay, but I refused to let him."

"So he's single, too? And he's still hot," Patsy exclaimed. "This is exciting."

"Not what I would call it," Cassidy said. Annoying. Frustrating. Scary. Thinking of scary reminded her of the night before, and knowing that Lang's attempted escape might make the news, she told her sister everything that had transpired the night before.

Patsy gasped. "Oh my God!" She grabbed Cassidy and hugged her. "That's terrifying. Oh my God! I can't stand the thought of how close I came to losing you!"

"I'm fine," Cassidy said.

But the collar of her robe must have slipped loose around her neck because her sister pointed at the bandages that Cassidy had somehow managed to keep dry in the shower. "You were injured." Patsy gasped again. "You could have been killed."

"I'm fine," Cassidy insisted again. She touched the bandages. "These are nothing. And Lang was caught. He didn't get away. Again."

"Because of Mark Colton," Patsy said. "He saved your life."

He probably had, but Cassidy didn't want to admit it. She felt much safer hanging on to her anger with him than letting herself feel any gratitude toward him.

"And you should have let him stay the night," Patsy said. "It is so scary how these traffickers have been abducting women. That could have been you last night, Cass."

"It wasn't," she said. "Lang was just trying to get out of the hospital." But she wasn't sure that he would have let her go once he had. He might have kept her like he and his partner had kept Fern with the intention of selling her off like a possession, like she wasn't a person.

Revulsion gripped her. "The police will make sure that doesn't happen again."

"You shouldn't be anywhere near him," Patsy said.

"I have to do my job," Cassidy said.

"But he hurt you!"

She touched her bandages. "I will make sure that I am never alone with him again. I'll be safe."

"Hopefully Mark Colton will see to that," Patsy said. "And he'll stick close to you."

But then Cassidy wouldn't be safe because nobody had ever hurt her like Mark had. She didn't want to give him the chance to do it again.

* * *

Sam slipped through his backyard to Susan's, pulled open the sliders and stepped into her enormous kitchen. She operated her catering business mostly from home unless she was working at a venue that had a kitchen.

The kitchen was warm and rich with the aromas wafting from her double ovens. "Cinnamon rolls," he murmured with appreciation.

She smiled up at him from where she stood at her sink. "I was going to bring you some, but I saw that Mark's SUV was still in the driveway."

"He's gone," Sam said. "And you should have stopped in anyways."

"I don't want to push myself on your sons," she said. After wiping her hands on a dish towel, she tucked a strand of dark blond hair behind one of her small ears. When they'd started seeing each other, she'd been as thin as Kate had been when she was sick. She looked healthier now and happier, too. Her blue eyes were so bright and beautiful.

"Dropping off cinnamon rolls would not have been pushing yourself on anyone," he assured her. "It would have been a treat."

She smiled. "I saved you some cinnamon rolls."

"I wasn't talking about the cinnamon rolls," he said. "I was talking about seeing you." And he was so glad that he'd started. Kate would have been furious with him if he'd continued on the way he had, isolating himself from everyone. She'd wanted him to live for the both of them after she was gone. She'd wanted him to be happy again. She'd even mentioned Susan to him, saying how she was such a special person who'd already suffered too much.

First the loss of her child. And then the acrimonious divorce with her vindictive ex. "You're the treat, Susan."

"You're a flirt," she said.

He'd forgotten how to flirt until he'd started to notice her as a woman rather than just a friend and neighbor. But once he'd woken up from his coma of grief, he'd figured it out. "I'm not a fool," he said. "I know how special you are. And my sons know that, too."

"They're just not ready to see you with someone besides their mother, and I respect that," she said.

Sam smiled. "Kate wouldn't have. She would have kicked their butts."

Susan chuckled. "She might have." She'd loved his wife, too. And she cared about his kids.

He sighed. "I'm worried about my boys."

"They'll come around," Susan said. "We just need to be patient."

"I'm not a young man anymore," Sam said. "I'm not going to wait too long before I kick their butts myself. But right now I'm worried about something else with them."

"What?"

"This whole human trafficking thing," Sam said, his stomach twisting in revulsion of it. How could anyone be so evil as to sell another human being?

"Jacob is investigating, right?" she asked. "But how does that involve Noah and Mark?"

"Well, Noah is more of a full-time investigative journalist who does search and rescue dog training and handling on the side," Sam said. "I'm sure he's still pursuing the story. And Mark..." His heart quickened when he thought of how his middle son must have put himself in danger the night before. "He stopped the trafficker, who was in the hospital, from escaping last night."

"Wow," Susan said. "That's great."

"Yeah, but it might have put a target on him now," Sam said. "Jacob called to warn him."

"So what will Mark do now?" she asked. "Will he leave Dark Canyon?"

"Not yet. He wants to make sure that we're all safe before he goes anywhere." Especially Cassidy. "But he'll leave eventually," Sam said. "He loves to travel too much to stay in anyplace too long, even home. But I'm worried that he's going to get hurt before he leaves." And Sam wasn't sure if it would be the traffickers or Cassidy Garner who hurt him this time.

Chapter 9

Worried that he might be too late, Mark sped the entire distance to Cassidy's town house, and his pulse was racing with fear nearly as fast as he was driving. He was just about to turn onto her street when he noticed the SUV parked in her driveway. And now his heart stopped beating entirely for a second with the horrific thought that he might already be too late.

But then he saw her, walking around the front of it, laughing and smiling at whoever was sitting in the driver's seat. And his heart started beating again, fast and furiously with relief and attraction and maybe with a little jealousy, too. The SUV had tinted windows, so he couldn't see inside. He couldn't see who had made Cassidy's face light up with amusement and affection. She opened the passenger door and jumped in so quickly that he couldn't see around her to whoever was behind the steering wheel. And then the SUV began to back up.

Instead of turning onto her street, Mark drove past and turned onto another one. Then he used someone's driveway to turn around again, so he could follow that SUV.

Just to make sure that she arrived safely at the hospital. That was all he cared about, not the driver of that vehicle. He didn't care who had made Cassidy laugh and smile like that. Their high school relationship had been over for more than a decade; they'd obviously moved on.

Or maybe he'd just moved around, but he'd carried her with him in his memories. Maybe seeing her again, with someone else, was what he needed to finally let her go. But first he had to make sure that she was safe.

So he followed that SUV but at a distance so that she didn't see him. She'd told him last night that she didn't need him to act as her bodyguard. But even though she didn't want him, she needed a bodyguard because he suspected that someone else was following her.

Or maybe it was just as she'd said last night, a lot of other hospital staff lived in her town house development. So it could have just been another employee heading to Baldwin Memorial for their shift. But still Mark tracked the nondescript white van that weaved in and out of traffic but always stayed behind the SUV in which Cassidy was riding. Mark couldn't see the driver of the van any more than he'd been able to see the driver of the SUV.

He considered speeding up to get closer, to see if maybe he could catch a glimpse of them in one of their mirrors. But as if the driver had sensed his interest, the van began to speed, too. And it made it through a traffic light that had just turned red while Mark had to slam on the brakes as a bus was already starting through the light that had turned green on their side of the intersection. A curse slipped out of his lips. And his frustration mounted as traffic continued passing in front of him even after his light turned green again. So many vehicles had turned between him and the van that he couldn't see it or the SUV Cassidy had been riding in either.

He had lost them both.

* * *

The minute Patsy drove off in her SUV Cassidy regretted having her sister leave her at the parking garage. She should have had her drop her at the lobby doors instead. But she needed to retrieve a box of candy bars from her vehicle before they melted. She'd promised her nephews that she would sell some at the hospital, so that they could earn money for their Boy Scout camping trip. With the trip coming up soon, she'd already given them the money for the bars even though she hadn't actually sold any yet.

She had to pick the twins up from school for Patsy this afternoon, and she didn't want them to see the box and know that she hadn't kept her promise to them. Yet. She would sell some bars today if they weren't already melted. Not wanting Patsy to know that the bars were still unsold, she'd just had her drop her off outside the gate to the parking garage. "So you don't have to pay," she'd told her.

"I don't think you should be walking by yourself in the parking garage," Patsy had said. "Not after what happened last night."

"That was last night," Cassidy had said. "It's broad daylight now. I'm perfectly safe, especially with so many people coming and going."

But the minute Patsy drove off and Cassidy walked around the automated gate, a chill rushed over her. A breeze blew through the concrete structure, but the wind wasn't cold. Something else was making Cassidy shiver. She was suddenly very uneasy.

Maybe because she had this strange sensation that someone was watching her. But of course she wasn't alone in the garage; other vehicles pulled in through that gate. But they pulled into parking spaces or passed her on their way to one.

Because she'd come in later in the day yesterday, she'd parked on a higher level of the structure. She headed toward the concrete steps that led up to it. And as she climbed them, she heard an echo of her footsteps.

Probably just someone walking up to an elevator or something. But the footsteps continued to echo hers. She stopped and waited for someone to appear. But the echo stopped as well.

"Who's there?" she called out.

Because someone was.

Now her voice echoed in the concrete stairwell, but nobody answered her. Maybe she had just imagined the footsteps. Mark had made her paranoid last night with his cynicism and his concerns for her safety. That was why she had almost pepper-sprayed her sister that morning.

She found herself reaching inside her bag now, fumbling around for that canister. But just as her keys had eluded her last night, the can eluded her now. Had she put it back in her bag after she'd taken it out that morning?

She'd had to get dressed fast so that she wasn't late for work and so that she hadn't made Patsy late for her job. Had she not put the can back in her bag?

But she found her keys instead. And the fob for her vehicle had an alarm on it. If she got close enough to it, she could sound that alarm and hopefully draw some attention.

If she was being followed…

But after standing still on the stairwell for so long and hearing nothing, she sighed. Mark had definitely made her paranoid.

She turned and started up another flight. And when she made it to the next landing, she heard the echo again. Heavy footsteps.

Someone had been standing in that stairwell below her, waiting for her to move again. She moved now. Since she was on the level where she'd parked, she pushed open the stairwell door and ran out into the parking structure. Hers was parked on the other end of the floor from the stairwell, closer to the stairwell that led to the hospital entrance that was inside the long atrium. She started running in that direction, hoping that there would be people walking up that stairwell, people who would hear her if she screamed. Because as she started across the floor, she heard the door creak open behind her. She whirled around to look back, but she couldn't see beyond the cars and the parking columns to see who'd stepped out behind her.

Who was clearly stalking her.

While she couldn't see who it was, she could feel them back there.

Coming for her.

Jacob wasn't sure who was more disappointed—he or Mae—that Mae hadn't found anything in the officer's coffee cup and on Lang's clothes. There had been no clue to the identity of the person who'd supplied the sleeping pills that had drugged the cop or the clothes that Lang had worn during his escape attempt. He suspected Mark would be even more disappointed than the two of them that they had no leads to whoever was helping Lang.

So Jacob didn't call him back. But he swung by the house where they'd all grown up. Mark's vehicle was gone already. He must have rushed out fast after their conversation.

And Jacob had a feeling he knew where Mark had gone.

From how concerned Mark was about her safety, it was

clear that Jacob's younger brother wasn't over his high school girlfriend. Mark was more worried about Cassidy than he was about himself.

Mark hadn't seemed to take Lang's threat seriously. And maybe it wasn't a serious threat. But it had made Jacob uneasy. And the way his brother had dismissed it made him even uneasier.

Jacob had to make sure that Mark stayed safe, and that Cassidy Garner did as well. But who could he trust to guard Lang and to help him investigate?

Right now Mae was the person he trusted the most within law enforcement. She was as determined to stop these traffickers as he was. Knowing that Lang had gotten his hands on a badge to fool Fern, Jacob wasn't sure if he should trust anyone else in law enforcement.

But he could trust his brother.

Although having Mark help out would put him in more danger than he might already be in.

And Jacob wasn't willing to do that. Mark had been away from the family for too many years while he'd been enlisted in the army. They'd gone for months on end without hearing from him, probably because he was out of reach on some dangerous mission.

As Ava had worried the night before, losing him here, at home, would be the ultimate tragedy. He should be safe now that he hadn't returned to the army. But as a bodyguard, he faced situations that were equally dangerous.

Even if Jacob didn't officially enlist him as a bodyguard in this case, he suspected that his brother was going to enlist himself. Or at least appoint himself as a personal bodyguard to Cassidy Garner, just as he had last night.

Jacob wasn't sure if that would protect Cassidy, though, or just put them both in danger.

Chapter 10

Damn it!

How had he fallen so far behind the other vehicles? Where had the SUV gone? And the van?

He was almost more concerned about that van. The traffickers, Leo and Billy Lang, had been driving a van; that was how they'd kidnapped Fern. And probably some other women who hadn't managed to escape like Fern had.

Mark slowed as he pulled into the driveway to the hospital. It branched off from there. One way led to the lobby, another to the ER at the back, another to the parking lots at the front, and another to the parking garage at the back.

Which way should he go?

An SUV was stopped at the road leading to the parking garage. A dark silver with the tinted windows, it looked like the one Cassidy had gotten into, but then in Utah, a lot of vehicles had tinted windows in deference to the heat of the sun. And this vehicle was heading away from the parking garage.

Would they have dropped her there?

He was tempted to stop, to try to get the person to roll down their window so that he could ask them that. And maybe also so that he could see who had picked her up from her condo. But what did it matter who had dropped her off? It mattered more who was with her now. If they had dropped Cassidy off in the parking garage, she could be in danger, especially if that van had followed her inside it.

And that wasn't safe.

He made a sharp turn onto the road leading to the parking garage. He sped to the entrance to the multilevel structure but had to stop at the damn gate. Impatience and concern gnawing at him, he rolled down his window and slammed his fist against the button for the ticket. Time stretched as the ticket slowly eased out of the slot. He yanked it free as soon as enough showed for him to pull. More long seconds passed as the gate slowly rose. He barely waited long enough for his vehicle to clear it before he sped forward.

He drove around each level, looking in every direction for a glimpse of Cassidy with her bright blond hair. She would be wearing scrubs like last night.

If only he knew what she was driving…

But why would she have been dropped at the parking garage if she had to start work soon? It didn't make sense.

That probably hadn't even been the same SUV that had picked her up. So many people drove them nowadays, everyone from law enforcement to soccer moms. He'd probably just overreacted and she was already in the hospital. Maybe she'd started her shift taking care of that slimeball Lang with his greasy hair and his desperation.

Lang knew he was in trouble, and he knew he had nothing to lose. That was why he had tried to escape last night. And that was why he would try again.

Mark needed to be inside the hospital with her to make

sure that Lang didn't try to use her again in his escape. He needed to make sure that didn't happen.

But according to Jacob, there were extra law enforcement officers guarding the human trafficker. Cassidy should be safe inside.

But if she was out here…

There was no one to protect her. While he'd glimpsed a couple of other people getting out of their vehicles or into them, they hadn't been wearing badges and guns. And even if they had been, they might not have been law enforcement. Just as Lang hadn't really been when he'd used a badge to get Fern to leave with him and his partner.

No. If Cassidy was out here for whatever reason, she wouldn't be safe. So he had to make sure that she wasn't somewhere within the structure before he parked and went into the hospital to find her. So he continued on to the next level.

It was farther up, so there were fewer people on it. But he finally caught a glimpse of bright blond hair and dark blue scrubs. But Cassidy wasn't just walking toward her vehicle or toward an entrance. She was running.

Panic rushed through him as he pressed hard on the accelerator, closing the distance between them. Then as he drew closer to her, he slammed on his brakes, threw the SUV into Park and jumped out.

"Cassidy!" he shouted.

She whirled around then, her face pale with fear, her blue eyes wide.

"What's going on?" He peered around then, looking for the reason that she was running. And he noticed a shadow moving through the garage, ducking behind vehicles, trying to disappear.

And he turned and ran off after it, as desperate to catch

them as they must have been to catch Cassidy. He wanted to know who had been chasing her, and he wanted to make sure that they wouldn't ever try that again.

A door opened, the metal slamming back against the concrete wall. And Mark caught just a glimpse of a black sweatshirt, hood pulled up, before the door slammed shut again. He ran faster and grabbed for the handle, intent on catching up, on stopping whoever had scared Cassidy.

He could hear her now. But she wasn't screaming. She was yelling his name. Had there been another person closer to her? Had he, in trying to protect her, actually left her unprotected?

"Mark!" Cassidy yelled his name despite how hard she was struggling to breathe. And it wasn't just her sprint across the parking garage that had winded her; it was the fear. For herself.

And now for Mark.

Last night she'd sent him off after Lang, but she'd known that all Lang had had were those scissors. This person, who'd chased her across the garage, could have had a gun. They hadn't fired it at her, but that would have drawn attention. They might have gotten caught.

But if Mark got close to them and it looked like he was going to catch them, they might fire that gun at him.

Was Mark armed?

He was a bodyguard, but she hadn't noticed a weapon on him last night. Of course last night he hadn't been on duty; he'd just been visiting Ava, or so he'd told Jacob.

Lucky for her that he had been. She was also fortunate that he'd shown up now, because she wasn't sure that she would have escaped from whoever had been chasing her. And just as she'd heard in the stairwell and across the parking garage, she heard the running footsteps now.

Had the person already done something to Mark? Were they coming back for her now?

She turned toward her vehicle again, knowing that she was closer to it than the entrance of the building. And she fumbled in her purse for her keys. But before she could pull them out, strong arms closed around her. And she screamed again like she had moments ago.

"Shh, it's me," Mark said, his voice a deep rumble near her ear, his breath warm against the skin of her neck. "It's me. Are you all right?"

Heat flashed through her body, and her pulse quickened even more than it had already been racing away. She still reacted to his closeness like she always had. And she didn't like that. She struggled in his embrace until he released her, then she smacked his shoulder. "You scared me. I thought it was the person coming back."

"You yelled for me," he said. "I thought I missed that there was another person closer to you."

She shook her head. "I only saw the one."

"You saw them?"

She shook her head again. "No. I really just heard them." So maybe there had been more than one.

"Why did you yell for me, then?" he asked. "I was chasing them. I might have caught them."

And that was why she had yelled. "You don't know that they weren't armed," she pointed out. "You could have been shot."

"You didn't see them, but you know they had a gun?" he asked.

As relieved as she was that he'd rescued her, twicc, she was also irritated with him. "I don't know if they did," she admitted. "But you've made me as paranoid as you are, so I was worried…"

"About me," he finished for her, and his mouth curved into a maddeningly sexy grin.

She glared at him. "And now I regret that. I shouldn't have stopped you from chasing after them."

"So I could have caught them?" he asked. "Or so that I might have gotten shot?"

Even as angry as she'd been with him when they broke up, she had never wanted him to be hurt. She sighed. "I wouldn't want you to get shot," she said.

And his grin widened.

So she added, "It would just make more work for me."

Instead of being offended, he chuckled. They had shared the same dark sense of humor; that was why they'd always had so much fun together. But the amusement left his face, and there was an intensity in his green eyes when he asked, "You are okay, right?"

She nodded. "I heard whoever it was following me," she said. "That was why I started running toward my car." But she wasn't sure she would have reached it had Mark not shown up when he had. She wanted to thank him for rescuing her. Twice. But the words caught in her throat. She had been angry with him for so long that she couldn't completely let it go. It had been hard enough to let *him* go all those years ago.

"What were you doing out here in the parking garage?" he asked. "Why didn't your ride drop you at the front door?"

"My ride wanted to drop me there," she said. "But I had to get something from my car before starting my shift."

"You shouldn't have been out here by yourself," he said. "It's too dangerous."

She glared at him again. "You're sounding like my dad again."

"I am not anyone's father," he said. "I sound like a bodyguard, Cassidy."

Defensive because she knew he was right, that she'd taken an unnecessary risk being by herself, she retorted, "I don't need a bodyguard."

"After a human trafficker tried to abduct you last night, I think you do," he said.

"So you've appointed yourself as my bodyguard?" she asked.

"You need one," he said. "And I'm between assignments at the moment."

She arched an eyebrow and couldn't help but needle him a bit more. "Wouldn't a good bodyguard be in demand?"

He laughed again. "You're not distracting me. We need to call the police and hospital security and report this abduction attempt."

"We don't know for sure what it was," she said. "They never caught up to me. Maybe I dropped something, and they were just trying to give it back."

"Did you drop something?" he asked.

"Well, no. I don't think so." But she struggled to admit that she was in danger, let alone accept it. "They could have found something and thought it was mine."

"Did the person call out to you? Tell you that they had something of yours?" he asked.

She shook her head. And when she'd stopped on the stairwell and called out to whoever was following her, they hadn't replied.

Mark pulled out his cell phone. "I'm calling this in as another attempted abduction of you, Cassidy."

"But, like I just pointed out, we really don't know that they would have grabbed me," she said. "We don't know what might have happened..." Had he not showed up when he had, had he not saved her again.

"It still needs to be called in," he said. "And hopefully there are cameras in the garage that will give us some video feed of what this person looks like."

"You do what you have to do," she said. "I need to get into the hospital. I'm already late for my shift." And she was never late.

He didn't touch his cell. "As Lang's nurse?" he asked.

The thought of treating the human trafficker sent a jolt of panic through her, just as she'd panicked when she'd heard those footsteps pounding the concrete behind her. The person must have been chasing her. As much as she didn't want to admit it, she probably was in danger.

"Yes," she replied. "I need to get into the hospital and relieve whoever had the last shift." And she turned toward the entrance to the hospital.

"So why didn't you go straight into the hospital when you got here?" he asked. "Why did you have them drop you at the parking garage instead?"

If she had been abducted, her reason for putting herself in unnecessary danger sounded silly now, so she just shrugged instead of replying.

"Why did you have to stop here first?" he persisted. "Did you leave something in your vehicle?"

She sighed and replied, "Candy bars."

"Candy bars?" he repeated. "Is that your lunch or something?"

"Boy Scouts," she said. "I am supposed to sell the candy bars for them."

"You're a Boy Scout now?"

She shook her head, but she refrained from mentioning her nephews. She didn't want to let Mark back into her life any more than he'd already let himself. But if he hadn't shown up last night and just now, she might not be here to spar with him like she was.

She shouldn't be fighting with him. She should be thanking him. She needed to thank him. But the words stuck in her throat. And then she remembered how she used to thank him for the things he'd done for her: with kisses. And she was so tempted to close the distance between them, to brush her mouth across his, to see if he tasted the same. If he kissed the same, with so much passion...

Where was the female nurse? Cassidy something. That was her name. Billy needed her on the shift if he had any chance of escaping again. While the bitch had stabbed him with that needle, she was still smaller and weaker than the male nurse treating him now.

He'd heard the burly guy grumbling to one of the officers about staying later than he was supposed to. The officers would be a problem, too. Well, depending on who the officers were.

But if he had that pretty nurse as leverage, they would have to back off. They would have to let him get away or risk seeing her blood spilled like he'd spilled it last night. That had just been a trickle, though. He might need to spill a river in order for them to take him seriously. To let him go.

Because he couldn't stay here.

He had to get out while he still had time. He wasn't going to jail, not that he actually expected to ever make it there.

The higher-ups wouldn't let him. They would be too

worried that he might make the deal that the district attorney kept offering and his lawyer kept encouraging him to turn down. Even his lawyer was working against him. So Billy had to protect himself, and that meant putting that nurse in danger again.

Chapter 11

Had she been about to kiss him? The way she'd been looking at his mouth, the sudden darkening of her blue eyes as the pupils dilated, made him think that she might have been. But then her cell phone rang, and she'd jumped at the sound.

He had, too.

They both had every reason to be jumpy after last night and what might have happened in the parking garage had he not shown up when he had. She might have been abducted and that was the least that could've happened given all that was going on around Dark Canyon these days.

Jacob wasn't as convinced, though. Instead of calling 911, Mark had called his brother. They both stood now in the security office of the hospital, watching the grainy surveillance video from the few cameras that were actually in the parking structure.

"This place needs more cameras," Mark grumbled.

"There are some in the stairwells and one on each parking level," the guard said defensively.

Cassidy had been defensive with Mark, too. She was so stubborn and independent that she hadn't wanted to admit to not being as careful as she should be, as she *had* to be, now that she was the nurse for the human trafficker.

Mark hadn't wanted her to report for that assignment, but she'd insisted on relieving whoever had been working the shift before her.

Even though Lang had injured her, she'd shown up for work. She was tough.

"The angles suck," Mark said, pointing at the grainy footage shown on the monitors.

The video of whoever had been following Cassidy up the stairwell didn't show his face at all. It just caught the top of his head, and with the hood pulled up over it, there was no way to tell what color his hair was or if he even had any. But from the width of his shoulders, he was male and muscular. If he'd caught up with her, he could have easily overpowered her no matter how hard Cassidy would have fought.

And she would have fought, just as she'd fought Lang last night. Was this person's motive for chasing her retaliation for that? For not letting Lang get away? Or had she been the intended target all along? Another female this crime ring wanted to traffic?

"We definitely can't identify whoever it is," Jacob said, his voice gruff with frustration.

"What about his vehicle?" Mark asked. "Go through the footage to see if you can find what he's driving."

The guard hit Rewind on one of the monitors. But it just showed the hooded person jumping over the gate, just as Cassidy had. It didn't show whatever vehicle he'd used to get there, but Mark had a feeling that he knew what the man had driven. A white van. If only Mark had been close enough to it to catch the license plate...

"Whoever he is, he definitely followed Cassidy into the garage and up to the level where she'd parked her vehicle," Jacob said.

His fear confirmed, Mark cursed. "She's in danger."

"Yes," Jacob said.

"You need to get Lang out of this hospital," Mark urged him.

"The doctors won't release him yet," Jacob said. "And his lawyer has already convinced a judge not to force his move into police custody until he's medically cleared."

"I wonder how he was able to afford such a good lawyer," Mark remarked.

"I've been wondering that myself," Jacob said.

"I'm also wondering how you're going to keep Cassidy safe," Mark said.

"We added extra security to the hospital staff," the guard said, still defensive.

"And we've assigned extra officers to make sure the suspect doesn't escape again as well," Jacob said.

"And yet none of them were out in the parking garage when Cassidy was in danger," Mark said.

"You were," Jacob said. "Are you going to be sticking around for a while?"

Mark sighed. "I wasn't planning on it." Until last night. And then everything had changed for him. He couldn't leave Dark Canyon for a new assignment until he was certain that everyone important to him was safe. And despite being broken up for over a decade, Cassidy was still important to him.

And not just to him.

He remembered that photo next to her bed of herself and those twin boys. With their brown hair and darker eyes, they hadn't looked like her. But that didn't mean that they weren't hers. She could be a mom.

A mom but not a wife. Or so he assumed because there had been no signs of a man sharing her home. And she wore no wedding or engagement ring. As much as he got some satisfaction and maybe a secret spark of hope that she was single, he was worried. Who would help her if she was alone in that house?

Or even alone with those little boys?

"So you're going to leave?" Jacob asked.

Mark groaned. "No, not now. I'll be sticking around for a while." And he would be sticking close to Cassidy whether she liked it or not. Maybe this would prove his most dangerous mission of all. And not just for his life but for his heart as well.

Cassidy hadn't known what to expect from Lang when she saw him. She'd thought that he might be furious with her for stabbing him with the syringe, for messing up his plan to escape last night. But since she'd taken over his care this morning, he kept smirking at her, like he was amused or smug. Like maybe he knew something she didn't, like maybe who had chased after her in the parking garage.

Fortunately she wasn't alone in the room with him since there was police officer with Lang at all times now. And when she wasn't in the room with Lang, Tyler had been reluctant to leave her alone, as if he was worried that someone else was going to grab her. Maybe in the parking garage, if not for Mark showing up when he had, they would have. Despite not having the security clearance yet, Tyler had even offered to take her shift for her. Even if he could have been approved that fast, he'd already worked a double, so she'd refused. She also hadn't wanted to feel like she owed him anything, because she had no doubt he would try to collect in the form of a date or drinks. There were also two officers guarding Lang now, with one stationed inside the room and another outside.

But despite their presence, she didn't feel safe. Not after what had happened last night and what had nearly happened in the parking garage.

While she didn't want to admit it, Mark was right. She had to be more careful. This wasn't the Dark Canyon she'd once felt safe in. This was now a place with a criminal element that preyed on women.

When someone knocked on the door, she gasped. And Lang laughed.

"A little jumpy, Nurse Garner," he said with that smirk.

He was way too cocky for someone who should be leaving for jail soon.

"Maybe that's the doctor coming in with your release orders," she said.

His sneer slid away, and he looked about to gasp now or choke. He shook his head. "No, not yet. I'm still too sick to be released," he said, his voice rising with a note of panic.

She smirked now. "That didn't stop you from trying to escape last night," she reminded him.

"But the infection—"

"Your fever's gone down," she said. "I think the antibiotics are clearing up your infection."

But when the officer opened the door, it was Jacob Colton who entered the room, not the doctor.

"You're wasting your time, Agent Colton," Lang said. "I'm not talking to you without my lawyer present."

"I'm not here to talk to you," Jacob replied to the trafficker. "Ms. Garner, I'd like to take your report now about this morning."

"What happened this morning?" Lang asked, but the

smirk was back. And Cassidy wondered if he already knew. Had he been behind it? Had he sent someone after her?

She ignored him and focused on the ISB agent instead. "Cassidy," she reminded Mark's brother as she followed him out into the hall. The officer at the door closed it behind them. And she breathed a sigh of relief at being away from Lang.

"Are you all right?" Jacob asked.

She wrapped her arms around herself and nodded. "Yeah, yeah, fine," she said. "Lang is just…he's acting so smug."

"Yeah, I hate that, too," Jacob said. "It makes me uneasy."

"You're not the only one," she said.

"And he's not the only reason you have for being uneasy," Jacob said. "Mark told me what happened in the parking garage. I'd like your side of things now."

She could have tried to downplay it like she had initially with Mark, but she told the agent the truth about the scare she'd had. Then she added, "From how smug Lang is acting, it almost feels like he knows about it."

"Nobody's been in to see him," Jacob said. "Besides officers and nurses and doctors."

She shivered as that admission made her even more uneasy. "So if he does know…" An officer or doctor or nurse had told him. And they would only know if they'd been there. Because she hadn't told anyone yet.

Even when Tyler had asked why she was late, she'd used the excuse of having left her vehicle at the hospital the night before and needing a ride to work.

She wound her arms tighter around herself. "Can I trust anyone, Jacob?"

"Like I told you last night, Cassidy, you can trust me and my brother," Jacob said. "It's lucky that he showed up when he did both last night and this morning."

She couldn't argue about that. In fact she shouldn't have been arguing with Mark at all, she should have been thanking him. And she nearly had thanked him like she used to, with a kiss, but the ringing of her cell phone had brought her back to her senses. Had snapped her back to reality.

And the reality was that they weren't teenagers anymore.

"Cassidy?" Jacob said, his voice deep with concern. "Are you all right?"

She sighed. "No. I was Fern's nurse. I know that these traffickers are dangerous." And Fern had been spared the worst of it. While Lang and his partner had abducted her, she had escaped before they were able to traffic her.

"They are very dangerous, Cassidy," Jacob confirmed. "So I think you should let Mark protect you. Let him be your bodyguard."

She wanted to deny that she needed one, but she couldn't do that anymore, not after the incident in the parking garage. "I… Is he even sticking around?" she asked.

"He wasn't planning on it," Jacob admitted. "But he's decided not to leave on another assignment until he knows everyone he cares about in Dark Canyon is safe."

"He doesn't care about me," she said. Or he wouldn't have left her all those years ago.

Jacob smiled at her. "I'm not so sure about that because he still loves to travel like he used to…"

She had once loved to travel, too. But since Patsy had lost her husband, the only places Cassidy had gone were with her sister and the boys. So to amusement parks and zoos. And those trips had had to coincide with school holidays.

"You must remember how much that was," Jacob continued. "So he wouldn't be turning down an assignment and sticking around Dark Canyon if he didn't still care about you, Cassidy."

But he wasn't the one who'd checked in on her now. His brother had. So where was Mark now? And did he really care?

Ava sat at her desk and watched as her cousin Mark paced the floor of her office. He fairly bristled with nerves. Fortunately he'd caught her between patients, so she had time to talk to him, to hopefully talk him down from whatever had him so on edge.

"Are you worried that if you sit down, you might start spilling your deep, dark secrets?" she asked.

"You don't have the security clearance to hear my deep, dark secrets," he said as if he was teasing her back.

But she was pretty sure that he was serious. "I wish you could talk to me," she said.

"I don't need to talk to anyone," he said. "I'm good, or I will be once Lang is out of this hospital."

"Me, too," Ava said, her pulse quickening with fear. "But I don't think I'm the one you're the most worried about. Is Cassidy the reason you're pacing my office like a caged animal?"

He kept pacing as he filled her in on what had happened that morning. And she gasped. "Oh no, that's terrifying. Cassidy must be so frightened."

"If she is, she doesn't really show it," he said. "She insisted on working anyways."

"She's strong," Ava said with admiration.

"She's stubborn," he said. "Just like she always was."

"It's one of the many things the two of you had in common," Ava said.

He sighed but didn't try to deny that he shared that trait with Cassidy. "Yes, it is."

"Is that the reason you broke up?" she asked.

He nodded. "Yeah, we were both too stubborn to compromise," he admitted.

"Do you regret that?" she asked. Her cousin had never gotten married; he'd never even been engaged, as far as she knew. So had he ever gotten over his first love?

He shrugged. "That's all in the past," he said. "I'm worried about the present right now."

"You're worried about Cassidy." So he obviously still cared about her.

"What do you know about her, Ava?" he asked. "Is she married?"

She shook her head. "No, I don't think so. At least not now."

"But she could have been married?"

She shrugged. "She just moved back to Dark Canyon three years ago, and we haven't really had a chance to catch up with each other." They were both always so busy. "Why are you so curious about her relationship status?" She fought to hold back a smile; she was pretty sure she knew why he was so curious. He was still a little bit in love with his first love, not that he would probably ever admit it to Cassidy or to himself let alone to Ava.

His body tensed a bit. "Well, that wasn't Lang in the parking structure. He had two officers guarding him since his escape attempt. So it had to be someone else. Maybe an ex or something."

Ava sucked in a breath as the thought of her own stalker struck her like a blow. She hoped that Cassidy wasn't living that nightmare as well, as so many women did.

"I'm sorry, Ava," he said. "I shouldn't have brought that up. Whoever it was is probably associated with Lang somehow."

"That doesn't make it any better," she said. "Until these human traffickers are stopped, a lot of people are in danger. Women and whoever else might get in their way."

Like her cousin, the bodyguard. Because it was clear that he intended to protect his old high school girlfriend from whoever threatened her, be it human traffickers or an obsessed ex. But in trying to protect her, Mark was putting himself in danger. Physically and maybe emotionally as well.

Chapter 12

Ava hadn't been able to answer Mark's questions, so he'd done some digging of his own. Not that his search had yielded much information.

Cassidy had just moved back home three years ago. And he couldn't find any permanent prior address for her. Where had she lived? What had she done?

He'd tried asking her about herself last night and again this morning, but she'd kept shutting him down. As she'd said last night, she hadn't wanted to do some high school reunion catch-up on each other's lives.

Maybe that was because she just didn't care about him, about how he'd done after their breakup, about where he'd gone. He was more than curious about her. He was as attracted to her as he'd always been.

Maybe more so now, because he knew how rare the passion they'd shared actually was. As a teenager, he'd naively believed that every relationship would be like his first one. He'd found out quickly how wrong he was.

But he'd been too proud to reach out to Cassidy again, especially after their last fight when she'd vowed she'd never wanted to see or talk to him again. So even today, after deciding that he would assign himself to be her personal bodyguard, he'd made certain to stay out of sight.

He wanted to protect her, but he also wanted to catch whoever had followed her that morning. And the best way to do that was to make sure that they didn't realize he was there.

So he skulked around the hospital, watching the doctors and nurses interact with her. At the end of her shift, a blond-haired male nurse kept chatting with her as she tried to get away from Lang's room.

"I'm in a hurry, Tyler," she told him. And when she walked away, Mark caught the look on the guy's face. He was more than annoyed. He looked angry with her.

Was that just hurt male pride? Or something darker?

Mark needed to find out more about Tyler. He would also check out the doctor from the ER who'd stitched her up the night before. That guy had acted a little more familiar with her than a mere coworker would.

And Lang could have someone who worked at the hospital helping him. Someone like that doctor or nurse. Someone who had access to his room.

Mark made a mental note to check into them both, but at the moment, he was discreetly following Cassidy from the hospital to the parking structure. He wanted to be close enough to jump in if she needed help but far enough into the shadows that he might catch someone else following her. Because the surest way to keep her safe was to catch whoever was after her and put them behind bars like Ava's stalker was. Cassidy walked to her small SUV, carrying her keys and a small canister of pepper spray. So she had taken his advice. Or maybe she was usually this careful just like she'd previously claimed she was.

He made sure that she was safely in her vehicle and driving off before he rushed over to where he'd parked his. He wasn't going to let her out of his sight again.

That wasn't easy, though. Cassidy drove like she was in a hurry. Or like maybe she knew he was following her and she wanted to lose him again, like she had eleven years ago.

So much for her bodyguard. Jacob had assumed that his brother would protect her. But she hadn't seen Mark since that morning in the parking garage. Maybe he'd figured she wouldn't want him sticking so close to her. And he would have been right had she not been so uneasy over the events of last night and this morning.

And over the way Lang had looked at her throughout the day. Maybe she should have insisted she be taken off nursing duty for Lang. But what if whoever replaced her wasn't as trustworthy? Tyler had offered to take over, but she wasn't sure that he would pass the clearance. She wasn't even sure what the criteria was that had gotten her approved to treat Fern and then Lang. But, as a traveling nurse, she'd passed some very in-depth background checks since some of her assignments had been in VA hospitals. Tyler had never worked anywhere but this hospital.

At least Jacob Colton had kept his word with extra security at the hospital. But she hadn't had anyone to walk her to her vehicle in the parking garage. And she'd had that strange sensation again of being followed or watched.

But she didn't hear or see anyone this time. So maybe she was just paranoid. She hoped that was the case since she had to pick up her nephews from school. And the last thing she wanted to do was put them in danger.

So she kept glancing in her rearview mirror, checking to see if anyone had followed her. But she didn't see anyone behind her.

Not even Mark.

She shouldn't have been surprised that he'd not kept his promise. He'd left her eleven years ago when they'd believed that they'd been madly in love, so of course, he would have had no qualms about leaving her now. No matter how much danger she might be in.

But that wasn't his fault. And she wasn't his responsibility either.

She was responsible for herself and for her young nephews. She pulled into the pickup line at school, waiting for the boys to run up to her vehicle like they usually did. They loved spending time with her as much as she loved spending time with them.

Sure, she missed traveling on her own, checking out places off the beaten path. But she would miss them, too, if she returned to travel nursing. If she left Dark Canyon…

She couldn't walk away from family as easily as Mark obviously could. When he left, he would once again be leaving his dad and his brothers and cousins, too. And some of them had been in so much danger lately.

Dark Canyon was far more dangerous than she'd ever realized. So she wouldn't have minded having a bodyguard around. A small hand pounded on the side window, and Cassidy jumped. Then she hastily unlocked the doors so the boys could pile into her small SUV. Their brown hair was mussed, their hazel eyes bright with excitement. "Hey, Aunt Cass!"

"Hey, guys!" she greeted them back, matching their excitement. "How was school?"

"Boring," Brian replied.

"Super boring," Alec added.

"Can't wait until the camping trip," Brian said.

"I can't wait more," Alec said, as usual trying to top

his twin. Brian had beaten Alec into the world by seven minutes, and Alec had been trying to get ahead of him ever since.

"I'm sure you're both equally excited about the trip," Cassidy said. She wasn't certain if it was the thought of camping that they were pumped up about or if it was spending time with their friends and with the dads that were chaperoning and helping the Boy Scout leaders with the trip. It had been three years since Brian Senior passed away, and they still missed their dad so much. Even though Patsy worked hard to be both mother and father, it just wasn't the same for them or for her.

A pang of sympathy struck Cassidy's heart. Moving home had been the right thing for her to do. She had to be here for her sister and for her nephews, but she would never be able to fill the void that losing Brian Senior had left in their lives.

"I am more excited about getting nuggets," Alec said.

"Yeah, nuggies!" Brian exclaimed.

She felt a twinge of guilt. She should have had something healthy waiting at home to feed them, but because she'd worked last night and this morning, she hadn't had time to put anything together. So she headed to their favorite fast-food restaurant, and as she drove, she kept glancing in the rearview mirror.

Someone was definitely behind her, but she couldn't tell if it was the driver of an SUV or of the white van that she felt watching her. Even though she could only see the vehicles and not the drivers, both of them made her uneasy since they kept following her with every turn she'd made after leaving the school pick-up lane. She was probably just being paranoid again and both those vehicles had kids inside who wanted fast food after school like her nephews. When she turned into the drive-through lane, the boys exclaimed, "No! Let's go inside."

"That's not a good idea today," she said. Maybe she was being paranoid, but she wasn't willing to risk her nephews' safety just in case one of those vehicles belonged to the person who'd chased her in the parking garage. If they went inside, one of the boys would inevitably have to go to the bathroom. And she couldn't enter the men's room with them, and if the person who'd followed her did…

She shuddered at the thought of either of them being in danger. "We're going to have to bring these meals back to my place and have some apple slices and milk with them."

They groaned, but they didn't argue with her. Fortunately the line was short, and they made it through quickly. But on the way back to her town house, she noticed the van again. So she opened the garage door; there was no way she was walking up to the front door. From now on, she was determined to be as cautious as she'd claimed to Mark that she was. No more unnecessary chances, especially not with her nephews. But before the door opened all the way, they were unbuckling their seat belts and jumping out of the vehicle. They ducked under the garage door and headed toward the door to the house.

But it was locked yet from Mark locking it last night. So they had to stand there until she pulled into her one-stall garage. Then she unlocked it and let them into the house. As she closed the door again, she had that sensation. Someone was watching her. And because they were watching her, they would have seen her nephews, too.

She could only hope that she hadn't put them in danger. She wanted to help her sister with the boys, not hurt them.

* * *

An opportunity had been missed that morning. But it would not be missed again.

He had been so close to her, but that damn Colton had rushed to her rescue like the white knight he wanted everyone to think he was. Fortunately Colton hadn't caught *him*. He would have to be more careful with his next attempt to pick up the pretty nurse.

And there would be another attempt.

But the next time it would be more thought out and planned so that she wouldn't get away. And so that Colton wouldn't rush to her rescue.

Just now, watching her from his van, seeing her at the school and with those little boys had gotten him thinking. He would have to be careful, though. Because he wasn't the only one watching her.

Colton was following her, too.

Had he seen him?

That couldn't happen. He had to get away with this. So he had to be smart.

Patient.

He could leave no room for error. Or for mercy.

Chapter 13

The picture was old. That was the first thing Mark noticed when the boys ran from the school to her small SUV. They definitely weren't as little or as young as they'd been in that picture of them snuggling with Cassidy. They had to be ten or eleven.

Ten or eleven was what they would have been had Cassidy had them after she and Mark broke up. If she'd been pregnant when they broke up…

She might not have known at the time of their big fight, but once she'd found out, she should have tried to contact him. She could have reached out to any member of his family; they'd all known how to get ahold of him when he'd been in boot camp. And even after he was deployed, there had been ways for people to get messages to him.

So he knew that she hadn't even tried. She'd deliberately cut him out of their sons' lives. Anger surged through him, making him want to confront her. But he didn't want his sons' first impression of him to be of an angry man yelling at their mother.

Mother. Cassidy was a mother.

He wasn't sure why she hadn't had them last night, but maybe because she'd been working, they'd stayed somewhere else. A former stepfather's?

Because Mark couldn't believe those kids weren't his. With their brown hair and either brown or green eyes, they didn't look like their blue-eyed blond mother. They looked like him. They had to be his kids.

Kids he'd never known about.

His stomach tightened with his anger and his dread. He had to talk to Cassidy about this, and he hated waiting. But while he waited outside in his SUV, he studied the neighborhood. When he'd been following her, he was pretty sure he'd seen the van that he'd noticed that morning. But then it had disappeared again.

Or maybe he'd just missed it because he'd been so distracted after seeing the twins. He didn't miss the silver SUV turning onto her cul-de-sac. As it pulled up, the garage door opened, and the twins ducked under the door and ran to the SUV just as they'd run to Cassidy's a couple of hours ago.

Again he couldn't see the driver as the boys jumped in fast and it pulled away moments later. When it did, he turned onto Cassidy's street and pulled into her driveway. He was shaking with fury as he hopped out and headed toward her front door. Once he was there, he jabbed the button for the bell and then pounded on the door as well. "Cassidy, it's me," he called out. "Let me in."

She opened the door and stepped back, her forehead furrowed with confusion. "What's the matter? What's going on?" And she peered around him as if worried that he'd been chased like she had been that morning.

He stepped inside, closed and locked the door behind himself.

"Is someone out there?" she asked, her voice a bit shaky. "I thought I saw someone following me, but I hoped it was just you."

Just you...

Like he was nothing. Like he was inconsequential. And to her, he must have been.

"How could you, Cassidy?" he asked, and his voice was shaking now with the fury he could barely contain.

Her forehead furrowed more. "How could I what?" she asked. "Leave the hospital without you? I didn't know where you disappeared to all day. I thought you changed your mind about protecting me. And I have things I need to do, responsibilities."

"Kids," he said. "You have kids."

Her lips pressed together in a hard line as she studied his face. Then she asked, "What are *you* upset about?"

Like he didn't have the right to be upset.

"What the hell do you think I'm upset about?" he asked. "You had my kids, and you never let me know that I'm a father. How could you, Cass? I know our breakup was messy, and we both said some things we shouldn't have. Or so I thought, but I guess I was right when I called you selfish back then. But I didn't realize that you could be so cruel and vindictive, too."

And maybe that was what was the worst part about this revelation, that she wasn't the person he'd thought she was, the woman he'd idealized all those years. While he knew she was stubborn and strong, he hadn't believed her capable of doing something as underhanded as keeping his children from him.

While he was so disgusted he felt like yelling at her, she started laughing. Like this was all a joke.

He had to get away from her before he did something he would regret. And he wasn't sure if that was yelling at her or kissing her. But he didn't want to risk either. So he reached for the door to unlock it and leave. But before he could turn the dead bolt, her hand covered his, sending a jolt through him. And he realized he was probably in more danger of kissing her than yelling at her.

What was it about her that no matter how furious she made him, he still wanted her? Despite what she'd done, how cruel she'd been to keep his children from him, he was still attracted to her. No, it was more than a simple attraction, it was almost like an addiction, one that he was powerless to overcome. When he'd appointed himself as her bodyguard, he hadn't realized that he was the one who might need protection. And from her.

Cassidy's laugh stuck in her throat, stopped up with the fury rushing up on her. She couldn't get over his ridiculous accusation. As if that wasn't bad enough, he was just going to leave after hurling the insulting claims at her.

Instinctively she'd reached out to stop him, so that she could explain. But now she removed her hand from his. She would let him unlock the door and let him leave.

"You haven't changed at all," she said. "You still run away when the going gets tough, just like you did that summer. Did you actually leave the army or just go permanently AWOL?"

He laughed now. "Permanently AWOL?"

"Well, are you ever going back?"

"Not to the army," he said.

"But you are leaving," she surmised. And now she was furious on behalf of the children he thought were his, that he could leave them just as easily as he'd left her all those years ago. "So much for being upset about not being part of your kids' lives, huh?"

"So it is true!" he exclaimed, and his voice cracked. "Those are my sons."

She snorted. "They're not mine, so I don't know how they could be yours unless you and my sister had a relationship that her late husband and I never knew about."

He narrowed his eyes as he stared at her, as if trying to determine if she was lying or not. "Those boys are really your nephews?"

She nodded. "Yeah, so did you and Patsy have a thing I don't know about?" Patsy had called him super hot, but she had no doubt that Patsy would never betray her or her late husband. She was just pointing out to him what a fool he'd been.

But he didn't look embarrassed; he looked amused and maybe relieved. His lips curved into a slight grin, and he shook his head. "No..."

"Then they're not your kids either," she said.

"I thought—"

Her anger erupted now. "And how dare you accuse me of being selfish and cruel and vindictive," she said, throwing his words back at him. "When Patsy's husband died three years ago, I gave up being a travel nurse and moved back to Dark Canyon to help her with the twins."

At the time it hadn't felt like a huge sacrifice. She'd wanted to be there for her sister and nephews while they recovered from their loss. But after staying in one place for the past three years with few opportunities to travel, she was getting antsy.

The boys were so active, though, that they would be too much for Patsy to handle on her own. While she had other parents who helped out from time to time, they weren't family like Cassidy. And Cassidy and Patsy's parents were both college professors who lived and worked out East, so they weren't able to see the boys except for a few weeks in the summer. They were no help.

"I'm sorry Patsy lost her husband," Mark said. "And that the boys lost their dad. That must have been horrible for all of them."

Tears stung her eyes, and she nodded. "It was. Brian was a very sweet man. He adored my sister and their sons. It's been a rough three years for them." As much as she tried to help, she couldn't replace her brother-in-law; she couldn't even begin to fill the hole his death, from a sudden heart attack, had left in the lives of his loved ones.

"And for you?" Mark asked. "What about you?"

"I loved Brian like a brother," Cassidy said, and her voice cracked a bit with the admission. She always thought of what Patsy and the boys had lost, not what she had lost. "But I wasn't around much until I moved back here three years ago."

"You were a travel nurse?"

She narrowed her eyes. "I didn't want to do this," she reminded him. "I didn't want to play catch-up with an old acquaintance."

"Why not, Cassidy?" he asked.

Because she hadn't wanted to let him back into her life. "Because we're not just old acquaintances, Mark."

"What are we, Cassidy?" he asked, his voice soft.

"Nothing now," she said.

"Nothing?" he repeated the word back at her and raised one eyebrow over one of his deep green eyes. "That's what we are? That's *all* we are?"

After he had saved her twice over the past two days, he was her hero, but because of his assumption that she would have kept his children from him, she wasn't feeling as appreciative about that as she previously had been.

So she raised her chin and nodded. "Yeah, nothing.

That's what you told Lang I was to you." And that had stung when he'd said it.

He shook his head. "Who cares what I told Lang? I want to know if you ever thought about me over the past eleven years," he said. "If you ever wondered where I was and what I was doing?"

She raised her chin higher and lied, "Nope. I never did."

He grinned slightly, as if he didn't believe her. He obviously knew how unforgettable he was. And she had tried to forget him; she had tried so damn hard.

"And you?" she asked. "Did you ever think about me? Ever wonder where I was?"

His grin widened. "Nope."

"Liar," she said, and she let her lips curve into the smile she'd been fighting.

"Takes one to know one," he replied.

"I did not lie about the twins," she said, just so that was clear. "We were not teen parents."

"We could have been," he said. "With as often as we made love, especially that summer."

"I was on birth control then, like I am now." Her pulse quickened with memories of the passion that had burned so bright between them. But she snorted dismissively of what they'd shared. "Teenage hormones..." Because she had certainly never experienced that fierce a passion again, not after that summer.

"Is that all it was?" Mark asked.

She shrugged. "If it was love, we would have figured out how to stay together," she said. "So it was just hormones that burned so hot and so bright that we got burned out, Mark."

"You were certainly hot," he said.

She arched an eyebrow now and put her hands on her hips. She still wore her scrubs. Her hair was up in a messy ponytail, and she had probably, during her shift, sweated off the little makeup she'd put on that morning. "You don't think I'm hot now?"

He held her gaze for a long moment before skimming his down her body. Then he met her eyes again, and his were dilated, the pupils big and dark. "You know you are. You had that ER doctor and that Ken doll nurse drooling all over you all day."

She narrowed her eyes. "You were watching me?"

"That's what bodyguards do," he said.

"But I didn't see you."

"That's because I'm really good at my job," he said.

She smiled. "And really modest, too." But her smile slipped. "I thought you changed her mind, that you took off again."

"Not while you're in danger," he said.

"Thank you," she said.

"For...?"

"For sticking around, for making sure I'm safe," she said. And then she thanked him like she used to. She stepped closer to him, rose up on tiptoe and pressed her mouth against his. The second her lips touched his, the heat ignited between them, as hot and bright as it had ever been.

His hands slid around her waist, but instead of pulling her against him, he held her back when she tried to wind her arms around his neck. And he lifted his head and blinked as if trying to clear his vision, like he was just waking up and he couldn't believe what he'd dreamed. "Cassidy?"

She didn't blame him for being surprised. She hadn't

exactly welcomed him back home or even thanked him for saving her life. But this wasn't just about thanking him.

This was about discovering if she had idealized her memories. If she'd made him out to be more than he'd been, and their relationship to be more than it had been, more than just a teenage romance.

"Yes," she replied to the question he hadn't asked with words. He'd asked it with the hungry expression in his green eyes. And she answered that hunger with her own as she dragged his head back down to hers.

She wanted this; she wanted him more than she could remember wanting anyone or anything in a very long time. And, after the close scrapes she'd had over the past two days, she knew life was too short to deny herself.

Her yes seemed to have unleashed the hold he'd had on his desire because he kissed her hungrily now, sipping at her lips, dipping his tongue into her mouth. Tasting her. Teasing her. She teased him back, sliding her tongue over his, nipping his lips lightly with her teeth.

And as she kissed him back, she tugged on his clothes, pulling his shirt free of his jeans then reaching for his fly. She wanted to release him, wanted him inside her.

He tugged on her scrubs, pulling down the pants, pulling up the shirt. And somehow she stood in her foyer in just her underwear. Good thing there was no window on or near her front door. He pushed down the cups of her nude-colored bra and he lowered his mouth to one breast. He closed his lips over the taut nipple then teased it with his tongue.

A jolt passed from her nipple to her core, and she moaned as she nearly came. All he'd ever had to do was touch her, and she came apart. But the tension wound tight inside her, and she was tempted to beg for release.

He dropped to his knees then and pulled off her panties. Then he made love to her with his mouth, kissing her intimately, sliding his tongue inside her. And as he did, he stroked her breasts and slid his thumbs back and forth across her nipples.

And she did come, screaming his name. Her whole body shuddered with the release. But it wasn't enough. She wanted more. She wanted him. She needed him inside her. So she dragged down his zipper and released him. Then she wrapped her hand around him, stroking up and down.

He groaned. "Cassidy…"

Then the last of his clothes were gone and he was easing between her legs, holding her against the wall. And they made love standing up, him supporting her weight as she wrapped her legs around his waist. And she wound her arms around his broad shoulders then fused her mouth to his, kissing him deeply while he moved inside her.

They made love in a frenzy. Him thrusting while she gyrated against him. It was wild and free but oddly synchronized, like an old dance they used to do but hadn't done in a while. The pressure built as the pleasure and the passion poured through her. Then another orgasm shuddered through her, more powerful than the last. And overwhelmed, she yelled his name.

Then his body tensed and shuddered against her as he found his release. And her name left his lips too in a groan that sounded as if he were in as much pain as he was filled with pleasure. "Damn…" he muttered between pants for breath.

"Damn," she agreed. Because she hadn't built up what they'd had in her mind. She hadn't idealized the passion that had burned between them. If anything she hadn't done it the justice it had deserved. And now she knew she was in trouble. And it had nothing to do with the human traffickers and everything to do with the man who'd appointed himself her bodyguard.

Patsy was only half listening as she watched the boys get ready for bed that night. She had to watch, or they would definitely *forget* to brush their teeth. But as concerned as she was about their dental hygiene, she was more worried about her sister. She hated that Cassidy had been in such danger the night before because of that horrible human trafficker. But Cassidy had assured her that there would be extra security at the hospital.

And Mark Colton.

He had come home. Patsy doubted he would stick around, though. He had the wanderlust as badly as Cassidy once had. But Cassidy had stayed for three years. Was that because she'd actually tired of traveling, like she'd once claimed when Patsy had asked her, or had she really given it up because of Patsy and the boys?

A pang of guilt racked her. She knew that she needed to talk to Cassidy about this again and to make sure that this time she found out the truth. But once she learned the truth, she might have to let her sister go, and the thought was almost as frightening as losing Brian had been. But she could survive without her sister living in the same area. She couldn't survive if she lost her completely.

"Aunt Cass was acting so weird today," Brian said.

"Super weird," Alec added.

"What? How?" Patsy asked. Her boys loved their aunt so much that they usually raved about the time they spent with her.

"She wouldn't go into the restaurant," Brian said. "Just

the drive-through, and then she wouldn't let us go outside at her house."

"She kept looking out the windows and checking the doors and stuff, too," Alec said.

"Even in the car, she kept looking in the mirror, but she wasn't looking at us," Brian said.

So Cassidy had been worried that she was being followed. By whom?

That trafficker was under police surveillance at the hospital. If he'd escaped, it would have been all over the news. So who had Cassidy been worried about?

"Ah, finish up brushing and head to bed," she said. "I'll be there in just a couple of minutes to read to you and tuck you in."

The boys groaned. "We're too old for bedtime stories," Brian said.

"Way too old," Alec said. "And we can tuck ourselves in."

"Okay, prove it," she said. "But I'm going to check on you."

Patsy left them hip-checking each other in the bathroom as they jostled for position at the one sink. The double vanities were in her bathroom instead of the hall one, which was ironic since she didn't need them anymore. It was just her. And she had thought it would stay that way. But now…

Now she might be more willing to move on from Brian than her sister had been to move on from Mark Colton. Though Cassidy would never admit that he was the reason she'd never become serious with anyone else.

She'd claimed that she hadn't had any other serious relationships because she never stayed in any place long enough for one. But she'd been back in Dark Canyon three years now, and Patsy wasn't sure if her sister had dated anyone since her return.

While Patsy…

She needed to have a conversation with her sister. But she wasn't ready yet for that; she just wanted to check in with her. So she grabbed her cell and made the call. It rang a few times then went to voice mail.

Cassidy could have been sleeping. She probably was after the night she'd had previous to working a day shift today. She had to be exhausted. But Patsy wasn't convinced. So she texted her, too.

I know you're probably sleeping, but you need to check in with me. The boys said you were acting weird. I'm worried. So if I don't hear back from you soon, I might call the police to check on you.

Or Mark Colton, if she knew his number. Patsy would have called him. But that would probably be a mistake. The last thing Cassidy needed was to get involved with Mark Colton again and then have him leave her like he had after high school. He'd broken her sister's heart so badly that it had never healed.

Chapter 14

Once had not been enough. After making love in the foyer, Mark had carried Cassidy upstairs to her bedroom. And they'd made love again.

And then again.

Despite not being teenagers anymore, they were as insatiable as they'd ever been.

But definitely not as indefatigable as they'd been as teens. Eventually they must have fallen asleep because Mark awoke with a start sometime later, and for a moment he didn't know where he was. Or what was real and what he'd just dreamed.

Had making love with Cassidy again just been a dream like the many dreams he'd dreamt of her over the years?

Was he actually asleep in his bed at home?

Almost reluctantly he forced his lids up and peered around the room. Light filtered into the space around a door, illuminating the soft pink walls and snowy white comforter lying near the foot of the queen-size bed. He wasn't in his room; he was in Cassidy's.

But the bed next to him was empty, the sheets rumpled. She was gone. But he could smell her on the sheets and on his naked skin. And then he could hear her, her voice drifting out from the door with the light shimmering around it.

"Don't call the police," she said.

Who was she talking to?

"There's nothing to be worried about," she said now.

That advice was too late for Mark. He was worried and not just about her safety. He was worried about his. He hadn't intended to make love with her. When he'd come up to her door hours ago, he'd been furious, convinced that she'd kept his kids from him for all these years. Heat rushed to his face with embarrassment that he'd jumped to such a wild conclusion.

But maybe it wasn't so wild given the way that he and Cassidy had ended things between them. With so much anger.

With so much passion.

That passion was still there. It hadn't been something that he'd exaggerated in his mind. If anything the passion was even hotter than he'd been thinking it was these past eleven years. So he knew he was even more likely to get burned the way he had back then, leaving him with scars that had never completely healed.

He'd been a dumb teenager when he fell for Cassidy the first time, though. Now he was older and wiser, and he wasn't sure if even that much pleasure was worth the pain that would inevitably follow.

But his body tensed in protest of the thought of walking away from her again.

The door creaked, and she stepped out of the bathroom back into her bedroom. She was wearing a robe with her hair down and tangled around her shoulders. "Good, you're awake," she said. "You need to leave."

He yawned and stretched, and the sheet fell down to

his hips. Her gaze slipped from his face down over his chest. And he grinned at her obvious reaction as her nipples pressed against the soft fabric of her robe. "Why?" he asked. "Are the neighbors threatening to call the police?"

"The neighbors?" she asked, her voice cracking.

"They probably heard us," he said.

Her face flushed bright red. "I, uh, I don't think they can."

"Then the walls must be pretty thick," he said because they had definitely made a lot of noise. He'd been right to worry that nobody would hear her cries for help if whoever was after her got inside her place. "So who was threatening to call the police?"

"My sister," she said.

"So maybe the walls aren't so thick if Patsy heard us," he said, teasing her. He liked making Cassidy blush. He liked even more that he had made her scream from the intensity of the orgasms he'd given her. And he wanted to do that again, his body hardening with the desire coursing through him.

Her gaze skimmed down his chest again and over the sheet that covered his lower body. And a soft gasp escaped her lips. But she shook her head. "Patsy was worried because the boys thought I was acting weird today."

He chuckled. "She was going to call the police because Auntie Cass was acting weird?"

"She was going to call the police because I didn't answer my phone when she called."

"Why didn't you?" he asked even though he already knew very well why she hadn't. Because he remembered when her cell had rung a while ago and what they'd been doing.

Her face flushed a deeper shade of red. "I was preoccupied at the time she called."

"Yeah, me, too," he said, his skin flushing with heat not embarrassment. Damn, he wanted her so badly again despite how many times they'd already made love. "Seems like an overreaction on her part."

"This morning, when she picked me up, I told her what happened last night," she said. And she touched the bandages on her neck.

And now anger coursed through him that Billy Lang had hurt her. Then fear chased after the anger as he considered what might have happened to her. That she might have died if those scissors had cut any deeper and hit an artery. "That shouldn't have happened," he said.

Jacob needed to figure out how it had, who had helped Lang, because Cassidy wasn't safe in the hospital until he did. It could have been an officer or a doctor or another member of the hospital staff who'd helped him.

"And Auntie Cass was acting so weird because *you've* made me so paranoid that I kept imagining someone was following me from the hospital," she said. "So I kept looking in the rearview mirror, and I wouldn't let the boys out at the restaurant or outside here once we got home." She shivered as if the thought of what might have happened to them chilled her.

He wanted her to come back to bed, to let him wrap his arms around her and hold her close.

But she wrapped her arms around herself and said, "But it was just you apparently."

He wasn't sure that it was just him who'd been following her. "Did you see my black SUV or a white van?"

A gasp slipped through her lips. "I saw both."

A curse slipped out of his lips, and he threw back

the sheet to jump up from the bed. "I thought I saw that van this morning, too, following you from here to work. And then after work, when you left the parking garage and headed toward the school, I thought I saw it again."

He needed to check all the doors and windows again, and he needed to call Jacob. Maybe he could tap into some traffic cameras in the area and get a license plate from that van. So he grabbed his clothes from the floor to get dressed.

"I need to call Patsy back," Cassidy said. "Make sure that she and the boys are safe."

"Whoever is driving that van is after you, not your nephews or your sister," he said. But he had his concerns, too. He could see someone like those traffickers threatening the people that Cassidy cared about to manipulate her into doing what they wanted, which was probably to help Lang escape.

"So you're certain they're not in any danger?" Cassidy asked, and she stared hard at him.

And he sighed. "I don't know for sure because I don't know who was after you in the parking garage and why they were."

"I really hope it was just somebody who thought I dropped something..."

"But if that was the case, they wouldn't have run away when I drove up," he pointed out.

So hopefully his presence alone would be enough to keep Cassidy safe. She was probably going to argue with him, but he wanted to stay the night. And the next night and the next until Lang was in jail and whoever was working with him or for him had been apprehended as well.

Once dressed, he headed toward the door to the hall. "I need to make sure everything is still locked up here."

"I kept checking earlier," she said. "That's probably another reason the boys thought I was being weird."

"I just want to make sure," he said.

"Don't you trust me?" she asked.

"This isn't about trust," Mark said. But he really didn't trust her not to break his heart again. "This is about making sure you're safe."

And to do that, he would risk his own safety.

Cassidy wasn't safe, but Mark was the person posing the greatest threat to her. And she just wanted him to leave. So she followed him down the stairs to the living room. "I checked all the locks," she said. "Nobody can get in here."

Mark snorted. "Somebody doesn't need to unlock a door or a window to get in here," he said. "They could just break it."

She shivered as she realized he was right. "But somebody might hear…"

"Like the neighbors heard us earlier?" he asked. "Like you said, these walls must be thick or somebody besides your sister would have called the cops earlier."

Now heat rushed through her as she remembered how many times she'd screamed his name as orgasms overcame her. The passion between them was as hot as it had ever been, maybe hotter because they were older and wiser and more experienced now. They knew what they were doing. He certainly did.

She hadn't been able to think at all, or she wouldn't have kissed him, let alone made love with him. She couldn't risk falling for him again. Because he wasn't staying. Once his family was safe, he would be leaving.

"I think I should stay here," he said.

"What?" she asked. "In Dark Canyon?"

"No," he replied as he moved around the living room, checking the windows. "In this town house with you."

Thunder rumbled and rain began to patter against the windows. The thunder felt like an omen…like a warning of something bad about to happen.

But Cassidy was worried that it was already too late for that. Making love with him, no matter how amazing it had been, was bad.

"I just wanted to thank you earlier," she said. "Not pick up where we left off years ago."

"That was quite a thank-you," Mark said. "But I'm not trying to permanently move in here. I just want to stay until I'm sure you're safe."

"I'm safe," she said. "The windows and doors are locked. And nobody's going to break in here to get me." Or so she hoped. But then lightning flashed, illuminating the area outside, and she saw a dark-clothed figure standing on her rear patio. A scream tore from her throat.

"What's wrong?" Mark asked with alarm.

And she pointed toward the patio.

"I'm going after him," he said, as if letting her know that she couldn't stop him like she had that morning in the parking garage. "Lock the door behind me." He pulled up the curtain rod, handed it to her, then he unlocked and opened the sliders.

She opened her mouth to stop him. But he'd already told her he wouldn't. So she just closed the door behind him and with a shaking hand, she flipped the lock up. Then she put the curtain rod back in place.

And she prayed that he would return, which reminded her of the last time she'd done that. Moments after their big fight, when she'd told him that she never wanted to hear from or see him again, she had prayed that he would come back to her.

But that prayer hadn't been answered. He hadn't come back to her then.

She hadn't seen him again for eleven years.

She hoped that wasn't the case this time. She hoped that he returned. And not just for her sake but for his.

Jacob never liked when his phone rang this late at night. Very rarely was it good news. But because of Mae—Dr. Copeland—there was the potential for a positive late-night call. She was still working on the little evidence they'd managed to collect from the scenes involving the traffickers. Maybe she'd found something.

But when he grabbed his cell from the bedside table, it wasn't her number lighting up his screen. It wasn't even a number that he recognized. He thought about letting it go to voice mail, but something compelled him to swipe to accept. "Agent Colton—"

"Jacob!" a female voice interjected. "This is Cassidy Garner."

"Cassidy, is everything all right?" Mark was supposed to be watching out for her. Unless that was why she was calling, to say she didn't want his brother's protection. Jacob wasn't sure why they'd broken up all those years ago. He'd just figured their teenage relationship had run its course, and they'd outgrown each other. But then Mark had never gotten serious with anyone else and apparently Cassidy was still single, too.

"No," she said. "It's not all right. I saw someone standing outside on my patio, and your brother went out to chase them down."

Of course he did.

"And he hasn't come back," Cassidy said, her voice cracking with fear. "I don't know what's happened."

Jacob jumped up from his bed. "How long ago was that?"

"Not that long," she said. "Maybe fifteen, twenty minutes, but..."

Thunder rumbled outside Jacob's place, and it echoed from the cell phone speaker. Then another sound came through the phone: pounding.

"Someone's trying to get in!" Cassidy gasped.

"Don't let anyone inside," Jacob said. "I'm on my way, and I'm going to see if a local officer is in the area." Because he had a horrible feeling that his brother needed backup. Now.

Chapter 15

Squinting against the rain pelting him, Mark chased after the shadow he'd seen on Cassidy's patio. Wearing all black with a hood pulled over their head, the person had to be the same one from the parking garage.

The person who'd chased after Cassidy was now the one being chased. But Mark couldn't catch up to him before he seemingly disappeared.

Where the hell had he gone?

He peered around the trees, trying to catch a glimpse of him. Was he hiding behind a tree? Or crouched under something? Or had he simply outrun Mark and gotten back to wherever they'd parked that van?

Or worse yet, had they doubled back to Cassidy's town house? Were they trying now to get in? Even if she had locked back up after he'd gone out the patio door, it was possible for someone to get inside easily enough.

All they had to do was break the glass in the patio doors or one of the windows, and Cassidy could be gone before he even got back to her place. Knowing that, fearing that, he ran as fast as he could. Blinded by rain and darkness, he stumbled and slipped on the muddy ground. But he kept running until he saw the lights glowing from her town house.

Then he rushed across the patio and pounded on the glass. He figured she would see him and know that it was him. But her back was to him as she held her cell phone to her ear. Hopefully she'd called the police because he wasn't sure that he was the only one who'd rushed back to her house.

The figure in the dark hoodie could be lurking around, too. And Mark tilted his head, listening for any indication. But he just heard the rain falling and the distant rumble of thunder. Lightning slashed across the sky, too, shining on him like a flood lamp.

Then the door opened, and Cassidy said, "I didn't know that it was you pounding on the glass. I thought it could be that person…"

"I was worried that they might have come back, too," he said. And he closed and locked the door behind himself. All the glass made him nervous, so he guided her back to the hallway toward the front of the house.

She held the phone out to him. "I called your brother," she said. "He gave me his card earlier."

"That was smart," he said as he took the phone and swiped it onto speaker.

"You chasing after someone without backup wasn't smart," Jacob said. "He could have taken out both you and Cassidy."

She gasped.

"I was fine," Mark assured them both, though he didn't know if Cassidy had been concerned for him or for herself. "I lost him, though, in the wooded area next to Cassidy's town house."

"I'm on my way and so is a local officer," Jacob said.

"Check for a figure running around in a black hoodie," Mark said. "Also check for a white van."

"Any better description? License plate?"

Mark swallowed a curse as frustration overwhelmed him. "Nothing on the plate. I didn't get close enough to read it when I saw it earlier today. I think it had something over it, like a tinted shield or something. As for the person, because of the hood I didn't see hair color or any of his face."

"His?"

"From the build, it's a guy," Mark said. "Probably six feet tall, pretty fit." Certainly strong enough to overpower Cassidy. That was why Mark had to stay with her and not just at the hospital. He had to move into her place to make sure that she stayed safe. He just hoped he would be able to get her to agree to it.

Cassidy did not want Mark to stay with her a moment longer than he already had. But then she remembered that man standing on her patio, and she reconsidered.

Patsy's call had already worried her. The boys had noticed how edgy she'd been, how paranoid. But she'd had a solid reason for that paranoia. Someone had been following her. Watching her.

Who and why?

Jacob had no answers when he showed up minutes after she'd called him. But at least he seemed to take her seriously whereas the local officer dismissed the person she'd seen as probably just a peeping Tom. And the way he looked at Cassidy made her very glad that she'd gone upstairs and replaced her robe with a baggy sweat suit.

"Peeping Toms can be dangerous," Mark pointed out to the officer.

The young man shrugged. "He ran off when you went

out to confront him, so it was probably just some horny teenage boy."

Mark shook his head. "I don't think so."

"Well, you're not a cop," the officer said. "What are you again?" And he glanced from Mark to his brother. Jacob was saying very little, though.

He still seemed upset about Mark going out alone to confront the intruder. Cassidy had been so afraid that he wouldn't return, that he might be hurt. And she realized that was one of the reasons she'd broken up with him eleven years ago.

Not only hadn't she wanted to follow him into the military, but she hadn't wanted him to join either. She'd been so afraid that he would get killed and she would lose him forever. But he'd been as determined to go as she'd been not to, and so she'd lost him anyways.

And while he wasn't in the army anymore, he still willingly put himself in danger as a bodyguard. So if she let herself fall for him again, there was every chance that she would lose him yet to death.

After watching her sister and the boys suffer through such a loss, she was not willing to risk it herself. She didn't think she was as strong as Patsy. Or maybe Patsy had just forced herself to keep living because of the boys, because they'd needed her so much after already losing their father.

Patsy and the boys needed Cassidy, too, and when Cassidy remembered how worried Patsy had been about her, she decided to let Mark stay.

"I'm a bodyguard," Mark said. "I've had to protect people from peeping Toms who turned out to be dangerous stalkers."

Jacob flinched at the word, and Cassidy remembered

that their cousin Ava had had a dangerous stalker. Ava was lucky she had survived, especially since her stalker had caused first a coma and then the death of Ava's fiancé.

"So you already have a bodyguard?" the officer asked Cassidy.

She sighed and nodded. "Apparently I do."

"That's good," Jacob said. "We will figure out who this is, but until we do, having Mark around will keep you safe." His forehead furrowed as he said it, though, and he glanced at his brother with obvious concern.

He was worried about Mark, too. So his family didn't like his chosen profession any more than Cassidy did. But Mark was headstrong and stubborn. And even though she might not have been the only one opposed to his plan to join the army, he hadn't cared what anyone close to him wanted. He'd gone off anyway.

He'd put himself in danger anyway.

Maybe he could live that way. And his family had to. But Cassidy didn't have to.

She would let him stay in her house right now. But she was not going to let him back into her heart. After his brother and the officer left, she told him as much when she said, "You can sleep in the boys' room."

His lips curved into a slight grin, but he didn't argue with her. He just nodded. "I'll grab my bag from my vehicle."

"You already brought an overnight bag with you?" she asked. "That was pretty arrogant of you."

He chuckled. "No, it's pretty practical of me. Sometimes I have to leave on a moment's notice for an assignment. I always carry an overnight bag with me."

A moment's notice. That was how quickly he might

leave again. And given the danger of the assignment, there was a chance he might never return.

She definitely had to protect her heart. "What happened earlier…" she murmured.

"We had mad, passionate sex," he said, his grin widening. "Just like hormonal teenagers."

"Yeah, that was a mistake," she said. "And it can't happen again."

"Oh, it could," he said, and he moved closer to her, his body brushing up against hers.

She could feel his erection pressing against his fly and against her. And her pulse quickened as heat rushed through her. But she stepped back.

"It could definitely happen again, Cassidy," he said.

She shook her head. "No. It can't."

"Why not?"

"Why not?" she asked. "There's no future to it. You're going to leave at a moment's notice when the next assignment comes up."

"I turned down the next assignment already," he said. "To make sure that you're safe."

"You didn't have to do that for me," she said, but she was touched that he had. And curiosity had her asking, "Where was it?"

"Australia."

A wistful sigh slipped out.

"Have you been?"

She nodded. "Five years ago I took a short trip there. Just a week, and it wasn't enough," she said. "I would love to go back…"

"What's stopping you?"

"I have responsibilities here, Mark," she said. "I'm not leaving my sister and my nephews."

"Ever?" he asked.

"Not while they need me," she said.

"So what? When the boys leave for college, you can have a life of your own?"

"I have a life of my own," she said. "It's just here in Dark Canyon."

He sighed as if he pitied her. "Dark Canyon will always be home," he said. "But I can't imagine staying here or anywhere forever."

"It's not forever," she said.

"Just until the boys grow up, then you'll go back to travel nursing?"

That was the promise she'd made to herself, but she didn't share that with him. "And what would you know about forever, Mark?"

He'd promised her that once. But it hadn't lasted, not when one of them would have had to make a sacrifice for the other.

"What do you mean?"

"You were never in danger in the army?" she asked.

He flinched as if remembering that danger or feeling that pain again. "Of course I was. I lost a lot of people I cared about, too."

"So you know there is no such thing as forever," she said. "Even as a bodyguard, you're always putting yourself in danger just like you did tonight."

"That's the job," he said. "I assess the risks. I can handle the danger. I survived my assignments as a bodyguard because I trust my boss and my team."

"What about the army?" she asked.

He sighed. "Turns out there was someone in the squad that couldn't be trusted."

"Is he why you left?" she asked.

"Coffey?" He shook his head. "I wouldn't have let him, or his commander father, chase me out. It was time. I lost too many friends to stay."

And he could have lost his own life as well. Even though he claimed it was safer to be a bodyguard, she doubted that because the role required him to put himself between the person he was protecting and the threat against them.

Right now she was the person he was protecting, and she hoped it didn't wind up costing him his life.

He'd had the opportunity earlier, or so he'd thought to get into the place while they were preoccupied. But they hadn't stayed preoccupied. And they'd seen him thanks to the flash of lightning.

But with the hood up over his head, they probably hadn't seen enough of him to identify him. The sweatshirt was soaked now, and so were his jeans and shoes. He turned up the heater in the van, blasting it out of the vents to warm himself up. But then he thought of them and his blood heated up with fury. Eventually he was going to get what he wanted.

He wouldn't give up until he did.

Chapter 16

Mark took the lid off the cup of coffee he'd purchased from the hospital cafeteria and lowered his face over it. He didn't drink it yet; he just inhaled the rich aroma. As he breathed it in, his head cleared a bit. He hadn't slept much last night, and it wasn't just because he'd hung off the end of the small bed in Cassidy's guest room. It was because he'd wanted to be in Cassidy's bed with Cassidy.

But she was right; they shouldn't do that again. It would only make it harder for him to leave. And eventually he would have to go back to work, or risk losing the job he enjoyed, and start traveling again. He missed it, missed exploring new locations and meeting new people.

"Are you drowning yourself in coffee or drinking it?" Cassidy asked.

Mark raised his face and glanced across the table at her. "I'm inhaling it," he said. "I can't believe you don't even own a coffee maker."

She shrugged. "I don't drink coffee." She held a clear cup with some goopy green junk in it. "I make healthier choices."

He shuddered. "That looks like slime," he said. "And coffee is healthy."

"For you?" she asked. "Isn't that the name of the guy who made you leave the army?"

"*E-Y*, not *E-E* on the end of his," he said. "And I didn't leave because of Rob Coffey. It was just time."

"You didn't enjoy it?" she asked.

"Not anymore," he admitted. "Not after losing so many..." Emotion rushed up, choking him, and he cleared his throat.

Cassidy reached across the table and covered her hand with his. "I'm sorry," she said.

He turned his hand over and entwined their fingers. "What are you sorry about, Cassidy?" he asked. "It wasn't your fault."

"That you lost your friends, no," she agreed. "I'm just sorry that they're gone, and you had to go through that."

"Thank you," he said, appreciating her empathy and her comfort. "For that and for not saying I told you so."

Her lips curved into a slight smile. "I didn't understand you choosing the service over us."

"I didn't understand you choosing college over us," he said.

"I wouldn't have done anything differently," she said.

He sighed. "Despite all the people I lost, I wouldn't have either." She was the first person he'd lost, and the loss that had hurt the most. But he couldn't imagine having lived his life any other way.

Except for last night. When they'd made love as passionately as they once had, he'd realized that they could have been doing that every day of their lives. But he had chosen to leave instead, to go off to boot camp. And because he had, he had saved some lives. He had helped some people that he wouldn't have if he'd just followed her around as she'd helped people.

"Ah, so this is why you keep turning me down for dates," a voice remarked.

Startled, Mark jumped, and coffee sloshed over the rim of the to-go cup, running over his hand. He swallowed a curse as his skin burned, but he was annoyed with himself that he hadn't noticed the blond-haired man walking up to them. Some bodyguard he was. But then Cassidy had a tendency to distract him.

She jerked her hand away from his and turned toward the person who'd walked up to them. This was the guy that Mark had seen hanging around her. He'd already made a point of learning his full name, but he looked at the ID badge clipped to his pocket.

"Ah, so this is Ty," he said as if he and Cassidy had talked about her coworker.

"Yeah," the man replied. "And you're the guy who nearly got her killed the other night, right?"

Mark smirked. "You mean stepped in to save her when everyone else just stood around getting in the way? Yeah, that was me."

The guy's handsome face twisted with a not-so-handsome grimace. "That's not exactly how that all went down," he said. "But I didn't realize you two knew each other so well."

"Cassidy and I know each other *very* well," Mark said, his voice and grin full of innuendo. "We go way back."

Cassidy's face flushed, and she shot Mark a glare. But then she sighed and said, "Tyler Gibbs, meet Mark Colton. Mark and I went to high school together."

"We did much more than that, Cass," Mark said, purposely goading her and her coworker, too.

"And here I thought Dr. Fink was the reason you wouldn't go out with me," Tyler said.

"Dr. Fink?" Mark asked as if he didn't realize he was

referring to the ER doctor, Francis Finkbeiner. But Mark had made a point of learning his full name, too, as well as everything else that he could about the physician.

"Yeah, didn't Cass tell you about him? He followed her here from some hospital where they met while she was doing her travel nursing and he was completing his residency," Tyler said, as if he relished sharing information with Mark that he hadn't known.

And he hadn't known how Finkbeiner and Cassidy had met. Maybe, like his cousin Ava had had, Cassidy had a stalker of her own. Or maybe she had two, given the way Mark had watched this male nurse follow her around.

"I understood Cass choosing a doctor over me," Tyler continued. "But…what do you do, Mark?"

Mark grinned at the man's implication that he wasn't good enough for Cassidy. Not that he was wrong. Cassidy was beautiful and passionate. And she was also very caring and self-sacrificing. She just hadn't cared enough about him to make sacrifices for their relationship. And that was why he had to be careful to protect himself while he was protecting her.

"Ah," Tyler said while Mark hesitated to reply. "You're between jobs right now?"

He nodded. "Something like that…"

"Mark is Agent Colton's brother and Ava Colton's cousin," Cassidy said.

"That's who he's related to, not what he does," Tyler pointed out, clearly unimpressed that Mark was a Colton.

Usually the Coltons got respect in Dark Canyon, especially since Mark's dad had once been the mayor. But apparently Tyler didn't care about that.

"Mark was in the army and now he's a bodyguard," Cassidy said, as if defending him.

As if he needed defending…

"Oh, so something like a security guard," Tyler responded dismissively.

Mark grinned. "Yeah, sure. So tell me, Ty, how do you think Lang got those clothes and managed to drug the cop watching his door?"

The guy tensed. "Why would you ask me that?" he asked. "I have nothing to do with security."

"But you must have some idea," Mark said. "Don't you think it must have been an inside job? Somebody who works in the hospital helping him?"

Tyler glanced at Cassidy. "What are you saying? Are you accusing Cass?"

"Since she was hurt, she's the last person I would suspect of being involved in Lang's attempt to escape custody," Mark said. "But why did Lang try to abduct her and not, say…you or Dr. Fink?"

Tyler gasped. "You can't seriously think I would help some creep like Lang."

Mark shrugged. "Why not?" he asked.

"Why would I help him?" Tyler asked.

"Money," Mark replied matter-of-factly. "That's the motivator for most people."

Tyler snorted. "Money? That guy is broke."

Mark narrowed his eyes and studied Gibbs a little more closely. "How would you know that?"

The man's face flushed, and he shrugged now. "I just… I…he doesn't seem like he has any…"

"But the people he works for must have very deep pockets," Mark said. "Or he wouldn't have the high-powered lawyer that he has. So those people might be willing to pay quite a bit to someone on the inside who could help get him out."

Gibbs let out a low growl. "Not me. I had nothing to do with that." He looked at Cassidy then. "You know that, right? I would never do anything that would put you in danger." He glanced back at Mark. "Some other people can't say the same thing."

"Dr. Fink?" Mark asked even though he knew the nurse was talking about him, about how he'd had the elevators and doors unlocked that night for Lang.

Gibbs snorted again. "As much as I don't like that arrogant SOB, I don't think he would either. He's got it too bad for Cass, and he doesn't need the money any more than I do."

"Just because you don't need something doesn't mean you don't want it," he said.

Gibbs glanced at Cassidy again. "Are we still talking about money?"

Maybe not. Mark sure as hell wanted her, but he had managed the past eleven years without her. Not that he hadn't thought about her, though.

Or that he hadn't missed her.

She stood up. "Well, *I* need to get back to work."

Mark suspected it wasn't because her break was over but because she hadn't appreciated how he and Gibbs had been talking about her. Hopefully she didn't think Mark had been interrogating the guy because he was jealous. His interrogation had had nothing to do with that though he might have felt a twinge or two.

And he felt a twinge now when the male nurse smirked at him. "She's pissed off now."

With how forcefully she dumped the contents of her tray in the trash, it was clear she was tempted to throw something. Probably him out of her place if he didn't explain himself. So he ignored Gibbs and rushed out of the cafeteria to catch up with her.

Cassidy didn't know why she was so mad, but she was. Mark had always had the ability to infuriate her without even trying, though. But she'd thought the volatility of their relationship had been because they were young and naive and, although she hated to admit it, also stubborn and selfish.

She was older now. Wiser. Calmer. Usually.

But she hadn't slept well last night and not just because she'd seen that man standing on her patio or even because she'd nearly been abducted twice over the past two days. She hadn't slept because she'd wanted Mark lying beside her. She'd wanted his arms wrapped around her, holding her close, keeping her safe.

Now she just wanted to get away from him. So she rushed to the elevators and fortunately found one standing empty with the doors open. She stepped inside and pressed the button for the floor Lang was on, but before the doors closed, a hand shot between them, pushing them back. And Mark stepped inside with her.

Clearly unrepentant, he grinned at her. "Well, that was fun."

"Yeah, now I know how a fire hydrant feels," she remarked.

He laughed. "Are you saying that Gibbs and I were acting like dogs?"

"Just acting?" She snorted.

"You should be flattered," he said. "Instead you're pissed off. Why?"

She shook her head. "You two weren't acting like that

about me," she said. "That was all about the two of you and apparently about Lang."

"Ah..." He stepped closer to her and touched her chin, tipping it up so their gazes met. "Are you jealous?"

She snorted again, amused despite herself. "Of Lang?"

He shrugged. "Of me," he said, and he arched one of his dark eyebrows. "You want me to be jealous because you've got guys drooling all over you."

She jerked her chin from his hand and took a step away from him. "According to you, that's not the case," she said. "They just want money from Lang."

He nodded. "That could be the case. I had to ask some questions to figure out if it is."

"Why?" she asked.

"Because that's how I do my job," he said. "I have to figure out who and what poses a threat to the person I'm trying to protect. Maybe nurse Tyler or Dr. Fink pose a threat."

She shook her head. "No. Neither of them needs money. They both work hard and a lot of hours."

"Then maybe they do need money," he said, "and that's why they're working so hard and so many hours."

She sucked in a breath. "I didn't think they did that because they had to..."

"But it's a possibility," Mark said. "But even if they are working for whoever Lang works for, that doesn't mean they're not drooling over you, too. So don't be insulted."

She sucked in another breath. "You think I'm insulted."

"I think you're mad, and I'm not sure why," he said.

"I thought you were acting like that with Gibbs because you're jealous," she admitted.

"And that made you mad?"

"You don't have the right to be jealous," she said. "You willingly left me over a decade ago."

He snorted. "You broke up with me and told me you never wanted to see me again."

She glared at him. "And yet here you are…"

Instead of being offended, he laughed. "Ah, Cassidy, I have missed you…"

Her heart contracted with his words, and she flinched. She'd missed him, too. Too damn much.

Billy Lang stared up at the ceiling of the hospital room, but instead of seeing the tiles, he saw himself getting out of here. Escaping to freedom, to a beach somewhere far from Dark Canyon, Utah.

He and Leo had talked about that so many times, what they would do with their money, where they would go. Mexico. Or maybe Costa Rica. They hadn't been sure about extradition. But that wouldn't have mattered if they hadn't gotten caught.

But Leo just hadn't gotten caught; he'd gotten killed. So it was up to Billy now to escape to live out their dream. To follow through with their plan. And he had to do it fast because he knew he was going to be released soon. The doctor had told him or warned him just a short while ago.

He wasn't sure who all was on the big boss's payroll. A lot of people were. Cops. Or at least one that he knew of; other people could be as well.

The door creaked open, and he turned to see the pretty blonde nurse walking in. But she wasn't alone. That guy from the other night trailed her like a puppy. That guy wasn't on the boss's payroll. Lang knew that for certain because he was a Colton.

"Hey, I don't want you in here," he said. "My lawyer

made it clear that nobody can violate my privacy like this."

"You lost your rights when you attempted to escape," Mark said. "Your lawyer knows that." Colton glanced around the small private room. "And there's supposed to be a guard in here."

Yeah, there was supposed to be.

"Where is he?" Colton asked.

Billy shrugged. "I have no idea. Must've had to take a leak."

Colton knocked on the door to the restroom. But nobody answered the knock. He opened it and glanced inside the small room. "I don't like this," he murmured. Then he turned toward the nurse. "You need to get out of here, go find the officer who was supposed to be in here with him."

She jerked her head in a quick nod and then rushed out.

And Billy laughed. "Now who's going to protect her when you're in here with me?" he asked.

"She'll be fine," the guy said, but he didn't sound as certain of that as he probably would like to be.

"But you don't know that for sure," Billy pointed out. "You don't know who you can trust and who you can't..." He understood how that felt; the one person he'd been able to truly trust was dead now. With Leo gone, he wasn't sure if he was an asset or a liability to the big man.

Or maybe he was just a loose end someone would have to tie up soon. That was why he and Leo had abducted Fern again; they'd wanted to tie up their own loose ends. That hadn't worked out like they'd planned, though. Leo was dead and Fern was going to testify against Billy, if he was around to go to trial. He had to escape before that; he had to escape before he went to jail because it was the only chance he would have to get away from the police and from the people he couldn't trust.

"You know what you're talking about," Colton said. "That night you nearly escaped that cop would have shot you if I hadn't been there."

Billy chuckled. "So you're trying to say I owe you my life? Is that it?"

"Maybe you do," Colton said. "So you can trust me. You can tell me who you're working for."

Billy shook his head.

"C'mon, you owe me," Colton persisted.

And Billy smiled. "Then consider us even," he said. "Because not knowing is a lot safer for you than knowing."

Colton stepped closer to the bed and stared down at him. "You're scared."

Hell, yes, he was. He nodded. "And you should be, too."

Chapter 17

A few days had passed since Mark's interaction with Billy Lang, but the man's ominous words haunted him. Fortunately the police officer who should have been in his room was found. Apparently Lang had told him that he'd needed a nurse, that he was in pain, and had sent the guy off in search of one. At least that was the story the officer told. Lang denied it.

And Mark didn't know which one of them to believe for certain. But he didn't like that Lang had been alone in his room. Had he made a call? Gotten a message out to someone?

Mark had called his brother to apprise him of the situation. But he hadn't heard back from Jacob since that call a few days ago, so he'd asked him to meet him here, at the park where Cassidy was watching her nephews' soccer game. He left her sitting on a section of bleachers with her sister, who'd been casting him disapproving glances, and walked over to meet Jacob near one of the park benches on the other side of the soccer field.

His stomach pitched a bit, maybe from all the caffeine he'd consumed that morning. He had bought a coffee maker for Cassidy's town house; it sat on the counter next to her blender that made those green concoctions of hers. As he walked over to his brother, he glanced back at the bleachers, making sure that she was fine.

She'd insisted that she would be when he'd called Jacob on the way to the park. "I'll be in a crowd of parents and grandparents," she said. "Nobody will try anything, and you won't be far away."

As the distance stretched between them, his uneasiness grew. But she was definitely in a crowd of parents and grandparents. And there was no way that her sister was letting anything happen to her. Or letting her go.

Maybe that was why his stomach pitched. Seeing how territorial Patsy was of Cassidy proved that Cassidy was stuck here, in Dark Canyon, helping her sister raise those boys. Patsy wasn't going to encourage Cassidy to live her own life, and Cassidy had too great of a sense of responsibility to leave town until the twins were adults.

"Did you lose your best friend?" Jacob asked when Mark finally joined him on the bench.

Mark released a shaky sigh as he realized that he had. Not today, though. He'd lost her eleven years ago. All through high school Cassidy had been his best friend. And even though Mark had made other friends in boot camp and in the squad, nobody had ever been as close a friend as she had been. Maybe that was why he'd missed her so much. That and the mind-blowing sex.

"Just making sure that I don't lose anyone," he said as he glanced across the field again. It looked as though the game could be getting over soon. "Did you find out anything about Tyler Gibbs or Dr. Francis Finkbeiner?"

"No criminal records for either of them," Jacob said. "So I don't have a reason to subpoena other records for them."

"Like bank statements and financials?"

Jacob nodded.

"The agency has some hackers we use from time to time," Mark admitted. "I can have them do some digging."

"You know that anything they find won't be admissible in court," Jacob said. "We need warrants and courts orders for evidence."

Mark nodded. "Yeah, but we need to know where the danger is coming from," he said. "That's why the agency uses these hackers. Evidence can be found a hell of a lot easier once we know where to look."

Jacob sighed. "That's true."

"I just wish I had gotten Lang to tell me more," Mark said, frustration gnawing at him again.

"Hey, I've tried, too," Jacob said. "I haven't been able to get anything out of him either."

"He's scared," Mark said. "I think he purposely made himself sick the other day because Dr. Finkbeiner was getting ready to sign his release papers." And he wondered how Lang had managed that. Had someone slipped him something to make him vomit like he had? Maybe that was where that guard had gone the other day, not to get a nurse but to get a reason for him to need a nurse and to stay in the hospital. Because it had been shortly after that that Lang had gotten sick.

"I'm not surprised," Jacob said.

"I'll definitely feel better when he's out of the hospital and in jail," Mark said. Then he wouldn't have to worry about Cassidy treating Lang anymore. She would be safe. Or so he hoped. He glanced across the park at her again. The game was wrapping up. Both teams were lined up for handshakes at the end, and the people in the bleachers were beginning to stand up.

"I don't know how safe Lang will be in jail," Jacob

admitted. "I still think a cop is involved. How else did he get that badge?"

"I already told you that Olsen guy made me nervous that first night," Mark said. "I was worried that he was going to shoot Lang *and* me."

"Olsen claims that he was nervous because you didn't identify yourself," Jacob said. "He suspected that you were helping Lang escape, and he wasn't sure if you had another accomplice around somewhere."

Mark snorted at the thought of him aiding and abetting a criminal. He hadn't even aided and abetted one of his own; he'd made sure that Coffey had paid for his mistakes. He just hadn't paid the same way too many other members of their squad had, with their lives.

"It's a plausible explanation," Jacob said.

"But he just happened to show up at the precise moment that Lang was escaping?"

"He pointed out the same thing about you," Jacob said with a smile. "And unfortunately, coincidences do happen occasionally."

"Luck," Mark muttered.

"What?"

"It was luck that I showed up when I did," he said. He couldn't imagine what might have happened had he not showed up. Lang probably would have escaped with Cassidy.

And what would have become of her?

Would she have been sold like Lang and his partner had intended to sell Fern? And what about the other girls who'd gone missing? Where were they?

"Do you intend to leave once Lang's been moved to jail?" Jacob asked.

"What? Why?" he asked, his heart beating harder at the thought of leaving.

"Well, he won't be around Cassidy anymore then," Jacob said. "She won't have access to him. That might be why someone tried to grab her in the parking garage and why he was standing on her patio. Maybe they intended to threaten or blackmail her into helping them."

Mark snorted. "Then they don't know Cassidy Garner. She won't be threatened or manipulated into doing anything she doesn't want to do."

"That might have been the case eleven years ago," Jacob said. He pointed toward where Cassidy stood across the park, hugging and high-fiving her nephews. "But now she cares enough about someone that threatening them could make her do something she might not want to do."

She hadn't cared that much about Mark, not enough to make sacrifices or even find a compromise with him. But she did love her nephews enough to give up the travel nurse job that she'd clearly loved doing. When he hadn't been able to sleep and had wandered around her town house, he'd found the photo albums with pictures from her trips. She wouldn't have given up something she loved like that if she hadn't loved the boys and her sister more. So if someone wanted to get to Cassidy, they would have grabbed her nephews or Patsy.

But someone was trying to grab Cassidy instead.

Why?

To get to Mark?

He cared about her. Too much. Much more than she'd ever cared about him. He couldn't sleep well at night because his body ached from wanting hers. His heart ached the most. Yeah, if somebody wanted to mess with him, then hurting Cassidy or his family would be the way to do it. Cassidy would be easier to get to, easier to hurt than his family, though.

The Coltons had all been through so much that they were tough. Cassidy was, too, but whoever was after her might not know that. They might not know her at all.

"You don't think..." Mark mused, but as he started to say it aloud, he looked for her again. Her sister was standing near one of the coaches, talking to him. But Cassidy and the boys weren't with them. She and her nephews had disappeared.

"Where the hell are they?" he wondered aloud. Had the very thing he and Jacob talked about just happened? He had to find them to make sure that they were safe.

Cassidy had needed this, the fresh air, the sunshine, the fun of watching her nephews play energetically, if not skillfully, as they ran up and down the soccer field.

And the distance from Mark. That was what she'd needed most. Because sharing her house but not her bed with him was driving her mad.

She wanted him so badly that her hands shook whenever he got close to her. She found herself staring at his mouth, at his hands. And she didn't know if making love with him that first night he'd stayed had been a mistake or not making love with him since was the mistake.

And she was beginning to think that it was the latter. She knew he wasn't going to stay, though. Because she was certain of that, she knew not to fall for him. But she could enjoy him while he was here.

"Aunt Cass! Aunt Cass!" Brian called out to her.

And she shook her head, clearing her mind and focusing on what the boys had asked her to do. Their mom had something for the coach in the back of her SUV, and they'd asked Cassidy to help them get it for him while their mom talked to the coach.

"Coach Chip is our Boy Scout leader, too," Alec said.

"And Carter's dad," Brian said. "Carter said his dad needed a new sleeping bag for our camping trip and Mom had the one she bought Dad for Christmas."

"He never got to use it," Alec said.

And pain struck Cassidy's heart. But the boys didn't talk about their dad with sadness anymore, just acceptance. He was gone, and while they missed him, they knew he wasn't coming back.

"Mom didn't want it to go to waste," Brian said.

"And she didn't want to use it herself," Cassidy said. Her sister wasn't a camper or a traveler like she was. They were very different, and they hadn't been particularly close until Patsy lost Brian.

"It's a Boy Scout trip, Aunt Cass," Brian said.

"Not Girl Scout," Alec added.

And she shook her head. "That's a little sexist of you two to say."

"Sex?" Brian whispered the word.

"Sex?" Alec repeated in a shout.

And heat rushed to Cassidy's face as some of the other people heading toward the parking lot glanced over at them. But they knew the boys and knew her, so they smiled.

If not for everyone else heading to their vehicles, she wouldn't have walked off with the boys without Mark. She didn't want to put herself in danger, let alone them. But she couldn't imagine anyone trying anything with so many witnesses.

And Mark wasn't far away. He also wasn't alone. His brother, the ISB agent, was nearby, too. They were safe.

She had Patsy's keys so as they neared the SUV, she clicked the switch to open the back hatch. Her sister's big silver vehicle was in a spot toward the corner of the parking lot near the street.

Vehicles passed behind it on their way out of the lot that was quickly emptying out. The boys waved and yelled at some of their friends as they rode off with their parents.

"We gotta hurry, Aunt Cass," Brian said, and he ducked between a couple of vehicles that fortunately stopped for him. Alec, of course, was right behind him.

"Brian!" Cassidy exclaimed, her heart beating fast. "Alec, you can't dart between cars like that!"

The boys were entirely too trusting that cars would stop for them, that people were good. She worried that they were going to wind up getting hurt if they weren't more careful and less impulsive.

Poor Patsy. She worried about her sons all the time. And while there was nothing Cassidy could do to make her sister worry less, she wanted to make sure that she wasn't the reason that Patsy worried more.

She waved for the vehicles that had stopped to pass her and then she joined the boys who'd climbed into the back of the SUV. The sleeping bag had rolled over their third row of seats that had folded flat up against the back of the second row of seats. She always teased her sister that she drove a school bus because her SUV was so much bigger than Cassidy's. It was just the three of them, so she didn't know why Patsy needed all the space. But then she and other parents shared carpooling duties so often that it made sense.

Everything Patsy did made sense. Cassidy wished she could say the same. But letting Mark move in with her didn't make sense. Sure, he wasn't staying; it was just for her protection that he was there.

But she could have stayed somewhere else herself. Somewhere safer. But where?

Not with Patsy and the boys. She didn't want to put them or anyone else in danger. So she had to get them back to their mother right now because with so few other vehicles in the parking lot, she had a sudden rush of nerves. Her skin chilled and prickled, and she felt like someone was watching her.

Once the boys climbed out of the SUV with the sleeping bag, she shooed them toward the park. "You guys run ahead." She pressed the button for the hatch to close. But it seemed to be moving so slowly, and then before it clicked, it started back up. The boys must have inadvertently pushed something into the track, so it wouldn't close.

As she started to lean into the back of the SUV, she noticed movement out of the corner of her eye. The lot wasn't as empty as she'd thought it was. And someone had definitely been watching her and probably waiting for the moment she'd just given them. A chance to try to grab her again. Fear rushed through her, so overwhelming that it momentarily paralyzed her. She couldn't move; she could barely think at the moment. All she could do was feel all the fear and the regret.

He'd been watching and waiting. But he hadn't expected another moment to present itself, not with how the bodyguard had been constantly at her side since that night she'd seen him on her patio.

So this was it; his best chance to take her. And he had to take that chance.

Chapter 18

Mark's lungs burned from running across the park. He'd outrun his brother who was trailing somewhere behind him. And he'd probably freaked out Patsy when he'd rushed up and asked her where her sister was.

"She just went to the parking lot with the boys to get something from my SUV," she'd replied. And then the color had drained from her face. "Oh my God, I shouldn't have asked her to—"

"It's fine," Mark had said. "I'm sure they're fine." But he wasn't sure at all, and he sprinted away from her the second the words left his mouth.

She might have called out something after him, but he couldn't hear her, not over the mad pounding of his own heart. Jacob was back there yet; whatever Patsy said had stopped him. But Mark wasn't interested. He cared only about finding Cassidy and the twins and making sure that they were all safe.

He shouldn't have left Cassidy alone, not even for a minute. As a bodyguard, he knew better. From his years in the army, he knew better; he knew how quickly a situation could become dangerous.

He sprinted toward the parking lot now, and as he drew closer to it, he came upon the twins. They were playing tug-of-war, with what looked like a sleeping bag, as they ran in his direction. "Hey, hey, guys, where's your aunt?"

One of them, he couldn't tell them apart, released one hand from the bag and pointed it behind him. "Back at Mom's SUV," he said.

Mark followed the direction the kid had pointed in, and the first thing he saw wasn't Cassidy but a familiar-looking white van. While Cassidy was lowering the hatch on the silver SUV, the van moved up behind her, blocking her from Mark's sight.

His lungs and legs burning, he raced to close the distance. Struggling to breathe, he somehow still managed to yell, "Cassidy!"

She must have seen the van, though, because suddenly she was running, too. She darted around the back of it and started toward him. As she did, the van made a sharp turn, tires squealing, and headed straight at her. The driver was clearly intent on running her down now.

And Mark was afraid that he might not reach her in time. And he and her nephews, who were screaming behind him, would have to watch as she was struck.

When she'd first spotted the van, Cassidy had frozen in place much too long. Long enough for it to drive up behind her and nearly block her in between it and the SUV. But she'd managed to scramble around the SUV's rear bumper and the rear of the van to escape.

But she'd heard the squeal of its tires as it turned; she knew it was heading straight toward her. And so was Mark from the other direction. He wasn't going to reach her in time, and if he did, they would probably both be run down. So she zigzagged across the lot as she ran.

Like when they made love, Mark seemed to anticipate when she would move and where that move would be, and he moved with her. So he reached her just as the van's tires squealed again.

She wanted to close her eyes and clench every muscle in her body for the blow that was bound to come. But she found herself unable to look away from Mark, their gazes locked as they both continued to run, this time in the same direction, away from that van.

Then Mark's arms closed around her, and he sent them hurtling across the asphalt. Rolling. But his body was wrapped around hers, taking the blows.

Cassidy closed her eyes now. And she could hear more clearly. Her nephews' screams. Mark's labored breathing. The frantic pounding of her own heart. And the engine of the van. But that sound was getting quieter, softer than the others, as it drove away from them.

"Are you all right?" a male voice asked, and it took a moment for her to recognize it.

It wasn't Mark's. He wasn't talking; he was still panting, though. So he could breathe. He couldn't be hurt that badly, could he?

Jacob Colton crouched down beside them, his gun pointed at the ground. He must have drawn it and scared off the driver of the van. "Mark? Cassidy? Are you all right?" he asked, his voice gruff with concern.

"Aunt Cassidy!" Brian yelled, tears in his voice.

"Aunt Cassidy!" Alec echoed his cry.

The fear in her nephews' voices echoed the terror that had momentarily paralyzed her. Hearing it from them compelled her to snap out of it now to reassure them. She cleared her throat and replied, "I'm okay. I'm okay."

She was more worried about Mark.

Though he was panting, he hadn't moved yet either.

His arms were wound so tightly around her, and he'd used his body to shield hers. She felt the hardness and the heat of him pressing against her everywhere.

"Were you hit?" she whispered to him. She wasn't sure why they'd gone rolling across the asphalt. But they'd landed in the grass just beyond the parking lot. "Are you all right?"

He expelled a ragged breath and nodded. "Yeah, yeah…"

"That came so damn close," Jacob said, his voice gravelly. "I thought the van hit you for sure."

"That was it," Mark said. "That's the van I was telling you about…"

Jacob glanced around, as if staring after it, or maybe confirming that it hadn't come back. Then he holstered his weapon and reached out to help them up.

Mark helped her stand up even while he stayed on the ground. And that fear coursed through her again. "Are you really all right?"

He nodded and expelled another ragged breath. "Yeah, yeah, just need a minute."

Slim arms wound around her waist as Brian hugged her. "Aunt Cassidy, I was scared."

"Me, too," Alec said. "I was so scared when I saw that van coming at you."

"It was chasing you."

"Oh my God!" Patsy exclaimed as she and the coach rushed across the grass toward them. "Are you all right? What happened?"

"I'm fine," Cassidy assured her sister and her nephews. But she turned back to Mark.

Jacob grabbed his brother's outstretched hand and helped him to his feet. Mark rolled his neck and shifted his shoulders and groaned. His shirt was torn and dirty, and so were his jeans. He really had taken the brunt of their tumble across the asphalt.

She wanted to throw her arms around him. She wanted to hug him and kiss him and thank him for saving her life once again. But she was still scared, scared at how instinctively he'd risked his life for hers. She was afraid because she knew that he didn't do this just for her but for anyone he was protecting. With a job like that of a bodyguard, he would always be putting himself in danger.

"Thank God you went to find her," Patsy said to Mark.

"You should've seen him," Brian said. "He ran so fast we couldn't catch up to him."

"He saved her or that van would've run her down for sure," Alec said.

"Who was that?" Brian asked. "Why did he try to run you down, Aunt Cass?"

She shook her head. "I don't know." She had no idea why someone would be coming after her like this. Was it all over those human traffickers? Over Billy Lang?

Or did she have some enemy she didn't know about? Someone who hated enough to try to kill her? She couldn't imagine anyone hating her that much. She was usually patient and kind with everyone; the only person who'd ever made her really lose her temper was Mark.

"You are really cool, Uncle Mark," Brian said.

And something shifted in her heart. She hadn't told her nephews to call him uncle. She wasn't sure why they had since Mark had just told them to call him Mark when he'd met them earlier that day. And as much as she had to agree with them that Mark was cool, she also worried about them getting attached to him. They'd already lost their father, losing another male role model would be hard for them. And they would lose him.

Because he wasn't sticking around, he would be off putting himself in danger somewhere else, after he stopped putting himself in danger for her. But she knew the only way that would happen was when they figured out who was trying to hurt her and Mark and his brother stopped him.

Jacob took the boys' statements and Cassidy and Mark's, too. But he learned very little more than he already knew about the van and the driver. He couldn't be upset with them, though, because he had not proven to be much of an eyewitness himself. He'd been so concerned about his brother and Cassidy Garner that he hadn't paid as much attention to the van as he should have. He'd just aimed his weapon at the windshield, intent on stopping the driver from running down his brother and the nurse.

The driver had swerved at the last minute and then careened out of the lot. And when Jacob should have been getting the license plate number, he'd glanced down at his brother and Cassidy instead, to see if they'd been hit. The way they'd gone rolling across the asphalt had scared him into thinking that the van had struck them.

But Mark explained that he'd been running so fast that when he grabbed Cassidy he had so much momentum that they just spun across the ground like a tumbleweed caught in a tornado. And because Mark had been moving so fast, he hadn't been able to see much before he'd caught up with her, just Cassidy running for her life.

His brother's voice cracked when he said that, and it was clear how much Mark still cared about his high school girlfriend. He'd risked his life for hers, and maybe he would have done that for anyone since he was a bodyguard. But the way Mark kept looking at her, and the fear on his face when he did, told Jacob that his brother still had feelings for Cassidy Garner.

She kept glancing at Mark, at his torn shirt and jeans, and there was fear on her face, too. But while Mark was afraid for her, Jacob wasn't sure if Cassidy was afraid for Mark, or if she was afraid of him.

Jacob asked her about the van and driver, and tears welled in her eyes. She sucked in a shaky breath and shook her head. "I just glimpsed it out of the corner of my eye, and I froze," she said. "I didn't know what to do. I was worried about the boys. And I didn't know what to do..."

"You're fine," Jacob reminded her.

"Because of your brother," she said. "I feel like such a fool that I didn't run away the second I saw it. He could have been killed trying to save me."

"That's the nature of his job," Jacob reminded her.

"I'm not paying him," Cassidy said. "He appointed himself as my bodyguard, and he could have died trying to protect me." The tears welled again, but she blinked them away.

"He's okay, too," Jacob said. He gestured to where Mark stood to the side with her nephews. The boys were clearly big fans of the bodyguard. Jacob was, too, of his brother and of the boys.

The twins might have given him the best description of the van and the driver. "He was wearing a black hoodie."

"It was tied tight around his face."

"He wore sunglasses, too."

"The van was white."

"And part of the plate was either an eight or the letter *B*."

"There was a three, too."

"And a seven."

"Great job," Jacob praised them. "You got more than I did."

"Me, too," Mark said. And he reached out to tousle their hair. "Great job, guys. You're going to help us catch this guy for sure."

"Can we shoot him then?" one asked.

"Alec!" their mother exclaimed. "Please don't talk about shooting people."

"But he tried to hurt Aunt Cass," the other twin remarked, as if defending his brother.

Jacob gestured for his brother to step away from the others. And once they had some distance, Mark said, "I don't blame them. I want to shoot this guy, too."

He probably wished that Jacob would have. "I didn't have a clear shot," Jacob said. "And shooting him might not have stopped him." Even wounded, he might have driven the van right over them. "This guy is dangerous, Mark. He must be really desperate to have tried to grab Cassidy from a park in the middle of the day."

"I'm not sure he tried to grab her," Mark said. "Or if he intended to run her down."

"Why?" Jacob asked.

"If I can't do my job, someone else will have to take over for me at the hospital," Cassidy said.

Jacob hadn't realized she'd walked up to them, leaving her sister and the coach to calm down her excited nephews.

"Of course!" Jacob exclaimed. "And maybe that person has already been influenced into helping Lang escape."

It made sense. "Who would take over for you at the hospital if you were taken off Lang's case?"

She sighed. "Tyler Gibbs has offered, but I'm not sure he would pass the clearance. I can find out if there's anyone else."

"Please let me know if anyone is angling for the job," Jacob said.

And as she stepped away to make a call, Jacob turned back to his brother. Mark didn't look as convinced as he was. "What? You don't think that's the reason?"

"I just keep thinking about what you said earlier. About if someone wanted to manipulate or coerce Cassidy into doing something, they would go after the twins."

"And?"

"He didn't go after the twins," Mark said. "He went after her."

"And that makes sense if they want her off the case," Jacob pointed out.

"Or maybe it has nothing to do with Lang at all," Mark said.

"So what would it have to do with?"

"Me."

"You think someone's after you and using Cassidy to get to you? Who would do that?" Jacob asked.

"My boss said someone was trying to find out where I am," Mark said. "I figured it was just an old friend or maybe someone I protected as a bodyguard. But maybe it wasn't a friend."

"But how would they know about Cassidy?" Jacob asked. "And she wasn't in danger until Lang tried to escape. I think this has everything to do with him. Not you."

Mark released a shaky sigh. "Yeah, yeah, I hope that's the case."

Jacob had a feeling that his brother would never forgive himself if he was the reason that Cassidy was in danger.

Chapter 19

Mark never intended to let Cassidy out of his sight again. But just in case the unthinkable happened and she somehow disappeared from view again, he had a solution. The same one he'd given his cousin Ryan to make sure that Fern stayed safe from the men who'd abducted and held her captive for so long.

He waited until he and Cassidy were safely back in her town house before he ran upstairs to retrieve the box from the duffel bag in his room. She'd come upstairs now, too, and was standing in her bedroom with the door open. He held the box out to her.

"What is this?" she asked, her eyes wide with surprise as she took the small box from his hand.

"Just open it," he said.

She lifted the lid from the small box and gasped. "A locket?"

"Yes." But it was more than that.

Her forehead furrowed. "I don't understand. Why would you get me anything? If anyone should be getting anyone gifts, I should be the one gifting you things. You keep saving my life, and you're not even getting paid for this job."

He smiled with amusement that she thought he cared about money. "I'm not protecting you because it's my job."

"Why are you protecting me, then?" she asked. "We were over so long ago. And you have other assignments you could be taking. You could be in Australia right now." And again there was that wistful longing in her voice. She obviously missed traveling.

"I still care about you, Cassidy," he said. "You weren't just my first love. You were my best friend."

Tears welled in her eyes, and she smiled back at him. "You were mine, too."

"I don't want anything to happen to you," he said. "That's why I want you to wear this."

"Oh..." The smile slipped away from her face, and the color drained from it as well. "I know what this is. You gave Ryan one of these for Fern."

"That's right, you took care of Fern, too," he said. Just like she was taking care of Billy Lang. Actually not just like, because the patients could not be more different. Fern had been an innocent victim while Billy Lang was a monster.

"Fern isn't just a former patient. She's my friend," Cassidy said.

"Then you know this locket saved her life," Mark said. "It can save yours, too, if something happens, if whoever is after you manages to abduct you."

She stared at the locket. "I won't need this because I'll be more careful from now on. I won't take any chances."

"I thought I could keep you out of danger," Mark said. "With my presence. But I wasn't that far away from you when this happened. And I could have lost you." Again. He'd already lost her once long ago.

"You don't have me," she said, reinforcing what he

already knew. "We're not a couple, Mark, and it feels strange for you to be able to track me twenty-four seven. I don't even share my location with my sister."

"Why not?" he asked.

She shrugged. "Patsy and I were never that close until Brian, her husband, died."

"And yet you made all these sacrifices for her." Sacrifices she hadn't been willing to make for him, but she clearly loved her nephews very much and her sister as well.

"She and the boys are family," Cassidy said as if that explained it all.

For him, it did because he was a Colton, and to the Coltons family was everything. His cousins were more like siblings to him, his aunts and uncles like extra sets of parents. And his dad…

His dad meant so much to him. For a while there it had felt like they'd lost him when they'd lost their mother. He'd been so devastated, so depressed. But he was happy now because of Susan Baylor. Would that happiness last, though?

And if it didn't, would his dad survive losing another woman he loved?

Mark had been devastated when he and Cassidy broke up all those years ago. And maybe that was why he'd never had another serious relationship. Not just because he'd been traveling and hadn't wanted to settle down but because he hadn't been sure he could survive losing another woman he loved.

"You have to wear this," Mark said. "For Patsy and the boys if not for me. How would they manage without you? I saw how upset they all were today. If something happened to you…" His voice trailed off as emotion overwhelmed him because now he wasn't thinking about their loss; he was thinking about his.

Even when he and Cassidy hadn't been talking, he'd still thought of her living her life as vivaciously as she'd been as a teenager. Smiling, laughing, joking around… happy. And thinking of her happy somewhere had made him feel better even in some of the horrible places he'd been sent on missions.

He moved around the bed and placed his hands on her shoulders. "Please, Cassidy, just wear the damn locket…" And he wrapped his arms around her, drawing her close, until her body pressed against his, against his heart that was still pounding madly from how close he'd come to losing her earlier today.

Mark wrapping his arms around Cassidy reminded her of how he'd done that earlier today. Of how he'd used his body to shield and protect hers.

He had saved her life once again. And in giving her the locket, he was trying to make sure she wasn't in danger again. That was the only reason he was giving her the locket, though. And when she'd realized that, disappointment had overwhelmed her common sense for a moment.

This wasn't a gift like the ones he'd given her during their relationship. And he had given her so many thoughtful presents. Blank photo albums for her to fill with pictures of them and their travels. Special bands that kept her hair back from her face but didn't pull it out when she tried to remove them. And jewelry. Not expensive items but things that meant something. Like a ring with his and her birthstones in it. And a locket with their pictures in it.

That was what she'd thought of when she'd opened the box. Of that old locket that had tarnished when she'd worn it. She'd kept all the items, like she had his flannel shirt, but she'd put them away in a box. She hadn't wanted to dwell on reminders of their time together. But she hadn't needed things to remind her of him.

He had never left her mind. Or her heart.

She laid her head on his chest where his heart pounded hard and fast beneath her cheek. "Thank you," she said.

"For the locket? I thought you didn't want me tracking your every movement?"

"Since you've been my shadow these past several days, you're pretty much already tracking my every movement." And she would have thought that would annoy her. But instead, with everything going on, it had made her feel safe.

He made her feel safe. Physically anyway.

Emotionally he scared the hell out of her.

So feeling both safe and terrified, Cassidy closed her arms around him, clutching him.

"I'm worried about this other shadow you have," he said.

"I am, too," she said. "That had been too close today. And if the boys had been hurt…" She never would have forgiven herself. "I know I need to be more careful, but I will wear the locket, too."

"Good."

"I wasn't thanking you for that, though," she said. "I was thanking you for saving my life again." She touched the torn sleeve of his shirt. "For putting yourself in danger for me."

He grimaced.

"Are you hurt?" she asked. He'd sworn at the scene that he was fine, but now she wondered. "You should take off your shirt."

He grinned. "*That* would make me feel better."

"Just so I can check to make sure you don't have any cuts or bruises that need treatment," she clarified, and she stepped back.

But when he unbuttoned and shrugged off his shirt, she forgot all about checking him for injuries, especially since there was just some light redness and a few small scratches. She focused instead on the muscles in his arms and his hair-dusted chest. And desire rushed up on her, momentarily choking her.

"See, I'm fine," he said.

He was fine. Very fine.

"I think you should take off your shirt, too," he said. "Let me check you for bruises."

"You protected me," she said. "I don't have a scratch on me."

He tilted his head. "I'm not sure that I can take your word for that," he said with a wicked grin. "I think I need to see proof."

She could have refused. Shc should have refused. But she found herself pulling up her T-shirt. Then she tossed it onto the floor, leaving her in just her bra and jeans.

He sucked in a breath, and his eyes dilated. He stepped closer and trailed his fingers down her bare arm. "I don't see any scratches here. But I should check your legs, too."

She arched an eyebrow but smiled. "That's a good idea," she agreed. "You better take off your jeans, too." And she reached for the snap of hers.

He sucked in another breath. "Cassidy?"

She unzipped her jeans and wriggled out of them. So now she stood before him in only her lacy bra and panties. She turned around, presenting her backside to him in the G-string. "See any scratches?"

He uttered a soft groan. "I don't see anything…" Then he trailed a fingertip over her butt cheek.

And now she was the one sucking in a breath as heat streaked through her and her skin tingled where he'd touched. Then she heard his zipper teeth hiss, and she turned back as he shucked off his jeans. His erection strained against his boxers. She reached out to release it, but he stepped back.

"Are you sure?" he asked.

"No," she admitted.

And he started to reach down for his jeans, as if to pull them back up.

"I want to do this," she said. "I want to make love with you."

She'd realized when he'd saved her life that she'd wasted the past few days. Instead of making love with him and experiencing all the pleasure that she could, she'd relegated him to one of the twin beds, leaving her own cold and empty but for her.

"But you said you're not sure," he reminded her.

She swallowed her pride and admitted, "That's because I'm scared…"

"Oh, Cassidy," he murmured, and he touched her face, cupping her cheek in the palm of one of his big hands. "I will do everything I can to protect you, to keep you safe…"

"I know that you think that," she said. "But what I'm most scared of is you…"

His green eyes glistened a bit, as if her admission almost brought him to tears. But he blinked and shook his head. "I would never knowingly hurt you," he said.

"I know," she said. "But I also know that you're going to leave again."

"Not until I'm sure you're safe," he said.

"But you will leave," she said. "You love your job. You love traveling." And she couldn't ask him to give up either for her. With as much as she helped Patsy with the boys and with as much as she worked, she didn't have the time to give to a relationship even if the man lived in Dark Canyon, too.

"You love it, too," he said.

"But I have to stay here," she said. Then heat rushed to her face. "Not that you're asking me to go with you. I know that. I know that whatever we had when we were young, puppy love, whatever it was, it's long over." For him. Unfortunately for her, after making love with him that first night he'd stayed in her town house, she'd realized she'd never really gotten over him.

"I've never felt about anyone else the way I feel about you," he said. "The passion between us, it's so damn incredible."

"It is," she agreed. And she didn't want to deny herself that passion, and that pleasure, just because she knew he was going to leave. Maybe, because she knew he was going to leave, she could protect her heart this time. She knew there was no future for them, so she wouldn't be disappointed when he left. "And I want to feel it again." And her desire was stronger than her fear.

She reached behind her back and unclasped her bra, letting it fall to the floor with their already discarded clothes. Then she pushed her panties down over her hips, so that she wore nothing now but the flush of desire on her bare skin.

Mark groaned and closed his eyes. "I don't want to scare you," he said.

"I know," she said. "So make me feel something else."

The passion that only he had ever made her feel. She stepped closer to him, brushing her bare breasts against his chest. Then she linked her arms around his neck and pulled his head down to hers. But she stopped with just a fraction of an inch separating their mouths, and she breathed in the air coming in and out of his slightly parted lips. He was breathing nearly as hard as he'd been when he'd run to her rescue earlier today. And he had barely moved. His chest expanded with each breath, his hair brushing across her nipples.

She emitted a soft moan at the sensation. And tension coiled inside her body.

He closed the distance between their mouths, kissing her deeply, hungrily. And as he did, his hands skimmed all over her body. He caressed every inch of her bare skin.

Her knees trembled, about to give out, and she tugged him down onto the bed with her. He wriggled around until his underwear was gone. And then she straddled him, taking him deep inside her.

His hands clutched her hips as she arched and moved against him. Then he raised his hands to her breasts, cupping and stroking them.

The pressure inside her coiled so tightly that she felt as if she might snap in half. Then he lowered one hand to her mound, and he moved his thumb across the most sensitive part of her.

And her muscles began to quiver inside as the orgasm started. She moved faster and harder, sliding up and down his shaft, rocking back and forth as the orgasm intensified. She kept coming, the pleasure so intense that she screamed and tears leaked from her eyes.

He arched off the bed, his whole body tensed. Then he growled her name as his big body shuddered with the release gripping him. She collapsed onto his chest that was rising even faster and harder now as he panted for air.

"Wow," he murmured.

"Wow," she agreed.

The passion and the pleasure were so intense. But so was the fear that gripped her again. Because even though she knew he was going to leave her again, she could feel herself falling for him.

Or maybe she'd never fallen out of love with him.

Billy Lang was getting mad, which was chasing away the fear he had been feeling. That fancy lawyer had promised him that he wouldn't go to jail. That somebody would get him the hell out of the hospital before he would be released into police custody. Well, thanks to Mark Colton foiling his last attempt, he was pretty much already in police protection with two officers posted around the clock in and outside his room.

How the hell was he going to escape now?

That fancy lawyer and the person who'd hired him were going to regret it if he went to jail because he was not about to spend the rest of his life in prison. He hadn't survived that crash just to live behind bars. He wanted to fulfill the dream he and Leo had had for that beach and the sunshine and the beer. And if somebody didn't help him escape soon, he was going to start talking. He was going to make a deal.

He considered calling Jacob Colton now. But he would wait a little longer. He would try one last time to get out before the doctor signed his medical release. And he would use whatever and whoever he could to help him escape.

Chapter 20

Mark wished he and Cassidy could have spent the rest of the weekend in her bed. But she had a shift on Sunday morning. So he was driving her to it. Fortunately she was wearing the locket he'd given her, so when he couldn't be with her in some patient rooms, he would still know where she was.

As long as Lang was in the hospital, she was in danger there. But was Lang the danger outside of it?

Were she and Jacob right in suspecting that someone wanted to get rid of her so another person could take her place as Lang's nurse?

He wanted to believe that, too, because then she would be safe once Lang was medically released to jail. But he had this odd feeling that he couldn't shake, this twinge of guilt that this might be his fault somehow.

"Lang should be getting released today," Cassidy said, her voice a little lighter with hope. "His infection has cleared up."

"He should have been released last week, but he suddenly got sick again," Mark reminded her. And that suddenness was so suspect. Was someone on the hospital staff working with Lang, keeping him sick enough so he couldn't be sent to jail?

Mark hadn't heard back yet from the agency about his request to have hackers check into some people from the hospital and around Dark Canyon. His cell rang then, as if thinking about the agency had inspired them to call. He could have called back, but if they had information, he needed to know right away, especially before Cassidy set foot in the hospital again.

So he clicked to accept the call, and his boss's voice emanated from the blue tooth in the SUV. "Hey, Colton, I've heard you're using agency hackers for your personal use."

"You were all right with that," he reminded his former sergeant because he'd gone through him with the request.

"Yeah, anything that will get you back on the job faster," Sarge said. "I have some tough assignments and could really use your help. You're good at figuring out where the threat is coming from."

Mark glanced across the console at Cassidy. "Not always." He hadn't figured out who was threatening her, and he hadn't figured out how much of a threat that she posed to him. Now that he was back in her bed, he wasn't sure he would ever want to leave it. Then he thought to ask his boss, "Did you ever figure out who was looking for me?"

"No. They haven't been asking around anymore."

Maybe because they'd found him. "Did you see them in person?"

"Not me. Whoever was looking asked one of the office staff about you."

"In the office? Were there security cameras on them?"

"Outside the office," Randy Howard replied.

"Let me send you a picture of Rob Coffey to show the person," Mark said. "See if that's who it was." He pulled onto the shoulder of the road, so that he could scroll through his phone and find a picture of Coffey. Then he sent it to his boss.

Cassidy leaned across the console and studied the photo, too.

He lifted an eyebrow, silently asking if she'd seen the guy. She shook her head. Not that she'd gotten a good look at the man who'd tried grabbing her and then running them down. But she might have seen Coffey around if he was here in Dark Canyon.

So maybe he was just paranoid. "Did you check out the people at the hospital I asked you to check out?"

Cassidy's eyes widened as she stared at him. Then she mouthed, *Who?*

"Francis Finkbeiner and Tyler Gibbs both have clear records and no strange financial transactions. And no messages that seem overly suspicious."

So the only real reason Mark had to dislike Finkbeiner and Gibbs was that they were interested in Cassidy, and he was jealous. Maybe he wasn't as good at assessing threats as his boss thought.

"Have the hackers found *anything* to help us figure out who's running this human trafficking operation?" he asked.

"They went through Lang and that Leo guy's messages and call logs. There was a couple of strange conversations with someone in law enforcement."

Mark tensed. "And who is that?"

"Victor Olsen, an officer with Wilson PD, Utah."

Mark grunted. "Yeah, I know him. And I'm honestly not surprised." That made so much sense. But even if Olsen was involved, he wasn't the big boss. Somebody else had to be. "We need to check Olsen's records, too."

"This is going to cost you," Sarge warned. "You need to get back to work."

"The faster this is all settled here in Dark Canyon, the faster I'll be back to work," Mark pointed out. And he glanced over at Cassidy again. But she'd turned away from him and was staring out the window.

"Yeah, we'll check into his records," Sarge confirmed. "Anybody else?"

"Susan Baylor," Mark said.

And Cassidy gasped and turned back toward him. Obviously she remembered Mark's former neighbor or maybe she knew her now. Susan was a pretty popular caterer in Dark Canyon.

"You think the trafficker could be a woman?" Sarge asked.

"Could be," Mark said.

Cassidy shook her head.

"But I doubt it," Mark said. "I just want to make sure that she's not a threat..." To his dad.

"Sure, we'll check her out too."

"And check out the people in her world, too, like Kenneth Baylor," Mark added. Her ex had been pretty cruel to her; Mark didn't want the guy hurting his dad because Sam was seeing Susan now. Some guys had trouble letting go of old loves.

Something he understood all too well.

Mark pulling off to the side of the road had nearly made Cassidy late for her shift. So she rushed ahead of him through the lobby, intent on relieving the nurse who'd had the shift prior to hers. She also needed some distance from Mark after the conversation she'd overheard between him and his boss.

Mark wasn't just any bodyguard; he was clearly a vital part of the team, an employee that his boss relied on and needed. That was not the only person who needed Mark.

Cassidy did, too. She reached up and touched the locket he'd given her, careful not to touch the panic button on it that would make him think she was in danger. Because of the locket he would always know where she was while she wore it, but she had no way of knowing where he was. And that made her feel like she had when he was getting ready to leave for boot camp.

Scared.

She'd been so worried that something horrible would happen to him while he was in the army. But she doubted that his life was any safer now that he was out. And was this Coffey person looking for him?

Why? If anything, Mark was the one with a reason to go after Coffey, not the other way around. It was Coffey's fault that Mark had lost his friends and nearly his own life as well. If anyone had a reason to seek revenge, it was him. But instead, he was focused on protecting her and figuring out who was running the human trafficking ring for which Billy Lang and his late partner had worked.

Billy. Her patient.

She'd rushed so quickly through the lobby that she hopped on an elevator before Mark caught up with her. She could have held open the doors and waited for him, but she was already at risk of being late. So she let them close and pressed the button for Lang's floor.

Mark knew where she was headed. And he had the locket to make sure that she didn't wind up anywhere else. Once the doors opened onto Lang's floor she nearly collided with Tyler Gibbs, who must have been waiting for an elevator. She held the doors for him.

"There you are," he said. "I was wondering if you were going to be late again." He glanced behind her. "You shook your stalker for once?"

"Stalker?"

"Yeah, the old boyfriend."

"Mark is a bodyguard," she reminded the man.

"So you don't need him anymore?"

"He's on his way up," she said. And she was glad of it now. Tyler was acting weird, almost possessive. "Are you on your way down?"

He shook his head. "No. Don't hold it. I'll make sure you're safe until you get to the police officer waiting outside the door. Isn't that what your boyfriend does…if he shows up?"

"He will," she assured him. "He was on the phone with his brother, the ISB agent." He'd wanted to fill in Jacob about what the hackers had learned about Billy Lang and Officer Olsen.

"Have you heard any updates about my patient?" she asked. "Is he on his way to jail yet?"

"Should be soon," Tyler said. "From what I've heard, he's fine. No reason for him to stay here anymore." He followed her as she walked to the nurses' station where she stashed her purse.

She'd been running too late to leave it in her locker in the employee locker room. As she stepped back from the station, a room buzzed for a nurse. Lang's room. "He wants something now."

She hurried around the corner to his hall. "Where's the officer who's supposed to be outside his door?"

Tyler shrugged. "I don't know. Maybe the other one sent him away when he showed up."

Other one…

She had a feeling she knew who it would be even before she pushed open the door to Billy Lang's room. Officer Olsen stood over Lang's bed with a syringe clutched in his hand. "What the hell are you doing?" she asked.

Lang lay limp against the bed, his face deathly pale.

"Tyler, get help." But even as she directed her colleague, she grabbed for her locket, pressing the panic button. She didn't trust anyone right now.

Except Mark.

She should have waited for him.

Tyler ran out, hopefully to get medical help and a security guard.

Cassidy had to check on her patient and edged closer to the bed. "What the hell did you do?"

"He attacked me with this," Olsen said. "He must have gotten it away from you."

"I just got here."

"Maybe from another nurse, then."

"Step back from his bed," she said because she was scared to get too close to the guy, especially when he was holding that syringe and the button on his holster was undone. He could quickly draw his weapon.

He could shoot her, especially if he wanted to eliminate a possible witness to what he'd done. Because she had a feeling that he'd just murdered Billy Lang, probably before the man could implicate him in the human trafficking ring.

Olsen couldn't have the nurse bringing Lang back from the dead. Not now.

So he grabbed her shoulders, holding her back from the bed. "He's gone," he said. "There's nothing you can do for him." And damn well nothing that he would let her do.

She tried to twist free of his hold. "What did you give him?" she asked.

"I don't know what was in that," he said. "But he's gone."

"He pushed the button for the nurse," she said.

"That was me," Olsen lied. "I pushed the button. Then I realized it was too late."

She tried again to get away from him, but he tightened his hold. Then he steered her toward the door. He had to get her out of here. He had to get out of here. Maybe he would try the same thing that Lang had.

But then he pushed open the door and found Mark Colton running down the hall toward them. She screamed. And he reached for his gun, wishing he'd shot Colton and Lang when he'd had the chance, where there would have been fewer possible witnesses.

Chapter 21

She pressed the panic button on the locket. Mark knew that wasn't something Cassidy would do unless she was definitely in danger. And he cursed himself for missing the elevator she'd taken up to Lang's floor. He'd been deep in conversation with Jacob and hadn't realized how far ahead of him she'd gotten in the lobby.

He'd taken the next available elevator up to the floor he'd seen hers go. It was good he'd checked instead of heading to the locker room floor where she usually went first. But even though he'd pressed the correct floor for his elevator, it hadn't been fast enough. He hadn't been fast enough.

And now, seeing her fear as the officer held her, he cursed Olsen. "Let her go!" he yelled. "I already called my brother. You're not going to get away."

Olsen had one arm wrapped around Cassidy, like Lang had had not long ago, while the other was on the handle of his gun, his holster already unbuttoned. He could draw his weapon and fire it before Mark could draw his. After what had happened that first day in the hospital, Mark carried it every day now. Jacob had authorized the hospital security staff to let him carry. But his was at the small of his back, clipped to his belt beneath his jacket.

Olsen could shoot him before he could draw it. Or worse, he could shoot Cassidy.

"You can shoot me," Mark said. "You can even shoot her, but there will be witnesses." That male nurse and the doctor were just around the corner from the hall where he, Olsen and Cassidy stood. "You're not going to get away."

"Who said I wanted to get away?" Olsen asked, his voice gruff. "I have no reason to run. I didn't do anything wrong."

"You killed him," Cassidy said, her voice cracking with fear. "You killed Lang."

Olsen shook his head. "No, no, I explained. He attacked me. It was self-defense."

Cassidy shook her head now, and she stared at Mark, as if compelling him to believe her. He did.

But he nodded as if he believed Olsen. "Sure, makes sense. He was desperate to get out of here. He attacked you to escape. Makes total sense. You can explain that to my brother. He should be here any second now."

When Mark had filled in Jacob on what the hackers found out about Olsen, he'd vowed to track the man down to question him. And when Cassidy had pressed the panic button on the locket, Mark had figured out where Olsen was. He'd begged Jacob to hurry.

"We need to check on Lang," Cassidy said. "Need to see if we can treat him."

And now Mark understood why Olsen was stalling; he didn't want them to treat Lang. He didn't want to risk them bringing him back to testify against him.

Damn.

"You know you can't refuse medical assistance to anyone, even a criminal like Lang," Mark reminded the officer. "That'll change your self-defense to negligent homicide, at the least. At the most…murder."

The color drained from Olsen's face. He was stuck, and he knew it. And knowing that could make him even more dangerous because he would have nothing left to lose.

But talking to the officer had distracted Olsen enough that he hadn't pulled his weapon yet. And he hadn't noticed Mark reach beneath his jacket or that he'd slowly moved closer until Mark reached out and pressed his gun against the officer's head. "Let her go. Now."

"You're assaulting an officer!" Olsen said. "You're going to jail."

"No, Olsen, I think you're the one going to jail," he said. And with his free hand, he tugged Cassidy away from the man's grasp.

She slipped back into the room, screaming for the others to come and help her. She was going to try to save a man after she could have almost lost her own life.

Because Mark was certain that Olsen would have killed them both if he'd thought he could get away with it. But he wasn't getting away now. And neither was Lang.

It should all be over now. The threat to Cassidy. But Mark couldn't help but think that it wasn't over. Not yet. Not by a long shot.

Lang had been down too long. Cassidy, Tyler and Dr. Finkbeiner had been unable to bring him back. And she cursed at the senselessness of it all.

"We did everything we could," Frank said, as if trying to make her feel better.

But she hadn't done everything she could have. She should have started CPR the minute she'd found him. But Olsen had pulled her away. Should she have fought the officer? Would he have actually shot her? She'd been so afraid that she hadn't known what to do, except press the panic button on her locket.

Mark had rushed to her rescue as he had so many times before. And she'd worried as much about Olsen shooting him as she'd worried about Olsen shooting her. But guilt overwhelmed her as she stared down at Lang's lifeless body. He might have had a chance if she'd acted instead of being paralyzed with fear.

"There was no saving him," Tyler added.

"How did Olsen get a syringe?" she wondered aloud. When he'd checked them out, Mark had found no evidence that Frank and Tyler had been involved with Lang's attempts to escape. But that didn't mean that someone else on the hospital staff hadn't helped.

"He said Lang got it," Tyler reminded her.

"And you believe him?"

"He's a cop," Tyler said. "I think your bodyguard boyfriend overreacted."

"I don't think so," Frank said, surprisingly coming to Mark's defense. "That cop had Cassidy by the shoulders, like he was going to use her as a human shield to get out of here." Frank shuddered.

Cassidy shuddered, too. That was how she'd felt, that Olsen and Lang had used her the same way, to save themselves. And they hadn't cared about her.

Mark had. He'd risked his life once again to save hers. But would an officer have killed her?

Could that officer be the person who'd first tried to grab her and then had nearly run down her and Mark in the parking lot of the park?

Part of her hoped that was the case because then this would all be over. But the other part of her realized that meant that Mark would have no reason to be her bodyguard anymore. He would have no reason to stay with her or to stay in Dark Canyon. He would take off on one of the assignments for which his boss needed his expertise.

And he would be putting himself in danger somewhere else, for someone else.

And Cassidy might never see him again.

Jacob felt no pleasure slapping cuffs on Officer Olsen. He hated that someone who'd sworn to uphold the law could so blatantly and amorally disregard it.

"You should be arresting your brother, not me," Olsen said in protest. If his hands had been free, he probably would have gestured at Mark who stood not that far away from them. "He pressed a gun to my head."

"Because you wouldn't let the nurse go and because you wouldn't let anyone treat Billy Lang," Mark said from where he stood near the open door to Billy Lang's room.

He'd already stepped inside it with Cassidy and the others, checking on Lang and finding out what Cassidy and Tyler Gibbs had seen. And he'd quickly filled Jacob in when he'd arrived a short while ago.

"There was nothing they could do for him," Olsen said, but he sounded more hopeful than certain.

"How do you know?" Jacob asked the question now. "What did you give him?"

"I… I don't know. He had the syringe," Olsen said. "He came at me with it."

"Lying in his bed?" Mark asked. "And he pressed the button to summon a nurse. He wouldn't do that if he was trying to escape."

"I pressed the button," Olsen said. "But then I started

thinking that maybe the nurse was helping him. Maybe she gave him the syringe to come at me."

Mark snorted. "Are you accusing Cassidy Garner of trying to help Lang? He could have killed her the first time he tried to escape the hospital." He touched his neck as if remembering the cuts Lang had given Cassidy.

"But he didn't," Olsen said. "I think they were involved somehow, working together..."

Jacob snorted now. "Nice try, Olsen. Cassidy Garner was vetted thoroughly before she was assigned to take care of the poor woman that Lang and his partner had abducted and held hostage. And I was there the last time that someone tried to come after Cassidy."

"Do you happen to own or have access to a white van?" Mark asked the officer.

"I'm not going to answer your questions," Olsen sputtered at Mark. "You're not in law enforcement."

"As a bodyguard, I kind of am," Mark pointed out.

"And I definitely am," Jacob said. "So answer my questions."

Olsen shook his head. "No. I want my union rep and my lawyer before I will say anything else to anyone."

Mark glanced into the room behind him. "You might want to talk before Lang starts talking."

"He's dead," Olsen said, and he sounded desperate to believe it now.

Then Cassidy, the doctor and male nurse stepped out. And the doctor shook his head. "We couldn't bring him back."

And Jacob caught the slight smile that crossed the officer's face. This definitely hadn't been the case of self-defense that he was claiming it was. But Olsen figured he might get away with it since there was nobody now to dispute what had happened in that room between the two of them.

Damn.

“You’ve got nothing,” Olsen said. “No reason to even book me.”

“We have plenty of reason,” Jacob said. But he couldn’t use the information Mark had given him about the text exchanges between Lang, his partner and Olsen. It would be inadmissible in court. He didn’t even want to let Olsen knew what he knew. He had to find another way to break him. Another way to make him talk.

Because no matter where Olsen fit into the human trafficking organization, he wasn’t at the top. He wasn’t the one who ran it all. And the only way Jacob would be able to stop the organization was to find out who was running it.

“Take him in and book him,” Jacob said to another officer who’d arrived at the scene with him. This was a Dark Canyon officer, not from Wilson where Olsen worked.

Cassidy and Mark stood beside Jacob, watching the officer walk away with the handcuffed Wilson cop. “Is it over now?” Cassidy asked.

“We’ll check into his whereabouts during the times someone tried running you down at the park and was spotted outside your place and here in the parking garage,” Jacob said. He needed to link Olsen to those attempts on her life in order to have enough leverage to get him to talk, because it was clear that he was just going to keep claiming self-defense over what had happened with Lang.

Cassidy shuddered as if frightened from him reminding her of the close calls she’d had.

Jacob reached out and touched her shoulder. "I'm sorry for what you've been through, Cassidy."

She smiled at him. "Not your fault."

"I was one of the people who vetted you to treat Fern and then Lang," he said. So he was partially responsible.

She shrugged. "I'm a nurse," she said. "I treat people no matter who they are. I wish we'd been able to save Lang."

"Do you know what was in that syringe?"

She shook her head.

"Or how he got it?"

She shook her head again but then she glanced at the other men who'd been in that room with her. They were walking away now. Even though Mark had checked them out, Jacob would, too.

"Do you think it's over now?" Cassidy asked.

"No," Mark said before Jacob could answer. "We don't know for sure why someone came after you, Cassidy."

"It had to be over Lang," she said. "And now he's gone."

So she should be safe. She shouldn't need a bodyguard any longer. Was that why Mark seemed so reluctant to believe that it was over for her? Because that meant it was over for them once again?

Chapter 22

Mark had fallen for Cassidy again. Or maybe he'd never fallen out of love with her. She'd always been in his head and in his heart. The one who got away, but really, just like last time, he was the one who had to leave.

She was telling him that now as they stood in her bedroom. They'd made love the night before, and this morning. And to Mark it had already felt like goodbye. So bittersweet.

And now she said, "You have no reason to stay, and I know that your boss needs you."

He cursed himself for putting that call with Sarge on speaker.

"And you don't, Cassidy?" he asked. If she said that she did, he would stay. He wouldn't leave her.

"A few days have passed since Lang died, and nobody has been following me or trying to get to me," she said. "It had to be Olsen who was behind everything that happened."

"That hasn't been proven yet," Mark said.

"It can't be disproven either," she said. "Jacob checked out his alibis and there is no way of knowing if he was really where he said he was any of those times. It had to be him. He was working for the traffickers. And they wanted me out of their way so they could get to Lang."

"But why?" Mark asked. "They managed to get to him with you around."

"But it took longer," she said. "If I hadn't been around, they might have gotten to him sooner."

Mark sighed because she was probably right.

"And since there have been no other attempts, there really is no reason for you to stay here," she said.

A twinge passed through his heart, like someone had struck it with a cattle prod. "No reason?"

"You have a job you love, and it involves travel," she said. "I have to stay here. It's just like eleven years ago all over again, when you had to leave for boot camp, and I wanted to go to college."

A grin pulled at his lips. "Except now you're not telling me how much you hate me and never want to see me again."

"That was immature of me," she said. "I was hurt, so I lashed out to hurt you, too."

"How did I hurt you?" he asked.

"You were leaving me," she said.

"You were leaving for college."

"But you were leaving for boot camp, for the army where you would be in dangerous situations," she said. "I was just going to college."

"And that's not dangerous?" he asked. "There are all kinds of dangers on college campuses. Mass shootings. Rapes. Muggings."

"None of those things happened to me," she said. "But I know you were in danger in the army, that you lost people you cared about."

He sighed, thinking of how many of his squad he'd

lost. "True, but life is dangerous no matter what you're doing or where you are. Look at the danger you were in as a nurse."

"Because I was assigned to treat a human trafficker," she said. "That was the only reason I was in danger. And he's dead. I'm not in danger anymore. But when you take your next bodyguard assignment, can you say the same?"

"I don't know what the next assignment will be," he said. He hadn't called Sarge back, but he needed to, or he might not have a job much longer.

"The very definition of a bodyguard is to protect someone else from danger," she said, "so that will of course put you in danger."

He couldn't argue about that because she was right.

"And while I'm older and more mature now," she said. "I am no more willing to wait around for you, wondering if you'll ever come home to me again, than I was willing to wait eleven years ago."

He flinched. "I'm sorry, Cassidy."

"Me, too." She reached up then and unclasped the locket around her neck. "Here. You can take this back. I don't need it anymore."

"Don't need it or don't want me able to track your whereabouts twenty-four seven?" he asked.

"I don't need it, Mark," she said. "And you can use it for someone else, someone like Fern."

"I wish you would keep it," he said. "I'm still not totally convinced that it was Olsen behind everything." Or maybe that was just what he wanted to believe so that he wouldn't have to leave her again.

"Then something would have happened over the past few days," she pointed out.

And the only thing that had happened was that they'd

spent more time together, in bed and out. And he wanted to go back to bed with her now. But she had plans with Patsy since she was worried that her sister was struggling with the boys being gone on their Boy Scout camping trip.

Cassidy was never going to leave Dark Canyon, not while her sister lived here and was raising her boys alone. As much as Mark admired Cassidy's selflessness and generosity in helping her family, he was also frustrated that the two of them could never make each other the priority that they should, that they would, if their love for each other was reciprocal.

"I'm still worried about you," Mark said. And it wasn't just because Olsen might not have been the person who came after her.

"After everything that's happened, I'm going to be more careful from now on," she said.

"I'm not talking just about that..." he murmured.

"Then why are you worried about me?"

"I'm worried because you're giving up the life you want to live in order to fill in for your late brother-in-law," he said. "I'm worried that you're always going to put yourself last, behind your family and your patients, and you're not being fair to yourself." Or to him.

"I worry about you," she said. "Because you keep choosing dangerous careers that put your life at risk. After seeing how much Patsy suffered over losing her husband, I can't put myself through that. I can't fall in love with someone who would willingly give up his life for someone else."

"But isn't that what you're doing?" he asked. "You gave up the life you wanted, the life you loved, for your sister."

She shook her head. "It's not the same thing, and you know it, Mark. I'm still alive."

"But are you?" he asked. "That spark is missing that you used to have, that excitement over exploring new places, meeting new people…that's gone."

She sucked in a breath. "That spark might be missing because I'm no longer a starry-eyed teenager, Mark. I'm an adult with adult responsibilities. You might not know what those are because you always put yourself first, what you want, over what those who love you want."

Now he sucked in a breath as her words jabbed him, making him feel guilty. "Ouch."

"Were you there for your dad when your mom got sick?" she asked.

"I was still in the army then," he said as if it was an excuse. But it really wasn't.

"So no, you didn't take time off, you didn't request a leave to help take care of her."

"I was unreachable when she first got sick," he admitted. "Nobody got word to me until a month later."

"Is that all she lasted?"

"No." That guilt intensified, making his heart ache now.

"So you could have come home after that mission?"

"I managed a few visits during that time." But they hadn't been long enough for him to really help or even to really say goodbye to his mother. But it had been so hard to see her suffering and not be able to help. He had no idea how his dad had survived it.

"Visits." She sighed as if with disappointment.

He groaned as the guilt overwhelmed him. "God, I guess I really am a selfish jerk. Dad kept insisting that they were fine. That he and Mom were doing okay without me, and they had neighbors and friends and Jacob and Noah. They didn't want me to give up doing what I love."

"And I do want you to give it up," she said, and she sighed again but this time it was as if the disappointment was with herself. "So maybe that makes me the selfish jerk." She shrugged. "I don't know anymore. You put your life on the line to save other lives. That isn't being selfish at all. I'm sorry." Then she moved closer to him, rose on her toes and kissed him.

That kiss ignited the passion between them that always burned so bright and hot. She still had that spark, and when it flicked against him, they started a fire. The clothes they'd put on just a short time ago were discarded so quickly it was as if they'd gone up in flames. And then they were naked on the bed they'd just made.

Mark's skin burned and tingled everywhere it contacted hers. She was the fire, scorching him with her passion. She kissed his neck and his chest, then tried slipping lower on his body. But he caught her shoulders and stopped her before she could touch his pulsating erection. He didn't want to be the only one feeling the pleasure. So he rolled her over onto her back, and then he made love to her with his hands and his mouth, kissing her everywhere.

She moaned with his every kiss, his every caress. Then she wrapped her legs around his waist and guided him inside her. They moved together as they always did, like they were one person, in perfect sync.

They were only that way making love, though. In every other aspect of their lives, they were out of sync. But not this. The tension gripped his body then finally broke just as she screamed his name, and her body quivered against his. They came together. But they couldn't stay together.

He had to accept that, and maybe he would finally be able to let her go.

* * *

He was gone when Cassidy awoke a short while after they'd made love. She wasn't sure if she'd fallen asleep because she'd been exhausted from their lovemaking, or if she'd been exhausted by the sleepless nights she'd had, worrying about this moment.

When he left her once again…

He'd left the locket behind; it was on the table next to the bed. She picked it up and ran her fingers over it, tempted to press that panic button. Because she was panicking over losing Mark.

He hadn't said when he was leaving Dark Canyon, but she knew that it would be soon. He had assignments waiting for him, a life of danger and travel that he loved. A life that she couldn't live with him.

Her chest felt hollow and empty; just like the last time he'd left her, he'd taken her heart with him. She loved Mark Colton, always had and probably always would.

She blinked back the tears that rushed to her eyes at the thought. And now she focused on the clock. She was going to be late to brunch with Patsy if she didn't hurry. So she quickly showered and dressed again. She even picked up the locket and clasped it around her neck. She'd like to blame that on being a habit, but she wanted to feel close to Mark even as he was slipping away from her. She blinked back another rush of tears and hurried downstairs. She was just about to step through her side door into the garage when she noticed the envelope that had been shoved under the front door.

Was it from Mark? Had he left her a card or a letter?

Was he going to admit that he loved her too?

But what good would that do? There was still no way

they fit into each other's lives. He was leaving Dark Canyon, and she couldn't.

But still she bent down to pick up the envelope. When she opened the flap, she found a photograph inside of the twins. But this wasn't a picture that their mother or even an acquaintance had taken.

It was from a distance. A picture of them getting into a big SUV. It wasn't Patsy's; it must have belonged to the coach. She could see him climbing into the driver's side while the boys and a friend climbed into the back. And in the glass of the back window, she caught a reflection of something. Maybe the flash from the bulb of the camera or phone used to take the picture. She flipped it over and read the note scribbled on the back: *I know where they are, and I will kill them if you don't meet with me. Don't call the police or they're dead. I'm watching you. And you better have this note with you when you show up.*

Panic squeezed her heart. The boys were out in a national forest, away from cell reception, with no way to get help or protect themselves from a mad man. She needed to call Mark. But if this person was truly watching her—and she believed that he was—he might go after the boys instead if Mark showed back up here. Because if this envelope had been here when Mark left, he would have found it. So the person who'd slipped it under her front door had waited until Mark left before he'd done it to make sure that she would be the one who found it.

Scared, she rushed back into the kitchen, set the picture on the counter and then she looked at it through her phone, blowing up the image. And she focused on that reflection in the back glass, making it big enough for her to see more clearly.

It was a man. A man she'd seen before. Rob Coffey.

Mark had shown her his picture. This was the man who'd been responsible for so many other people dying. Obviously he felt no remorse over most of his squad losing their lives. And therefore he would have no compunction against killing her nephews.

Losing them would destroy Patsy. So Cassidy had no choice. She had to meet with this man. She had to do whatever necessary to keep him away from her nephews. But how could she keep Alec and Brian safe without losing her own life?

Mark.

But clearly that was what Coffey wanted. He wanted to hurt Mark, as if it hadn't hurt him badly enough losing so many of his friends. Now Coffey wanted Mark to lose her. He didn't want to just talk to her; he intended to kill her.

Mark Colton was about to pay for what he'd done. He'd destroyed Rob's life, taking away his livelihood and his father's respect. Not just his respect for Rob but the respect his father, the commander, had earned from everyone else in the army. Covering up Rob's mistake had cost his dad his career just as the disclosure of that mistake had cost Rob his.

But he'd lost more than his career and his relationship with his father. Some of the squad's families were suing him for wrongful death. He had nothing anymore. No job. No relationships and no money.

Mark Colton had taken everything away from him. And now Mark would lose what mattered most to him: Cassidy Garner.

Chapter 23

Mark had called his brothers to meet him at home for brunch. He was going to let them, and their dad, know that he was leaving, and also what the hackers at the agency had discovered. Sarge had kept up his end of their deal; he'd gotten the information Mark needed in order to know that his family would be safe in Dark Canyon.

He knew who the human trafficker was. But he wanted to share that information with his brothers and his dad at the same time. Because Dad needed to know as much or maybe more than his brothers did.

And now that Mark knew he had no reason to stick around, he had to honor his promise to come back to work. His boss was thrilled about that. Mark wished he felt the same. He enjoyed his job, and he loved traveling. But he wasn't as excited to do it as he'd once been. Instead he had this hollow, lonely ache inside, and he knew from experience that it would never entirely go away. This was how he'd felt the past eleven years, like something was missing.

His heart.

He was leaving it with Cassidy, just as he had all those years ago. And he couldn't help but wonder, like he had all those years ago, if he was making a mistake.

Was he being selfish and uncompromising? Probably. Was there a way to have a life with Cassidy here in Dark Canyon but still work?

Since she hated how he put himself in danger for others, probably not. He didn't know how to do anything else. He was a soldier and now he was a bodyguard.

"Hey!" Noah snapped his fingers in Mark's face, and the dogs who'd been asleep at his brother's feet raised their big heads. Dancer was a yellow Lab, Ripley a chocolate one. Noah had trained them so well that they were some of the best search and rescue dogs around when they weren't being couch potatoes at home with Noah and Sabrina now. "You called this meeting. What's up?"

"Did you find out anything from the hackers your agency uses?" Jacob asked.

Mark nodded. "That was the deal with my boss. I wasn't coming back until I knew you would all be safe here." Especially Cassidy. But even though Mark knew now who the human trafficker was, he wasn't sure that would make Cassidy safe.

He wasn't sure that the human trafficking had really had anything to do with what had happened with Cassidy, with those attempts to abduct her and run her down.

"So who is it?" Jacob asked, his voice sharp with impatience. "What did they find out?"

Mark glanced around the kitchen that was empty but for them. "I wanted to tell you all at the same time," he said. "And then I'll forward you the file that my boss sent me."

"Send it to me, too," Noah said. "I want to expose these bastards to the world."

"I'm still going to have to find evidence that can actually be used in court to convict whoever it is," Jacob cautioned them both.

"But once you know who they are, it'll be easier," Mark said.

Jacob nodded. "Yeah..." He glanced around the kitchen. "Where is Dad? We're in his house, and he's not here." He grimaced. "Is he at Susan's?"

Mark shrugged. "I don't know. I just got home a little while ago myself."

"You were at Cassidy's?"

He nodded. "Saying goodbye." Though he wasn't sure that he'd actually uttered the word.

"Dad knows about the brunch, right?" Noah asked.

Mark nodded. He'd bought doughnuts and cinnamon rolls from a bakery on his way home. They sat on the table along with mugs of coffee. "Yeah, I'm sure he'll be here."

"He might be worried that we're staging an intervention or something," Noah suggested.

"For what?"

"For his relationship with Susan," Noah said. "We haven't been all that receptive to him moving on from Mom. At least I haven't."

"Me neither," Jacob said.

Mark sighed. "It's hard to think of him with someone besides Mom."

"But your mother is gone," their dad said as he walked through the French doors Mark had left open to the patio. "And she made me promise not to wallow in grief after she was gone. She wanted me to live and love again."

Mark felt a twinge of guilt. "That sounds like something Mom would say."

Jacob nodded. "It does."

"Yeah," Noah agreed.

"Your mother even talked about Susan," Sam said. "She loved her as a friend. She admired her too for how strong she was in dealing with her grief over the loss of her son and in getting away from that bastard ex of hers."

"Ken Baylor really is a bastard," Mark said. "He's also the human trafficker."

Noah and Jacob both gasped in shock. But his dad didn't look at all surprised.

"The hackers found that the former lieutenant governor, Baylor, has the foster care records and addresses of several of the missing women. He's also been getting kickbacks from some prominent businessmen."

"Son of a bitch," Noah murmured.

Mark nodded.

"I'm still going to have to find admissible evidence to tie him to this," Jacob cautioned them.

"You will," Mark said. "Now that you know where to look." He turned toward his dad. "You suspected, didn't you?"

Sam nodded. "Yeah, Ken Baylor is an amoral, sadistic son of a bitch. He put poor Susan through hell." He turned toward Jacob. "I can't wait until you put him away for good."

"I've got to call Mae," Jacob said. "See if she has an idea where to start."

"Wait for just a second," Sam said. "Susan and I would like you all to have dinner with us tonight. Here or at her house, if it wouldn't be too uncomfortable for all of you."

Guilt niggled at Mark again. "I'm sorry, Dad. You deserve to be happy, and if Susan makes you happy, that makes me happy."

"Are you happy?" his dad asked. "Because you don't look it."

"I'm leaving today," Mark said. "I have to go back to work."

"You're leaving?" Sam asked.

Mark nodded. "I have a job that I've neglected for too long already."

"What about Cassidy?" his dad asked.

Mark shrugged. "We can't make it work any more now than we could when we were teenagers."

"That's too bad," Sam said. "I always thought you two were perfect for each other."

"Speaking of perfection, can I bring Sabrina to dinner?" Noah asked.

Their dad chuckled. "Of course." He turned toward Mark. "And bring Cassidy."

Mark shook his head. "No. We already said our goodbyes." Without actually saying them. To get the focus off himself, the turned to Jacob. "Why don't you bring Mae?"

"Mae?" Jacob asked, his voice cracking.

"Ah, Dr. Copeland, the person you bring up in every conversation," Mark teased.

"That's just because we work together," Jacob said. "That's all we are, coworkers."

Mark snorted. "I don't talk about my coworkers the way you talk about her."

"The way you've always talked about Cassidy Garner, with that sappy look on your face," Noah said. "She's the reason you've never gotten involved with anyone else. You never got over Cassidy."

"I've never gotten involved with anyone else because I've never been in one place long enough to make a relationship last," he said.

"You know...they have these things called long-distance relationships," Noah said. "That's when two people love each other but they have busy lives that separate them, but they make certain to always make time for each other, too. You don't work twenty-four seven. You could make time for Cassidy."

He could and he would if that was what she wanted. But she hated that he kept choosing jobs that put him in danger. She didn't want to lose him like her sister had lost her husband. He shrugged. "It's not what she wants."

His phone dinged with a text. "That's probably my boss," he said, but when he pulled out his cell, he saw that the message was from Cassidy. No, it was a picture. She'd sent him a picture she'd taken of a picture that was sitting on her countertop next to a to-go cup of coffee.

Cassidy didn't drink coffee. She must have taken the cup out of the trash where he'd put it that morning. She was trying to tell him something. Then he studied the picture. There were two images. One of the front and another of the back. He read the note first, and then he studied that image.

"Damn it!" All this time it had been his fault that she was in danger. And now it wasn't just her life that was being threatened but her nephews', too. So he had no doubt that Cassidy was already on her way to the meeting that Rob Coffey had summoned her to.

He knew why Rob wanted to meet with her. To kill her. That was going to be his revenge against Mark for exposing his incompetence; Rob was going to take away the person who meant the most to Mark.

Cassidy was scared but resolute. She had to do this, especially after she'd scared Patsy. "Get to the boys," she'd told her when she called to cancel their brunch date. "Make sure they're safe."

"They're with Chip," Patsy said. "They're safe. He loves them like his own."

"Chip?"

"The coach," Patsy said.

"The coach loves them like his own?" Cassidy was missing something here, but she didn't have time to delve into this more. "Just make sure they're all safe." And Cassidy intended to do the same.

She would meet Rob Coffey where and when he wanted. She just hoped that Mark would get there in time to save her like he had before. But he didn't have much time. She was due to meet Coffey in just a little while.

She followed her phone directions to the address he'd given her. It brought her through the canyon to an abandoned warehouse on the other side. It was secluded, and the parking lot, with its cracked asphalt, was empty.

Was Coffey even here yet?

And what about Mark?

Cassidy reached for the locket she'd clasped on that morning. And she touched the panic button. Would Mark be close enough to pick up the signal? Or had he already left Dark Canyon on his way to his next assignment?

She almost wished that he had because she had a feeling that this was a trap. Coffey didn't want just her; he wanted Mark, too. He'd had to know that she would reach out to him, that she would forward that picture. That was probably what he wanted, so that he could kill them both.

But since he'd threatened her nephews, she didn't dare take a chance. She loved them too much to risk their lives. Hopefully Patsy had tracked them down to make sure they were safe.

Cassidy knew that she wasn't. But still she pushed open the door of her vehicle and stepped out. Then she started walking toward the warehouse, her heart pounding fast and furiously with fear for herself and for Mark. If he couldn't save her this time, he would never forgive himself. And if he tried and failed, they would both die.

And she thought with regret of all the time they'd wasted, all the years they'd spent apart when they should have been together. But it was too late now to make up for the lost time, especially now that she felt her time running out.

Jacob hated this last-minute plan that his brother had thrown together. But the note Cassidy had forwarded to him didn't give him much time.

"It's a trap," he warned his brother in a whisper through the speaker on his cell phone.

Mark's voice, also in a whisper, emanated from his cell speaker. "I know."

But for Cassidy, it was obviously a trap that Mark was willing to walk into. He was willing to give up his life for hers. And Jacob didn't believe that it was just because Mark was a bodyguard.

This was because he loved Cassidy Garner. He'd always loved Cassidy Garner. But watching through the binoculars as she walked toward the old warehouse, Jacob had a terrible feeling that Mark was about to lose her forever.

"This is too damn dangerous," he said in protest.

"Yeah," Noah's voice came through their three-way connection. "Dad's going to be so pissed if we don't make it home in time for dinner."

Jacob didn't appreciate his youngest brother's attempt at humor. But Mark actually chuckled.

"We've got this," he said.

Jacob wasn't as convinced. He'd wanted to call in more help than him and his brothers and the couple of bodyguard coworkers who'd been close enough for Mark to call in as backup. But Mark had reminded him that Ken Baylor was still a threat. And he probably had other cops on his payroll besides Victor Olsen. They couldn't trust anyone but themselves and Mark's friends. But the person they couldn't trust the most was the one who'd lured Cassidy here: Mark's enemy.

The man intent on hurting him knew him well enough to know the best way to do that was to hurt the woman Mark had always loved. So Jacob wasn't sure that his brother would be able to save her this time. And if he couldn't, there would be no saving Mark.

He'd loved Cassidy for so much of his life that losing her would destroy him even if trying to save her didn't kill him, too.

Chapter 24

Mark hadn't had a lot of time to come up with a plan. So he wasn't sure if this one would work, or if it would only put himself and Cassidy in more danger.

From the vantage point he'd found in the warehouse, he could see everything in the surrounding area and within the warehouse itself. He saw Cassidy park her vehicle and start walking toward the warehouse where Coffey was waiting for her.

Coffey intended to kill them both. Mark had no doubt that was *his plan*. One Mark had to thwart, just as he had thwarted Coffey from getting away with his negligence that had cost so many lives. And the only real punishment Coffey had faced for that was losing his job and his father being forced to retire early. Neither of them had suffered the consequences that the other squad members and their families had.

They hadn't lost their lives.

Mark had to make sure that Coffey didn't take more lives, like Cassidy's and his. And just in case the man intended to hurt the boys, he'd sent a couple of his bodyguard coworkers off to the woods where the Boy Scouts were camping. Cassidy cared more about her nephews than she cared about herself.

Because here she was…

Just as Mark had known she would be; he hadn't called her because he'd known there was no talking her out of showing up. If there was the smallest chance that Coffey might carry through with his threat to hurt those boys, she had to be here. Her family meant everything to her, even more than her own life.

And that was what Cassidy meant to Mark: everything. Even more than his own life…

He cursed himself for letting it slip to his squad about Cassidy, about how much she'd meant to him. About how he'd never moved on from the girl who'd gotten away. That was why he hadn't had the serious relationships and the families that most of the other members of his squad had had.

Even Rob Coffey had been married and to his high school sweetheart. He had probably understood better than most how much Mark's first love had meant to him. How Cassidy was really his only love.

He couldn't let anything happen to her for any reason but most especially not because of him. He wouldn't be able to live with the guilt. But he suspected Coffey didn't intend to let him live any more than he intended to let Cassidy live.

He'd lured them both here to kill them.

Cassidy's legs shook as she walked toward the warehouse. She had the locket around her neck, but it wasn't the only protection she had. She also had a small canister of pepper spray inside her closed hand. She knew this was a trap for her and for Mark.

But she wasn't walking into it blindly. She knew how much danger she was in.

As she drew closer, a sliding metal door creaked open, rust falling like dust from the surface of it. A man stood in the opening. He wore a black hoodie, but the hood wasn't up now. She could see his balding head. And she could see his cold, dark eyes.

"And there she is," he said.

She nodded. "I did what you said. Now you have to assure me that you won't hurt my nephews."

He chuckled as if amused that she was trying to make him do anything. "You really are the girl who got away," Coffey said. "From me several times and from Mark. And this time he won't have a chance to get you back again."

He intended to kill her. She had already suspected as much but hearing him admit it chilled her to the bone. He was so cold-blooded.

"I asked you about my nephews," she reminded him. "You promised you will leave them alone if I met you."

"This isn't about those kids," Coffey said. "It isn't even about you. It's about him." He swung his arm around him now, and he had a gun in his hand. "This is about Mark Colton, that sanctimonious bastard."

It wasn't Mark's fault that his squad members had died; it was Coffey's. But she wasn't about to point that out to him. She was going to try instead to figure out how to get herself out of here.

Alive.

But her pepper spray wouldn't be much protection against the gun. Coffey could shoot her from a distance while she had to get close enough to direct the spray into his eyes. But getting closer to him was also going to put her in even more danger.

So she wasn't sure what to do. She just knew that she'd

made a mistake in coming here, in meeting a man as evil as Rob Coffey.

She'd made a grave mistake. And she was worried that it wouldn't just cost her her life but that it would cost Mark his as well.

Because she knew he was here.

She could feel his presence just as she had always been able to tell when he was near. Her pulse quickened and her skin tingled and heated. Mark was here.

And then he confirmed it when he said, "This isn't about her, Coffey. You can let her go. This is about you and me."

His voice echoed around the empty metal building. Where was he? How close?

And when she looked up, looking for him, Coffey moved closer to her. Suddenly the barrel of his gun was pressed against her temple.

Even if she used the pepper spray against him now, he could pull the trigger. He could shoot her in the head, leaving no chance for her survival. So she wasn't able to protect or save herself right now.

And she didn't see any way that Mark could either. She was going to die and with so many regrets. So many years she'd lost with the man she loved because she'd been so afraid of losing him.

But in pushing him away, she'd lost him anyways.

And now she was about to lose her own life, too.

Hearing Mark Colton's voice filled Rob with rage. That rage had been the only thing keeping him going over the past year. Rage and the quest for revenge against the man who'd ruined his life.

And he was so close to getting it. This was even better than running them down in the parking lot like he'd tried. Because now Mark knew who'd come after him and why, that this was all his fault.

"Come out, you coward!" he shouted as he pressed the barrel of his Glock against the girl's head. His finger twitched on the trigger. He'd already slid off the safety. It would be easy for him to kill her now. "Come out of hiding, Colton!"

"You're calling me the coward?" Colton asked, his voice echoing around them. "You're the one who tried to shirk responsibility for what you'd done, who'd tried to get Daddy to clean up after you like he always did."

Fury surged through Rob again, boiling now, so that his skin heated and sweat trickled down his brow, into his eyes. He squinted against it, trying to see in the shadows into the warehouse.

Where the hell was Colton?

"It would have been all over," Coffey said. "But you couldn't let it go. You had to report us."

"Yeah, lives were lost," Mark said. "Because of you. People deserved to know what happened to the people they loved."

"What about me?" Coffey asked. "I lost people I loved. My dad won't talk to me. My wife divorced me. I lost people I loved, too. And now so are you…"

His fingers were getting sweaty, too, sliding on the trigger. He was going to shoot her. He intended to shoot her. "I'm going to kill her first, so you can watch. And then I'm going to kill you."

And then himself because he had nothing left, no reason to live.

Chapter 25

Mark could see the sweat rolling off Coffey. He could also see how the guy was shaking. Mark was sweating and shaking, too. That damn gun was pressed so tightly against Cassidy's head that she couldn't move. She didn't even look like she was breathing. Her face was deathly pale. And he was afraid that she was going to pass out.

Or maybe that would be for the best. She needed to get out of the line of fire.

"This is between you and me, Coffey," Mark said, and he dropped down from the rafters where he'd been hiding. He wasn't the only one up there, though. So he was hoping Coffey wouldn't look up.

"You can let her go now," Mark persisted. "She didn't do anything to you."

"No," Coffey agreed. "But she means everything to you."

Mark didn't want to deny that, but he had to. "She's an old girlfriend," Mark said. "That's all."

Coffey snorted. "Bullshit." Then he swung his gun toward Mark. "That's bullshit."

Mark shrugged. "You already cost enough innocent people their lives, Coffey. So you need to let her go."

Coffey shook his head, and he moved the gun barrel back to Cassidy's head.

He should have tried to take him out when the barrel had been away from her temple. But the guy was moving too fast, was too shaky. And with good reason, too. He had to know that Mark wasn't alone here.

"You're not going to get away with this," Mark warned him.

"I don't care. You think I've had any life since you got me dishonorably discharged?" Coffey snorted again. "My life is over. You put all those deaths on my head. What are three more?" He swung the gun away from Cassidy again, toward Mark and then to his own head.

"You don't want to go out like this," Mark said. "The deaths of our squad members were accidents." Though he hadn't always believed that. "Murdering Cassidy and me won't be an accident."

"No, it won't," Coffey said. "Just as trying to run you down wasn't. You ended my life. I want to end yours."

"You don't," Mark said. "You want to end the guilt and the pain you're suffering, and I get that. I feel guilty, too, that so many of my friends died. I wish I could have saved them. I know you do, too." He really didn't know any such thing, but he was willing to give the man the benefit of the doubt while he kept him talking.

He had to distract him.

"You couldn't save them," Coffey said, "and you won't be able to save her." He pressed the gun barrel to her temple once again. And his finger was all twitchy.

"What about you?" Mark asked. "Can I save you from yourself? Can I make you see that this isn't the way? Your dad is already upset with you." Now that the truth had come out. "How do you think he'll feel if you take yourself out like this? Like a coward."

Tears welled in the man's eyes at the words, and Mark knew he'd struck a nerve. A dangerous one. Because Coffey swung the gun back toward him. And he might have taken a shot but there was suddenly a blast of toxic fumes.

And Coffey and Cassidy started coughing. Then Coffey dropped to the ground. Sarge, up in the rafters yet, had gotten his shot. It wasn't a kill shot. The bullet had just gone into the shoulder of the arm that had been holding the gun. Coffey dropped his weapon, and then he dropped to the ground, writhing in pain as he coughed and sputtered.

And Mark rushed forward. After kicking the gun away, he closed his arms around Cassidy, holding her against his wildly pounding heart. She was alive.

But even though she was alive, he was worried that he'd still lost her. What had just happened must have proven to her how dangerous his life was and how much danger he regularly put himself in.

Frank flushed out Cassidy's eyes. "What the hell happened, Cass?" he asked. "How'd you get pepper spray in your face?"

"I sprayed it at the guy who had the gun," she said. So that he wouldn't shoot Mark because Mark had clearly been inciting him, trying to get him to turn his weapon on him and away from her.

"The guy that went up to surgery with a bullet in him?" Frank asked. "That guy?"

She nodded.

"That's why the police are here again." Frank groaned. "I thought it was all over once Lang died."

And she had a sudden rush of fear. "You weren't…you didn't help Olsen get that syringe, did you?"

Frank gasped and stared at her with eyes wide with shock. "What? Hell, no." Then he sighed, and his face flushed a bright red. "Not intentionally. But I might have inadvertently distracted one of the nurses. She came up to me later and confessed that she couldn't find a syringe of morphine. It was for a terminal cancer patient. High dose. She admitted that a cop had been around, flirting with her just before she stepped away to talk to me. That must have been when Olsen got it."

"Have her tell the police that," she said.

He nodded. "I will. I just didn't want her to get in trouble."

"That's sweet of you," Cassidy said, and she smiled at him. Clearly he was interested in another nurse now and not her.

He smiled. "She's the sweet one. I'm glad I came to Dark Canyon and met her."

"I am, too," she said. "Because I would hate to think you came here expecting something to happen with us."

His face flushed. "I might have hoped, but I figured out back when we dated that you were still hung up on someone else. Mark Colton?"

She could have denied it, but she nodded. "Yeah, but it's not going to work out this time either." Seeing him in action, how good he was at his job, she knew she couldn't ask him to give it up. Just as she helped save lives, he was doing the same. But he had to put his in danger in order to do it, like he'd done today for her.

Frank leaned closer and whispered, "Maybe you need to tell him that." And he pointed toward Mark who'd just slipped between the pulled curtain and the wall of the ER bay.

Frank left them alone then, and they stared at each other.

"I'm so sorry, Cassidy," Mark said. "I never wanted to put you in danger. I just wanted to protect you."

"I know," she assured him. "And you did. I'm fine."

He pointed at her eyes. "Except for the pepper spray."

"Yeah, when I sprayed it up at him it came back down in my face, too." And it had stung so damn much that her eyes were still watering.

"Thank you," he said. "You saved my life."

"I would say we're even, but you've saved mine more than once."

"Because I was the one who put you in danger," he said. "And I am so sorry about that."

She reached out and grabbed his hand and squeezed it. "Coffey put my life in danger. Not you. This was all his fault."

"All of it, Cassidy?" he asked. "Because you don't seem willing to take a chance on us."

Her heart ached with yearning to do that.

"We could try long distance," he said. "We could take trips and spend time together when I'm between assignments."

It was so tempting. But then she remembered how broken Patsy had been over losing Brian senior. And she shook her head.

"So I guess coming to dinner at my dad's tonight is out, too?" he asked, his voice light as if he was teasing her. But she detected a serious question in there.

She pointed to her face. "Not like this. I just want to go

home and sleep." And cry. Because she felt like she was being ripped apart to let him leave her again.

Relief and love overwhelmed Sam as the last of his three sons walked into the house. Jacob was already here. And Noah had brought Sabrina, who was wearing a beautiful engagement ring. And now Mark.

He was fine. Jacob and Noah had left with him earlier today, and there had been such urgency and fear in all three of them that Sam had worried that they weren't just going to miss dinner but that they might never come home again.

But here they all were and with Susan, too. She passed around appetizers while he opened a bottle of champagne to toast his youngest son's engagement to the beautiful Sabrina, who glowed with happiness and love for Noah.

"No Mae?" Mark asked Jacob.

Jacob shook his head. "No. We're just colleagues, nothing more. What about Cassidy? You didn't invite her?"

Mark sighed. "I invited her, but she wouldn't come." His shoulders slumped, and the look that crossed his face reminded Sam of how he must have looked when he'd lost their mother. Devastated.

"She's been through a lot, and not just today," Jacob said, as if trying to console his brother.

Sam suspected Cassidy wasn't the only one who'd been through a lot. Mark had, too. Mark had been worried about Cassidy losing her life, but even though she'd survived, he'd still lost her anyway.

He found himself reaching out to wrap his arm around Susan's shoulders.

Her face flushed red, and she looked nervously at his sons, as if she expected them to protest his display of affection for her. But he didn't care what his sons thought at the moment. Finding out just how evil her ex was had unnerved Sam. He was worried about her.

And he understood how Mark must have felt earlier today when he'd learned that Cassidy was in danger.

"Don't give up so easily," Sam said to Mark.

"What? She really doesn't want to come to dinner. She got pepper spray in her face and—"

"I'm not talking about dinner," Sam said. "I'm talking about the rest of your life. You know you want to spend it with Cassidy. Figure out how to make it work, where you can compromise."

Mark shook his head. "I don't know, Dad. She hates what I do for a living. And it's all I know."

Sam snorted. "You know a lot of things. And I'm sure there's a way to be in the bodyguard business without being on the front lines all the time. Compromise, son, that's how relationships work."

A look of yearning and hope crossed Mark's face now. "I wish…"

"Stop wishing and make it happen," Sam said. "Love, real lasting love like you have with Cassidy is worth every sacrifice."

Mark nodded. "You're right. I see that now. I just don't know if Cassidy will be as convinced."

"You won't know until you talk to her," Sam said.

"I'll make you a to-go box for you and for her," Susan offered.

"Thanks, Susan," Mark said, and he leaned forward to kiss her cheek. "And thank you for being there for my dad and giving him a reason to be happy again."

Tears filled Susan's pretty eyes, but she blinked them away and smiled at his son. "He has done the same for me."

Mark stayed just long enough to toast the newly engaged couple before heading out with the meals Susan had boxed for him and Cassidy. And Sam hoped that this mission was as successful for Mark as the last one had been and that not just their lives survived but their hearts as well.

Chapter 26

Until his dad had suggested it, Mark hadn't seen a way to compromise with Cassidy. But now it was all so clear to him. And on his way to Cassidy's town house, he'd called Randy Howard, his former sergeant and current boss, to make sure that it could happen and that he wouldn't have to find a whole new profession.

But if he'd had to, he would have. Cassidy meant more to him than his job. Nearly losing her today had proven that to him. But that didn't mean she felt the same way about him.

When he got to her town house, he parked his vehicle next to Patsy's big silver SUV. Fortunately Susan had packed enough food for more than two people; there would be plenty to share with Patsy. But he also wanted to talk to Cassidy alone. And he wasn't sure that Patsy would let that happen, especially if she knew that he was reason that her sister and even her children could have been in danger.

He drew in a deep, bracing breath, and then he rang the doorbell. When Patsy opened it, he half expected her to slam it in his face again. But instead she reached out and closed her arms around him, tightly hugging him.

"Thank you," she said, "thank you for saving my sister today."

"I think it's more like she saved me," he said. "She's incredible."

"Yes, she is."

He glanced over her shoulder down the hall toward the living area. "Where is she?"

"Upstairs resting her eyes," Patsy said. "I just didn't want her to be alone."

"Are the boys home?"

"Tomorrow," Patsy said. "I didn't want to cut their camping trip short. They were having too much fun."

"That's good."

"And they were mad at me for embarrassing them showing up like I did," Patsy admitted.

"I'm so sorry that you had to go through that," he said. "And I'm sorry that Cassidy had to, too."

She took the bag that dangled from his fingers. "Smells delicious. I can plate this up while you talk to Cassidy. And then I can make myself scarce…if she wants me to."

While Patsy wasn't mad at him, she clearly wasn't sure how her sister felt about him. He nodded, left her in the kitchen and headed upstairs to Cassidy's room.

"Who's here?" she asked when he walked into the dark bedroom.

"It's me, Cassidy."

"Mark?" She lifted her head from the pillow to peer at him in the shadows. "Did you stop by to say goodbye on your way out of town?"

"I don't want to say goodbye, Cassidy," he said.

"You have a job you love," she said. "And you love traveling for it. Our lives are just not compatible."

"You really aren't willing to give long distance a try?"

he asked. "I understand that you have to stay here for Patsy and the boys. But I can make this my home base, too."

"So you would come home to me in Dark Canyon but only if you survive your assignment?"

"I won't be on the front lines anymore," he said. "I called Sarge and worked out a new position. I'll go out in the field but only to assess the threats and set up the security plans. I won't be the actual bodyguard anymore."

She sucked in a breath. "You're willing to give up being a bodyguard."

"I would still be in security," he said. "I would still be protecting people. I just wouldn't be the one who might take a bullet for someone."

"Like you tried to take one for me today," she said.

"You saved me, Cassidy. I don't want to leave you again," he admitted, emotion making his voice gruff as the thought of leaving her overwhelmed him.

"I don't want you to leave," she said. "I never wanted you to leave me."

"I hope that sometimes you'll be able to travel with me, for business and for pleasure. I know how much you miss it. And I know how much I've missed you all these years. I love you, Cassidy, and I don't want to give you up. I want to figure out a way to make our relationship work."

"I'm just not sure this is fair to you," Cassidy said, and there were tears streaming from her eyes.

He didn't know if that was because of the pepper spray or because she was overcome with emotion, too.

"What's not fair?" he asked.

"You'd be giving up the job you love and making Dark Canyon your home base, and with Patsy and the boys, I still wouldn't be able to travel that much with you. And when you're here, I would still be busy with them." Her voice cracked now. "I can't make the sacrifices you're so willing to make. And I'm so sorry…"

"Cassidy," he said, his heart breaking for her. He started to move toward the bed, but someone suddenly grabbed his arm. He'd been so intent on Cassidy that he hadn't heard Patsy come upstairs.

"Let me talk to my sister, please," Patsy said. "Just wait in the hall a minute."

He wasn't sure if there was any reason for him to wait; it didn't sound as if Cassidy was willing to give their relationship a shot no matter what compromises he made. Maybe he should just leave, and not just her town house but Dark Canyon.

After Patsy pulled Mark out of the room, she stepped back inside and closed the door behind herself. "What are you doing?" Cassidy asked. And fear gripped her that she might not see Mark again. He'd agreed to make the sacrifices he hadn't been willing to do as a teenager, but Cassidy hadn't met him halfway.

"What are you doing?" Patsy asked. "Why wouldn't you jump at what he's offering you? You have been in love with Mark Colton all of your adult life, Cass."

She had been, so she nodded.

"Life is too short, Cass, so we have to make as much time as possible for the people we love."

"That's why I can't do this…" Cassidy said. "I have to be here for you and the boys."

"The boys and I are fine on our own," Patsy said. And her lips curved into a slight smile. "But we're not really alone anymore. I've been seeing Chip."

"Chip?"

"The coach. He lost his wife a few years ago, too, so we

both know how precious life and love is. And we're helping each other with our kids and with our broken hearts."

"That's great. Why didn't you tell me you were dating again?"

Patsy sighed. "It didn't feel like dating at first, and I wasn't sure I would be able to open up my heart again after losing Brian. But I got through that, so I know I can get through anything. I'm strong and I'm resilient and I don't need you to keep making sacrifices for me and the boys. We love you, but we know you have a life of your own, one you stopped living when Brian passed. You have to start living and loving again, Cassidy. Don't let Mark go. You'll regret it even more than you did last time."

Her sister was right. So Cassidy threw back her blankets and rushed for the door. But Mark wasn't standing out in the hall waiting like Patsy had told him to. Maybe he'd thought there was no reason to wait, that she wasn't willing to make any sacrifices for him.

But the thing was, she wasn't making any sacrifices. She was getting everything she ever wanted in the relationship he'd proposed. She was getting him. She caught him at the front door. "Stop, please."

He stopped with his hand on the knob, but he didn't turn around. "Why?"

"Because I love you," she said. "I have always loved you, and I don't want you to leave me again."

His body tensed.

"I know that there will be some assignments that you might have to go on alone," she said. "But I want to go on as many with you as possible. I want to travel with you and live with you and share our lives."

He turned then and scooped her up his arms, holding her close to his madly pounding chest. "I love you."

"Okay, lovebirds," Patsy said, and she had her hand over her eyes. "Let me get out of your way."

As she passed them, they both touched her shoulder. "Thank you, Patsy," Mark said.

"Thank you," Cassidy said.

Patsy patted her hand. "Thank you for all you've done for me and the boys. Now live your life."

Once the front door closed behind her, Mark carried Cassidy back up to her bed. They made love once with the fervor and passion they usually made love with and then they made it again gently, staring into each other's eyes. Love flowed as fiercely as the passion.

Cassidy had never felt as complete or as happy. Once she could catch her breath again after the ecstasy, she laid her head on Mark's bare chest and let out a long sigh.

"So I take it we're not breaking up this time?" Mark asked between pants for breath.

She laughed. "Never. And I am really excited about traveling with you again."

"After what happened today, Sarge gave me another week off," Mark said. "If you can get some time, we should go to North Dakota and catch up with some of my Colton family members who live there."

"North Dakota?"

He nodded. "If that doesn't sound very exciting, we can go someplace else."

"Anyplace I go with you, I am sure it will be exciting, and I'll go wherever you want," Cassidy said. She trusted him and trusted their love. It had already lasted more than a decade.

Thanks to his brother Mark, Jacob knew who was responsible now for the missing women and for the deaths.

He just had to find a way to prove it before Baylor realized they were on to him. And even though he'd said earlier that day that he would call Mae to help him find that evidence, he hadn't called her yet. Sure, the text from Cassidy to Mark had stopped him. And then there had been the dinner with his brothers, his dad and Susan and Sabrina, too.

The dinner had just wrapped up a short while ago, and Jacob had insisted on cleaning up for Susan to make up for not being as welcoming as he should have been to her. And so he'd sent her and everyone else out onto the patio while he loaded the dishwasher and wiped down the counters. He hoped he'd thanked Susan enough and complimented her enough and not just for cooking for them. She really did make his father happy again, just as Sabrina made Noah happy.

And hopefully Mark would be happy, too, and Cassidy wouldn't reject him again. He glanced through the patio doors to where Noah and Sabrina sat with the dogs; they shared one chair, cuddled up against each other. His dad sat close to Susan, too, his arm wrapped protectively around her shoulders.

She kept glancing fearfully around, as if she was still afraid of what her ex might do. She had every reason to be afraid. And so did everyone else.

And that was the other reason that Jacob had hesitated before calling Mae. Kenneth Baylor was a very powerful and a very dangerous man. And Jacob didn't want anyone he cared about to get hurt.

Epilogue

Mark felt like a teenager again. Carefree and happy. And madly in love with Cassidy Garner. He kept his hands over her eyes as he guided her from the public parking area to the remote campsite he'd rented in Lewis and Clark State Park near the North Dakota Badlands. In the distance, he could hear the soft babble of the Gamache Creek that emptied into lake Sakakawea.

She stumbled over a rock on the path, but he caught her, holding her close against his body to steady her. And his pulse raced in reaction to the heat and softness of her body.

And he was glad now that he'd picked the remote site farther from the other campers even though it was farther from the lake. He needed some time alone with Cassidy, especially after spending time with his Colton relatives who lived in North Dakota. He wanted her all to himself again. And he didn't want to worry about whatever might be going on with his family.

Not yet.

Right now he just wanted to focus on Cassidy and on making her happy, which was really all he wanted to do for the rest of their lives.

"Mark, where are you taking me?" she asked. "Should

I be worried that you're going to walk me off a cliff or something?"

"You can trust me, Cass," he assured her.

She reached up and squeezed his forearm. "I know. I do trust you with my life and with my heart, too."

"I'm so happy that you do," he said. He'd worried that they might not ever regain what they'd lost so long ago. But they had never really stopped loving each other, and now that love was even stronger.

Finally he stopped and pulled his hands away from her eyes. "Here it is..."

Her lashes fluttered as she lifted her lids. And she stared for a long moment before saying anything.

"If you don't like it, we don't have to keep it," he said. He should have bought her a ring instead, but for some reason he'd thought this would be an even better gift to start their lives together. "I know it's not like your old van—"

"Thank God for that," she said. And she rushed toward the small van camper he'd bought. "I hope it has a bathroom."

"It does," he assured her. "And a working air conditioner."

She pulled open the side door and jumped inside the camper. "It's so perfect!" she exclaimed. As she peered around, her smile widened.

"You're perfect," he said. "So beautiful..."

She turned back to him. "You're perfect. This..." She spread her arms around the small space.

"Should I have bought a bigger one?" he asked. "Should we have more room?"

She shook her head. "No. I like being close to you." And she wrapped her arms around his neck and pulled his head down to hers. Then her mouth moved across his, and she kissed him deeply.

The passion burned hot between them, as hot as it had ever been and as hot as it would always be.

Cassidy awoke an hour later, satiated and happy. Happier than she could ever remember being. But she reached out to find the bed next to her empty. Mark was gone.

But she had no fear that he'd gone far and that he wouldn't return. She trusted him to never leave her again, and if he had to go away for work and she couldn't accompany him, she knew he would come back to her. That he would always come back to her.

But he wasn't gone. She could hear the deep rumble of his voice as he talked to someone. And when she raised her head, she could see him through the open door of the camper. And behind him, she could see the towering buttes and rolling hills of the Badlands.

Mark stood outside talking to someone on his cell. Probably Sarge. Or maybe one of his family.

"You're going to win that playoff game for sure," Mark said. "I have no doubt that you will play your hardest, Alec. Brian. Both of you will play equally as hard. Oh, hi, Carter, yes, you will, too. All of you…"

He wasn't talking to his family; he was talking to hers. No. Theirs. The boys loved Uncle Mark, even Chip's son, who was like a brother to her nephews now, like another nephew to her. Patsy and Chip were engaged, and because they knew how short life could be, their engagement was going to be short, too. Cassidy was going to be her maid of honor.

"We'll see you soon," Mark said. "We won't miss your game." Then he slid his cell back into his pocket and turned toward the camper. His gaze met hers, held, as he stepped inside to join her. "Guess we'll have to cut this trip short," he said.

She smiled. "It's fine. We'll make another..." And another. They both loved to travel. "Thank you..."

"For what?" he asked. "The camper? You really like it?"

"For everything," she said, her heart swelling with love for him. Just when she thought she couldn't love him anymore...

"I would have bought you a ring," he said, "instead of this, but I was worried it might be too soon for me to propose. I want you to be sure that we can make our relationship work this time."

"I have no doubt that we can," she said. "We're older and wiser. And we know how special what we have is..."

"So after that playoff game, maybe we should go ring shopping," he said with a grin.

And Cassidy reached for his hand and tugged him back onto the bed with her. Maybe she was just making up for the eleven years they'd been apart, or maybe she would never get enough of him. "I love you so much..."

"I love you, too."

* * * * *